Three Days

By

Bob Looker

Three Days

First published in Great Britain in 2013
By R J M Looker Publications

Copyright © Robert J.M. Looker 2013

A CIP catalogue record of this book is available
From the British Library

ISBN-13: 978-1492830665

Printed by CreateSpace. An Amazon.com Company
Available from Amazon.com and other book stores

Dedication

This book is dedicated to my Uncles Trigger and Jack,
both of whom were members of the Auxiliary Forces.

Chapter 1
We need an edge

It was ten o'clock in the morning of Friday 5th September 1940, when General Emmerich Huber knocked on the door. There was a short delay before he was told to enter the office.

As well as the Generalfeldmarschall, there were two other people in the room. The first was an SS Officer and the second man wore a black leather coat, had on a small hat and, tucked under his arm, was a brief case. Viktor assumed that this man was from the Gestapo.

"What do you want?"

"The SS Paratroopers we dropped into Kent, yesterday, have been captured."

"What do you mean captured?" Generalfeldmarschall Lars Eberuardt screamed.

"We've just received messages from our command post and an agent, in England. The SS Paratroops have all been captured, Sir." Huber said.

"They were supposed to be the elite of the SS. They were put through two months special training for what? How could such battle hardened fighters get captured by the English?"

"Sir, I don't know. I have asked Obersleutant Viktor Junker to send me a report. I should know all the details by tomorrow morning."

"I want that officer in my office today. I'm having dinner tonight, with the Fuhrer and he'll want to know what went wrong." Lars Eberuardt demanded.

With that said Lars stood up and turned his back on those assembled. This was his way of saying they were dismissed. Once he had heard the door close he returned to his desk and picked up the telephone to speak to his wife.

He told her that he would not be home for a day or two. Then he sat there for a while, deep in thought. He stood up and strode around his office, trying to think of what the Fuhrer was likely to ask.

This was a catastrophe. The setting of the final date for Operation Sealion had been dependant on the success of these troops. Once they had established themselves, in the English country side, the invasion could begin and at the appropriate times, these men would carry out the tasks they had been sent there to do.

Without such people in place, to ease the advance of their troops, it could result in a disastrous humiliation for the German Army, if they were to be forced back across the English Channel. They had a very small window in which to carry out the invasion. If they missed it, then it would mean they may have to postpone the invasion until the spring of 1941.

In the mean time General Huber was making his way to his office. Once there he got his secretary to get Obersleutant Junker on the telephone immediately.

5

It was about five minutes before his telephone rang and he was informed that Obersleutant Junker was on the line.

"Viktor, you're to report to my Office, in Berlin." He ordered.   In the next three hours."

"But I can't get there today. I'll be there first thing tomorrow morning." Viktor said.

"No, Viktor, I need you here in the next three hours. I have to report to Generalfeldmarschall Eberuardt in four hours.   Get an aeroplane and be here." Huber ordered.

"They'll never give me a flight."

"Your authority is Generalfeldmarschall Eberuardt.   It is him you are coming to report to, anyway."

"Do you know what happened over there?"   Huber asked.

"The only thing I have been able to find out, is that, although they were dressed in civilian clothes, they were not actually like those worn by the British.

Only the Officers and Senior Ranks spoke any English.   The rest spoke no English at all"

"Why was that?"   Huber asked.

"The SS General ordered that only SS paratroopers were to be used.   I had lined up ten other paratroopers who could speak good English but I couldn't use them." Viktor said.

"Well you remember that when you report.   Now get off and get here as quick as you can." Huber ordered.

Viktor picked up his telephone and asked to be put through to the camp commandant, at the nearest Luftwaffe air station.   It took a few minutes to arrange this but then his phone rang and he spoke to the Camp Commandant.

He used Generalfeldmarschall Eberuardt's name as authority and was told that if he could get to the air station in the next half an hour, he had a plane that could get him to Berlin in an hour.   Viktor thanked the Commandant and said that his name would go into his report to the Generalfeldmarschall.

He left his office on the run, having already picked up his briefcase and nothing else, all the papers he needed were in there.   The staff car was waiting at the door, to the building.   He instructed the driver to drive as fast as he could to the airfield.

Because this mission had failed, he felt that only he should go to Berlin.   Viktor had thought of taking Major Axel Wolf with him, as he was involved in the training for the mission, but thought better of it.   As this was an SS failure, their General would be looking to pass the blame on to someone and he didn't feel that Axel had done anything wrong.   He, himself, would have to face the music, about the failed operation.

Within the desired half an hour, He was being driven onto the air station and the driver was directed to take him to a specific aircraft, waiting by the runway. As he got out of the staff car, a man in Luftwaffe uniform came marching up to greet him.

"You nearly missed the flight. If the gate guard hadn't rung forward, the plane would have taken off without you." He said as he held out his hand to shake Viktor's hand.

"Sorry, a bit of traffic hold up, as we left our barracks. Thanks for holding the plane." Viktor said.

"You have a Heinkel 'Blitz' as your taxi today. That'll get you to Berlin within the hour."

Viktor saluted the camp commandant and ran over to the plane and was helped up, into the cabin.

This plane was quite a small transport plane and had about eight seats in the passenger compartment of which three were already occupied. The pilot turned around and asked if he was ready. Viktor said he was so the pilot released the breaks, revved up the engine and moved the 'Blitz' onto the runway. Once he received clearance from the tower, he opened up the engines and they gained speed as they roared down the runway.

Once they were air born, Viktor opened up his briefcase and took out his papers. He needed to read everything three times each. He did not want to have to fumble his words in front of the Generalfeldmarschall. He had to be sure of his facts. He knew that he did not have the full information as to what went on, in England, but he had told Axel that if any new information came in, while he was on his way to Berlin, he was to telephone it through to General Huber's office, in Berlin.

Having read through all the information he had and that included all the notes on the training, before the mission, he decided that he needed to have a plan ready, to recover the situation. He knew that he had ten good soldiers and each one of them could speak perfect English. They had all been brought up speaking English as their first language. He studied the maps of the English coast and, with his knowledge of the invasion plans; he thought that he could develop a new plan, one which would recover the situation.

Before he was told that they were about to land in Berlin, he had made notes for his new plan. The one he would pitch to the Generals. After all, the potential gains that these ten men could make, for the invasion, would far outweigh the dangers of not carrying it out.

As the Heinkel taxied to a halt, Viktor was putting all his papers back into his briefcase. He thanked the pilot for the flight and then moved to the door. Once the small steps had been moved, below the door, he stepped down from the plane.

When he started to walk towards the main building, a staff car came across the runway, from the side of the building and drew up beside him. The rear door opened and he could see the face of General Huber looking out. He beckoned for Viktor to get in.

—

7

As soon as he was seated and even before he had closed the door, the driver drove off, at speed. Viktor was just about to speak and tell the General all about what had happened, when the General signalled for him to say nothing. It was then that Viktor noticed, in the reflections from the windscreen, that the driver had SS badges on his uniform.

Within the three hours, that the General had given him, Viktor was stood in his office, in Berlin. The Generals aid had handed Viktor several sheets of paper, as he walked through the outer office. These must be updates from Axel.

"Viktor, in twenty minutes we have to report to Generalfeldmarschall Eberuardt. He will want to know what happened and how it could go so dramatically wrong. You had better have the answers or you and I will be in a lot of trouble." Huber said

"I just need to read the reports Major Wolf has sent me and then I'll be in a better position to give you a full report." Viktor said.

"Go and sit over there." Huber said, indicating a small table, on the other side of his office.

Viktor walked over to the table, sat down and took his papers out of his brief case. He quickly read the new information that he had just received. It was as he had warned.

The SS were not right for the job. Had they all spoken English, then they may have stood a chance but this failure caused their arrest and capture. He could now stand by the fact that the mission failed because the SS would not listen to him and Axel. They wanted the glory but would not listen to the risks.

Just as Viktor was about to get up and walk back to the General's desk, the office door opened and in walked the General's aid, flanked by an SS Officer and two SS Soldiers, all not only fully armed but with their weapons drawn and, apparently ready for use.

"The Generalfeldmarschall will see you now." The SS Officer said.

This was not so much a request to a very senior officer but an order. This was the way such SS Officers behaved, around the Headquarters. In their minds, the SS was by far the senior arm of the German Military and as such what they said went. This brought great resentment from all the professional Military Officers. The SS had no Staff Officer military training and very little understanding of how to actually fight a war.

General Huber stood up and picked up his cap and put it on his head. Viktor did likewise and followed the General out of the office. The SS Officer led the way, General Huber and Viktor following and the two SS Guards, marching behind them.

It did not take them long to reach the office of Generalfeldmarschall Eberuardt. The SS Officer halted outside the large doors and knocked. This was not a request to be allowed to enter but more to inform those inside that he was about to enter, with his 'prisoners'.

They entered the largest office that Viktor had ever seen. Around the walls were large paintings of German or Germanic Officers, in full uniform, painted with fighting going on behind them. Most likely from famous battles that they had won. Also there was a wall with two large maps. The first one was of France and Southern England.

The second one was of the Eastern front. He could feel the power that emanated from this room.

"General Huber. What have you to report about this fiasco?" Eberuardt asked.

"Generalfeldmarschall, Obersleutant Junker has just arrived from his headquarters and has all the facts for you." Hubert said, introducing Viktor.

"Junker, I know what has happened, and so does the Fuhrer, but what I want to know is why?"

"Sir, at the start of the training, when the men had been posted to me for training, it became obvious to both my training officer and my self, that the men were not suitable for the mission."

"They were SS Soldiers. All SS Soldiers are suitable for the most dangerous missions and especially one so important to the success of the Fuhrer's plan to over run England." A General, with SS markings on his uniform, protested.

"It was not that they were not good soldiers, Sir, but that they could not speak English and we were expecting them to land and live, with the English, until such time as the Fuhrer gave the go ahead for the invasion." Viktor said.

"Obersleutant, you are lying. The Officer could speak English." The SS General retorted.

"With due respect Sir. He could just about speak English but not well enough to pass as English, as the plan dictated."

"What did you do about that?" Eberuardt asked.

"I reported this to the General, there, but he insisted that only those SS soldiers were to be trained. I had said, in my report to him, that I had ten paratroopers, that I could get, who spoke perfect English. They had been brought up with English as their first language and would be perfect for the mission." Viktor said, directly to the Generalfeldmarschall.

"Is that true? General Wannemaker." Eberuardt asked.

"This was a SS mission. Only SS soldiers were to take part." Wannemaker said.

"So because of you, twenty good soldiers were sent to their death and Operation Sealion could be cancelled because of it?" Eberuardt commented.

"Sir" Viktor said, addressing the Generalfeldmarschall.

"I believe that if we used the ten men, that I mentioned earlier. I could put together a mission that would ensure that we were able to succeed in the invasion." Viktor said.

"Explain yourself Obersleutant."

"Well Sir. The British are now expecting us to invade, using the Dover Straits. The one thing that we need would be a port. The obvious one is Dover but that is too heavily defended. There is a good port, further along the coast, at Newhaven." Viktor stated, having walked over to the large map of England and pointing to the place he was referring to.

"That port is too close to Portsmouth and the Royal Navy." Huber said.

"I understand that there is a port at Hastings." General Wannemaker said, trying to get himself back in with the Generalfeldmarschall.

"No Sir, there is no port at Hastings. There is only a beach launched fishing fleet there." Viktor stated.

"We don't have two months to train these men. We have about ten days to get them there and ready for our invasion." Eberuardt stated.

"A week is all I need to prepare these men. They are all good soldiers. All they need is some training in how to use explosives. Also it will give them time to get use to speaking English again. All the training will be carried out in English. Major Wolf speaks good English." Viktor said and waited for a response.

"Wait outside, Obersleutant." The Generalfeldmarschall ordered.

With that, Viktor saluted, turned and marched out of the office. He stood in the corridor, accompanied by the two SS Guards, for about fifteen minutes. Every time he started to walk off down the corridor, one of the guards would block his way, the same would happen if he went in the opposite direction. He was going nowhere.

All of a sudden, the door opened and out walked General Huber and the other officers. The SS Guards walked off with their Officers and Huber escorted Viktor back to his office.

"Well the Generalfeldmarschall fell for you plan. The SS General was not happy, but he had no choice but to agree. All you have to do is ensure that the plan works or both of our heads will roll." General Huber said.

Chapter 2
A good place to start the invasion

Before Viktor left General Huber's office he made contact with Axel and ordered him to get all the ten men, on their list, brought to the headquarters, no later than mid-day, tomorrow.

"Viktor, what has been going on? I've had SS following me everywhere I went, since you left. Then all of a sudden they all disappeared. What's going on?" Axel asked.

"I'll explain when I get back, tomorrow morning. In the mean time set up a quick training program for these ten men. They need to be familiar with the Schmeisser and the Luger. They also need to be trained on how to use explosives." Viktor said.

"How long have we got?"

"Just seven days, at the most." Viktor replied.

"What if I can't get all these men?" Axel asked.

"Then get some off that reserve list, but the priority is on the first ten. They are more likely to bring about the success we need." Viktor said.

"They'll be here, I promise." Axel said.

For the next hour, Axel was very busy on the telephone and sending and receiving messages around the various paratroops' regiments, where the ten men were thought to be serving. It was possibly the hardest work Axel had done for some years. Once he had contacted the appropriate Regiments, he then had to persuade the Commanding Officers that it was in the Third Reich's interest that they release these men. They would get a personal message from Hitler, for their cooperation.

Only one man, from their original list, was not available. He had been killed, in battle, only three days earlier. With that he searched down the reserve list to find a man who would match the skills of the missing soldier. He found one, Unteroffizier Jan Martin.

The reason he was not on the original list was that it was ten years since his first language was English. It was, on average, only three years the other nine.

All the soldiers were ordered to report for special duty, at Major Axel Wolf's barracks, no later than twelve o'clock, the following day. They were to get Priority One transport, on the authority of Generalfeldmarschall Lars Eberuardt.

For the remainder of that night, Axel spent the time setting out a training program for the ten men. The first thing was to get them to the camp tailor and have them measured up for the clothes that they would be wearing on the mission.

Next he wrote an order for the armourer to ensure that the following weapons were made available and that there was a nearby range, where the men could practice, with the weapons.

Other than a Luger for each man and nine Schmeisser machine guns, he also requested that the armourer gets hold of a sniper rifle, with telescopic sight. If possible he should get a gun carrying case for this weapon.

The second bit of the training was how to use explosives. That was his personnel expertise. He was about the best man with explosives, in the Wehrmacht. That is why he had been chosen as the man to train the SS soldiers, who fowled up the last mission. He was going to make sure that this bunch of soldiers, were not going to be brought down, as easily as the SS.

From the moment they walked in the barracks, they would be ordered to only speak in English. Any one caught speaking in German, even swearing, would be punished.

Axel thought that it was very important that they regained their language skills, as soon as possible and that they were comfortable in the English language.

At four o'clock in the morning, Axel returned to the Officer's Mess and to his room. He did not bother to undress, he just took off his boots and lay down on his bed and was soon fast asleep.

On his way into the Mess he had asked the duty steward to ensure that he was woken up, no later than seven thirty, in the morning. Being dead to the world, Axel had forgotten his request and was not at all happy at being woken up, just after falling to sleep. Once he was told the time, he dismissed the steward and asked that he could have breakfast in thirty minutes, in his room.

The steward left his room with the intention of returning with the officer's breakfast, in half an hour.

Axel was half way through having his wash when his bedroom door opened and in walked Viktor. Seeing that Axel was already up, he sat on his bed and waited for him to finish shaving.

"Did you get it all done? Did you get all the men we wanted?" Viktor asked.

"Yes, all but one, Leopold Maurer. He was killed, in battle, three days ago. I have replaced him with Underoffizier Jan Martin." Axel reported.

"When do we expect them?"

"They have all been told to report, no later then twelve o'clock, today." Axel said.

"Good. Let's go and have breakfast, I have a lot to tell you, before we get to the office." Viktor said.

Once Axel had finished his ablutions, got dressed and replaced his boots, the two of then walked to the dinning room, just as the steward was carrying a covered tray, towards the corridor that would have led him to Axel's room.

He did not need telling, he returned the tray to the kitchen and then walked up to the table where the two officers had just sat at and asked if they wanted breakfast. They gave their orders and he went back to the kitchen to get what they had ordered.

Once the steward had left, Viktor told Axel what had happened in Berlin. He explained how he had come up with the new plan. He felt that this could save the project and, most importantly, their lives.

It was for this reason that the SS were following Axel.

If it was decided in Berlin, that the two of them were responsible for the failure of the mission, they would both have been arrested, court marshalled and, most likely shot.

Viktor quickly outlined the plan he had left with General Huber. It would be put before Generalfeldmarschall Eberuardt and if he approved it, then they would start putting it into operation, today. That was why it was important for him to get all the men on their list.

Axel listened to the plan and realised that it had two main advantages, over the last one.

Firstly the men would be operating in an unexpected part of the English South coast, along way from known centres for the British forces. Secondly, the men being used were properly trained soldiers and who would expect such a group to land by sea.

After they had eaten their breakfast, the two of them walked over to their barrack block. They had been allocated a separate barrack block, when they were training the SS soldiers. This had given them a certain level of secrecy, as it was separate from the rest of the camp. It also allowed all those, in training and their instructors to inter mix, not just while carrying out the training but in the down time, as well. In this way the trainees could clarify training issues, away from the training classrooms or field training. It had not worked particularly well with the SS as they did not mix well with others, outside the SS.

Their offices were on the second floor of the first building, at their disposal. Axel's was quite a large room, but he needed this for all the maps and plans that he always need to display and work on. Viktor's office was much the same size as Axel's but far more formal. Being an Obersleutant, he had a certain status to uphold. It was here that any meetings were held, about the missions. It was here, also, that he had confronted General Wannemaker about the unsuitability of most of his SS troops, for that failed mission.

When he rounded his desk he noticed a message, sitting in the middle of his leather surrounded writing pad. 'Plan approved' signed by General Huber.

"Axel, it's approved." Viktor shouted out, hoping that Axel could hear him.

Instead of holding their meeting in Viktor's office; Viktor went into Axel's office, where all the maps were situated, and they worked for the next three hours to pad out the details of the plan. By the time they had finished, they were not really in a fit state to carry out any training or introductions with the ten men they expected to arrive in a couple of hours. They named this mission, Operation 'Tramp'. This name came from the nickname they had given the officer, who would be leading the operation.

They decide that they would make use of one of the barrack rooms, downstairs, to have 'forty winks'. Neither of them had slept much last night and today was likely to be another long one.

After all, these ten men's lives would depend on them both being good enough to ensure that the training they were about to receive, was up to the highest standard.

Because of the timing of the actual invasion was drawing very near, they still required a small force to be landed in England. To be there to assist the successful landing of a significantly large army and its support troops, so that they could secure a sufficiently large bridgehead. In that way they ensured that they would not be driven back into the sea.

For this second landing they chose to concentrate on a relatively short part of the English South coast. They would make sure that these men could deliver, not only a secure landing area but, most importantly an undamaged port. For this reason they had chosen an area from Eastbourne, then East along to Newhaven.

The most important attribute they needed from the men they sent, was not their military skills but the fact that they spoke English like a native. They hoped that in the short time they had, once they gathered the team together, they could train them how to use explosives and be able to shoot effectively.

They were lucky, in the officer they selected, Hauptmann Simon Krause. He had been brought up in England, while his father worked for a company in Enfield. He had been brought up bilingual. He went to an English school but, at home, he spoke only German. A man like this was invaluable for the mission.

The other nine men spoke English, without a German accent. Three of them, Underoffizier Jan Martin, Obergefreiter Karl Braun and Gefreiter Richard Hartmann were brought up in America, two, Wachtmeister Fritz Jung and Underoffizier Hans Lange, in Canada and the other four, Unterfeldwebel Hans Schmid, Gefreiter Steffen Koch, Obergefreiter Simon Baecker and Fahnenjunker-Gefreiter Erich Drechsler from around the world but all went to English speaking schools

Another fact that was coming to light was that although the SS were wearing civilian clothes, they were not English clothes. They would have to find a way around that.

An immediate order was sent to the German Embassy, in Dublin. The Ambassador was asked get one of his agents to purchase sufficient clothes, of the type listed, for these men. He was given the sizes they required. In this way the camp tailor would have less work to do to ensure that the clothes fitted each of the men, correctly.

It took, nearly to the day before the men were due to leave for England, for the clothes to arrive in Calais. In the mean time, they were given similar clothing to wear, so that they got use to them.

From the moment Axel, greeted the soldiers, he spoke to them in English. His was more German school boy English but he spoke it well and would have allowed him to get about in England, but not at the moment, with a German accent.

The men were ordered to speak only in English. It was important that they could converse in perfect English and for it to be natural to them.

Few of them had spoken any English, since they returned to Germany in the late 1930's, so they were a bit rusty.

Axel told them that if any of them were heard speaking German, all ten of them would be expected to do twenty press ups, each. They were not happy with this punishment, especially when they were told that applied to them the whole time they were in these barracks, in training or not.

Another thing that they were not happy about was the fact that they would be expected to use their English names, while training. The names had been specially chosen so that they were similar to their German names, in that way they were less likely to get caught out.

Once they were in England, if they allowed themselves to slip into German, it could mean that they were either shot, or arrested and imprisoned for the rest of the war. It was explained that it was because of this failure, of the previous mission, that they had been called up at such short notice.

Only Hauptmann Krause was permitted to speak German, and then only while talking to the High Commanders of the mission.

While the Wehrmacht soldiers were being trained for their individual tasks, the German navy was ordered to capture an English fishing boat. This was not a welcome diversion from their normal work but as this order came from Berlin, it was carried out.

On Tuesday 10th September 1940, an E-boat was dispatched to find and capture an English fishing boat, preferably one that operated along the south coast of England. Once they located one, they had little difficulty in boarding the vessel and taking control. The crew were interned in a German prisoner of war camp.

By that afternoon Leutnant zur Tobias Schiffer was handed the fishing boat and ordered to take it out and get use to how it sailed. He was given three men. One was a ships engineer and the others were just normal ratings.

Tobias made sure that the boat was seaworthy and that it was fit to sail across the channel, with the men and equipment he had been told he would be carrying.

He soon found that this was a very small boat and with the men and equipment he would be carrying, he would not be able to carry any crew, just himself.

Once he returned to port, he reported his findings and his worry about not being able to even carry the engineer. He was firmly told that only these men and their equipment were important. He would have to cope, the best he could. With that he returned to the boat and went down to the cramped engine space.

To call it a room would be an exaggeration. The navy engineer gave him a full briefing as to how the engine had been behaving, while they were out at sea and advised him how best to cope, if the engine played up.

On the Wednesday, the 11th, he took the boat out by himself, to see if he felt comfortable in being able to get these men over to England. The engine seemed to run well, provided that he did not go above half throttle.

That meant that it may take a bit longer than had been planned. He would have to ask that they left earlier, to ensure the mission was on time, when they reached the dropping off point.

If he missed the high tide then he would not be able to land the men, until the next high tide.

For the rest of the day, he spent his time going over the charts he had been given of the channel and, more importantly, the area that needed his particular skills, taking this fishing boat into the estuary and up the river.

At the final briefing for the mission, Tobias was invited to attend the final half an hour. What they had discussed before his arrival was top secret.

Whatever the men would be doing, once he got them ashore, was of no importance to him. This final half an hour was concerned with the loading of the boat and the time they would be leaving the port of Calais.

The original orders had been for them to leave at nine o'clock, in the evening of Thursday 12th September 1940, arriving in the Cuckmere River at five o'clock the following morning.

This is where Tobias spoke up. He reported that as he was responsible for the fishing boat and that he could not take any crew with him, he would need to go much slower, to ensure that the engine was able to get them there safely.

Generalmajor Eberhardt was not at all happy at this change but after a long discussion with Viktor, who was in actual charge of the mission, it was decided that Tobias could have his way and the party would leave the port at five thirty, that evening.

That final day was then a hectic one for the camp tailor, to ensure that each man had the correctly fitting clothes and that the 'Tramps' clothes looked sufficiently well worn and dishevelled.

At four thirty, the team of saboteurs arrived at the dock side and started to load their equipment onto the fishing boat. Tobias had not been told that, among the things he would have to stow in the hold, was a motor bike. He could see no way in which that was going to get through the hatch.

Tobias took Hauptmann Krause to one side and explained that he did not think that bringing a motor bike on the boat was a good thing, as it would have to be stowed on the deck. Krause said that it was very important that they carried it and so he detailed off Gefreiter Koch to go and find some tarpaulin, so that they could ensure that it was covered and, hopefully kept water proof.

Once everything was loaded and stowed on board, Tobias asked Viktor for permission to set sail. This was given and so he instructed the men on the dock side to release the ropes. He had already given orders for two of his 'passengers' to bring the ropes on board the fishing boat, once they were released.

On the way over he got together three of the men and told them that he needed them to do some special work, once they were coming into the river mouth.

He had two knotted ropes, and on the end of each one was a weight.

Tobias showed them what he needed them to do and the signals he required them to give. It took about half an hour to complete the training.

In the mean time Krause had taken the helm and was steering the boat on the compass heading that Tobias had told him to follow. With the training completed Tobias returned to the wheel house and checked that they were still on the course he had set.

After a further half an hour, Tobias changed course and headed north. Now he was heading directly towards the English coast. After an hour, he took readings, from the stars and plotted his exact position. He was very pleased, he was on course and he could now turn east. He could now keep a good distance from the coastal patrols, before he needed to head north again and, hopefully, he would arrive just off Beachy Head.

Day one – Friday 13th September 1940

Chapter 3
Give me the Baltic any day

Bringing the fishing boat into the mouth of the River Cuckmere was a lot more difficult than Tobias had though it would be. The men on board were not sailors, with the exception of him self. He had worked on fishing boats since he was ten years old but where he sailed was the Baltic Sea, not the English Channel.

They had achieved the first objective of crossing the channel and so far had reached a point off Beachy Head, before daybreak. The reason Tobias had been chosen for this mission was his excellent navigational ability.

He had brought them to within half a mile of the lighthouse before they could even make out the shape of the cliffs above the lighthouse.

Tobias now steered the fishing boat off towards the gap in the Seven Sisters range of cliffs that marked the estuary of the River Cuckmere. It was now that his knowledge of the charts and overall seamanship would be put to the test.

The river mouth was narrow and reportedly to be fairly silted up. They had planned to arrive at high tide. In that way they should be able to get the keel of the boat over the silt and then sail a short distance up the river.

He had planned it well and was aware of the load he would be carrying, when he made his calculations. If everything went well he would be able to bring the boat up the river a bit, unload his cargo of men and equipment and get back into open sea before the tide turned and his boat was trapped in the estuary. Being lighter when he left the river mouth would mean that he needed less water under the keel to sail out to sea.

The sun was just coming over the horizon as he approached the river mouth. This gave him just enough light to see where he was going. He looked at his watch and saw that he was just about on time; soon it would be high tide. He steered the boat towards the river mouth.

At the bow were two men, one on each side, holding weighted ropes. Tobias had arranged a system of signals from these men that would tell him how much water was under him as he approached the silt. He gave the signal for the men to start testing the depth of the water. Provided the weight did not reach the bottom, before all the rope had followed it, then there was sufficient depth of water, with some to spare. If the weight did reach the bottom, then the man would hold up his arm to lift the weight off the bottom. As soon as he felt it come of the bottom he would stop. Holding up his arm, so that Tobias could see how deep the water was.

By watching the men he was able to adjust the direction of the boat. At one time the man on the starboard side lifted his hand very high. This brought an immediate reaction from Tobias, he swung the wheel over to bring about a change in direction but before the bow moved to far he brought it back again.

He knew that at this point the passage was very narrow so if he went too far he wound find the same signal coming from the port side man. Tobias watched both men constantly now; each one of them were raising their arms but not enough for Tobias to need to change direction. He had planned this well, he needed to see the arms raised so he knew exactly where he was. He had spent several days practicing this approach, adjusting the rope length to exactly what he wanted. All this work was now paying off.

By the time they were into the river, the light had increased so that they could see exactly where they were going. It also meant that they could be seen.

All the German soldiers had been given English names and dressed in English clothes. For the last two weeks they had been working in clothes like these, talking English and calling each other by their adopted names. Now they were about to find out if all their training, their English and clothes would hold up to scrutiny.

Simon Johns, their Hauptmann now took charge of the landing. Tobias had done his job by getting them into the River Cuckmere, now it was time for the soldiers to take over and do their part.

Chapter 4
The binders working now

It was day break on Friday 13th September 1940 and Jack Fintch had been up for some time. Jack hadn't been called up for war service because he was in a reserved occupation. He was an agricultural engineer and was needed to help in the war effort of the farmers, who had to work much harder to produce more food for the country. Although many of the younger farm workers had enlisted, to fight for their country, some, like Jack, were needed to 'fight' on the land.

Without the farm equipment being kept in good order, the farmers would not be able to meet the requirements of the Ministry of Food. The ministry was forever increasing the amount of food they needed the farmers to produce, from each acre of land. In many cases they were required to bring unproductive land in to use. It was only from this extra effort that the country could hope to feed itself.

It was not that easy, during harvest time, for him to get a full night's sleep. Due to the scarcity of people in his trade, he was required to support up to twenty farms, in the area. If anything went wrong with any farm equipment, then he had to ensure that it was repaired as soon as possible.

Last night his brother-in-law, Frank Clark, had reported to him that, while cutting the sheaves of wheat, the blade of the binder had caught a large flint and been buckled. This then got jammed into its guiding rail. As a consequence the binder was out of action until the blade was free and ready for cutting again. The tractor, used to pull the binder, had an early night. The land girls could also get home early, as there were no sheaf's of wheat to stack.

Time was always precious, it was important that no crops were wasted and that as much cereal was got to market as possible. There were a few land girls, to help out but as this was the first harvest of the war, proper, the extra workers had not yet been organised properly.

It was because of this that any fine days were used to their fullest and today was forecast to be a very fine day so they would be able to get out into the fields earlier than usual, provided Jack could repair the binder.

Due to the importance of Jacks job, he was not only allowed to drive a van but also had extra petrol coupons so that he could get about his work more efficiently. Jack's van was about ten years old, but he had kept it well serviced and repaired, over this time but it was starting to show its age.

Because of the harvest he had not been able to carry out some preventative work on his van, he was just keeping his fingers crossed that it did not fail him, before he could carry out the repair.

Jack worked for Mr Savage at Bishop's Farm, in Bishopstone, on the Newhaven side of Seaford from where he was this morning. Today he was working on the binder belonging to Mr Young at Chryston Farm, in a field near Seaford Head, overlooking the Cuckmere estuary.

Most of the farmers could keep their machinery in reasonable shape but, if anything broke or was outside their own skills, then they would need the services of a skilled agricultural mechanic, and the local man was Jack Fintch.

He had arrived at the gate to the field, in his van, at about four fifteen. The sun had not yet started to appear on the skyline over Beachy Head. Once the gate was open, he drove into the field and over to the deserted binder, on the far side of the field. He was hoping that he would not need to use his brazier to get the blade out of the rail; if he did then harvest would be a little late today.

Jack had a good range of tools in his van, those he or the farmer had purchased, others either he or the local blacksmith had made for him. If you are working by yourself, out in some deserted field, you need the right tools with you and ones that allow you to work with both of your hands. It is no good needing to work on something and not having a hand free to carry out the repair.

It didn't take long for him to find the offending blades. They were set three teeth in from the right hand side of the row of cutting blades. Each tooth was a separate item, bolted on to the guide rail. It was the edges of these teeth that did the cutting. These two teeth were well and truly buckled and one of the retaining bolts had been sheered off, during its confrontation with the flint and the guards. He would need to replace one of the teeth but the other one could go back on once he had hammered it flat again.

He was lucky that it had been Frank that had been in charge of the binder, when this happened. He had known others who would have continued on and totally destroyed both the cutting blade and the guards, requiring them all to be replaced. Today he would have about an hours work to remove the teeth, take out the whole blade, replace the teeth and ensure that the guard was not damaged, otherwise it would also need replacing.

He was lucky, with this particular binder as it had been well looked after and as a consequence, all the nuts and bolts were easy to undo. This made his task much easier as it was not long before he had the cutting rail out of the machine. His next task was to remove the bent guard and refit it with one that he carried in his box of bits and pieces. One of the teeth was bent, beyond repair but the second one was easy to hammer straight and refit. He always carried spare teeth, in his van, so was able to replace the damaged one, from his box of spare parts.

22

Once he had checked that the teeth were fitted, he slid them into the guide rail and ensured that they moved to and throw easily. When he was satisfied that everything was OK, he took the cutting rail back out and spent the next ten minutes sharpening all the teeth, ready for their work, later today.

Normally they would only need sharpening every two weeks, during harvest, but he knew that this would be due within the next few days. While he had them out it was more effective to do the work now.

After three quarters of an hour, as he was reassembling all the parts, he noticed a fishing boat making its way up the River Cuckmere.

Jack had lived in these parts for about ten years and never seen such a thing. Fishing boats normally sailed into Newhaven port, just a few miles further west, along the coast. He could understand it if a gale was blowing but it was a clear morning, with light winds and the sea seemed to be relatively calm.

As he looked he noticed that there were several men on the deck and the boat appeared to be being manoeuvring towards the river bank, two hundred yards, upstream. Were these black marketeers?

Jack put down his tools and lent the blade against the binder. In his van he had several secret compartments, to protect items that he didn't want to fall into any thieves hands.

He went to one, he had made just under the dashboard. With a slight slide to one side the compartment door opened, downwards, and out dropped a telescope.

With the scope in his hands he returned to the binder and stood with the machine between himself and the fishing boat. Leaning on the drivers seat he could open the telescope and rest his arms so as to keep it as still as possible. It took him only a moment to focus on the fishing boat and the men on it.

He watched with puzzlement at what was going on. These men did not look like fishermen; they appeared to be dressed more as farm workers, travellers and the like.

Once the fishing boat had been brought alongside the river bank, two men jumped out, each holding a rope. They pulled on their ropes, until the boat was firmly against the bank. They then sat down and braced themselves, so as to hold the boat firm.

Once this was completed, the rest of the men, on board, started to unload the boat. What was being unloaded was not fish, as he might have expected to be unloaded, if these were black-marketers, but they were taking off suitcases, bicycles and a motor bike.

Jack got very worried when he noticed that one of the men had over his shoulder what looked like a gun bag. From this range, he was not sure but it was a gun of some sort.

The man who had this was dressed as a farm worker but the bag was not the sort used to carry a shot gun. So what would such a man want with another type of weapon? Why were they landing from a fishing boat at this time in the morning?

He continued to watch the men unload their items from the fishing boat. Once this was completed, the two men, who had been holding the ropes, stood up and, once they had coiled up the ropes, threw them back on board the boat. The boat drifted into mid-stream and the captain then turned it around and headed back out to sea. While this was going on, the men gathered around a man, who looked more like a tramp than anything else.

After about ten minutes the group started to disperse and for a spit second Jack thought that he saw one of the men giving the 'Tramp' a Nazi salute. He was not sure what to make of that, it puzzled him some. Was the man having a joke, at the tramps expense or was this for real?

Just as he was about to look at where the men were going he heard the sound of someone coming over the field, on a bicycle and ringing his bell.

Jack turned around and waived to the man to stop the noise. It was Frank, coming to see if he had been able to repair the binder. If so then he could tell the rest of the workers that they would be harvesting today.

Frank had known Jack for many years and they had developed a signal system, between them. Usually it was so that they could catch rabbits, pheasants and the like but was just as useful now there was a war on and an invasion possible.

As Frank joined Jack he was handed the telescope and Jack indicated the men by the river.

"What do you make of those?" asked Jack.

Frank looked from one to the other, as they gathered their belongings and headed towards the road, at Exceet Bridge. Like Jack he found it unusual to see so many men at this time of the morning.

He couldn't understand the mixture of men, farm workers; a fisherman, a tramp and what looked like a couple of travelling salesmen.

"What are they doing there?" he asked.

"I don't know, but they were landed by that fishing boat," Jack said as he pointed to the boat, just reaching the sea currents and swell.

They looked at each other, with all the reports of the Germans readying to invade England, had it started or were these men the advanced guard?

Frank was the first to speak,

"You finish the repairs to the binder and then go and give John a message to pass on to the Sussex Patrol. I'll go and tell Mr Savage what we've seen. I'll tell him that you will come to the New Barn at eight o'clock. There you'll give him the details of what you saw." He said as he looked at his pocket watch.

Jack looked at his pocket watch. He had quite a lot to do and getting the message to John would take a while but he felt he had enough time to do all this, as well as getting to the rendezvous at eight.

With that done, Frank got back onto his bike and peddled fast across the field, through the gate and onto the road. Jack did not stop to watch him go, it was important that he finished his work, so that the harvest could be continued today.

Having done all the hard work, earlier, all he had to do now was put everything back together, test that it worked and leave it for the farm workers and land girls to arrive later.

In the mean time Frank was well on his way to find Mr Savage, at Bishop's Farm. Although Frank did not work for him, it was him that needed to know about these men and decide what action should be taken.

For most civilians, such a sighting would be reported to the police but for Jack and Frank they were not just civilians, they were members of the Auxiliary Forces, a Top Secret branch of the Home Guard.

If the truth were known, they were not even in the Home Guard, although they did posses Home Guard uniforms, with the insignia of the 203rd battalion. No such battalion ever existed.

These men were in the British Resistance. Both Jack and Frank belonged to the Bishopstone patrol. It was a small unit with just five members. Their leader was Jack's employer and the other members included the post master and another farm worker, from the area.

Their occupations gave them good covers for their movements, if the Germans did invade it would allow them access to their secret hide-a-ways with the arms and explosives they would need to wreak havoc on the invading German Army.

They had been recruited several months earlier and each had undergone training, at the Auxiliary Forces training centre at Coleshill House.

The training consisted of how to use the various weapons, which were to be put at their disposal and, the fun part, explosive training. Some of it was how to use plastic explosive but other included home made explosives and Molotov cocktails.

Because of the early hour, it was about six o'clock when Frank arrived at the farm house. Mr Savage was still in the house and had not yet gone off to one of the fields on the farm.

"Mr Savage, we have a problem with the binder." Frank reported, when he was shown into the farm kitchen by Mrs Savage. This was a code word that they had arranged if there was something to do with the war that needed urgent attention.

"I'll come over to the barn and you can show me," said Mr Savage as he picked up a slice of bread and butter.

Frank didn't wait for Mr Savage, he headed out to the barn and when he arrived he ensured that there was no one else around. What they had to discuss was not for preying ears.

By the time Frank had ensured privacy, Mr Savage had arrived.

"What's the problem Frank?" he asked.

"Sir, I was up at the Head to check whether Jack had repaired the binder for Mr Young. The cutter had been damaged by a flint when we were bringing in the harvest, yesterday."

"Yes but why did we need to talk?" asked Mr Savage again.

"Jack spotted some men being landed by a fishing boat, at the river bank."

Frank let that sink in for a moment then continued, "These men were all dressed in different clothing, some looked like farm workers, others as travellers and one, who looked like a tramp."

"You seem to think the tramp is important, don't you Frank?" said Mr Savage.

"Both Jack and I do, Jack said that one of the men appeared to salute him as they departed." Frank reported.

From briefings they had received from, the Sussex Patrol Leader (the group of regular soldiers who were there to offer support for the various Auxiliary units), they were expecting the Germans to invade along this part of the coast, sometime in the next month.

Could this be an advance party or a group of saboteurs? They had heard that a group of German Paratroopers had landed in Kent but had soon been rounded up.

"Where did they go?" Mr Savage asked.

"They headed towards Exceet Bridge, some on bicycles, one on a motor bike and the rest on foot." Frank said.

"But where did they go, from there?"

"I didn't stop to find out and Jack had to finish off his work, so that we could get harvesting again today." Frank said. "I did tell Jack to go and report what we had seen to John, so he could get the message to the patrol."

"Good thinking Frank, I'd better get in touch with the police and inform them. Now you get back to your farm and get on with the harvest. Then come back here and we'll plan what we need to do." Mr Savage ordered.

"I told Jack to meet us at New Barn at eight o'clock, after he had done his errand. I though that would be a better place to meet, less people to overhear what we were up to," said Frank.

"OK, I'll be at New Barn at eight o'clock then," said Mr Savage.

Chapter 5
Funny place for an airfield

Jack took fifteen minutes to complete repairing the binder and testing it, to ensure that the cutting blades ran smoothly. During this time he had kept an eye on the men who had landed by the river, as he worked. They had all disappeared out of his sight now. He had made a quick mental note of the number of men, rough descriptions and their mode of transport. But he made a particular note about the 'Tramp'.

Having finished his work, he now collected up all his tools and put them in the various boxes and secured them in the back of his van. This was to ensure that he could find them again, the next time they were needed. The telescope he put back into its secret compartment. He made one last look around the area, moved the binder backwards, to ensure that he had left nothing underneath.

Jack got behind the steering wheel, but before he started the van's engine he reached into the glove compartment and took out his notebook and pencil. Now he could make a note of what he had seen. He included brief descriptions of each of the men and a particular note about the 'Tramp'. That salute was starting to worry Jack. Happy that he had done a good job, he then drove off, over the field, to the gate. Once through the gate he got out, fastened it behind him and drove off.

Frank had said that he was to report all that they had seen to John, his younger brother, in Jevington. It was a bit out of Jacks way. He still had to get back home, in Seaford for his breakfast before returning to Bishop's Farm for the meeting at eight o'clock. The farmer at Folkington Bishop's Farm was waiting for him to come and repair a tractor, but that would have to wait until after the meeting. His initial priority was to deliver this message to John.

One thing had been drummed into all members of the Auxiliary Units was that their identity was to remain secret, if, by any chance, anyone, outside the 'force' found out about them, it was their duty to arrange for that person to be killed, if the Germans ever did invade England.

One person already high on their 'hit list' was the Chief of Police. He had interviewed all members of the Auxiliary Forces and was the only person who knew the identity of all the members of the Auxiliary Forces units, in East Sussex. It didn't matter if the person was a member of their own family. Utmost secrecy was to be maintained. It had only been at a very recent briefing, by their unit leader, Mr Savage, that Frank and Jack had known John was involved in their work.

They were told that John had been recruited for two reasons, one he was to be a link between the various groups, in East Sussex, and the Sussex Patrol.

The second was that he was to ensure that the special Auxiliary Forces hideout, in Holt's wood, in his village, was not disturbed. This hideout had been specially designed so that it could hold twenty men, at a time.

It was stocked with sufficient food for these men, to last a month. There was also an extensive arsenal, so that they could replenish any arms or explosives, which they may have had to discard, when leaving their home area.

John had not been told about any of the members of the various groups but would recognise them if they gave the password – 'Hare'. He would reply – 'Rabbit'.

As Jack thought that what he was reporting was very important, instead of using the dead letter drop, a secret drop down shelf, hidden in the village telephone box. He would have to find John and hand him the message. Jack couldn't wait to see his brother's face, when he gave him the password.

Once he joined the main coast road, instead of heading left towards Seaford, his home and breakfast, he turned right, towards Eastbourne. With that he was heading down the hill towards Exceat Bridge. As he drove down the hill he noticed two men, on bikes, coming up the hill, towards him. From what he had seen earlier, they appeared to be two of the men he had noticed, disembarking from the fishing boat.

Both men were dressed as travelling salesmen. One of the men waived out to him so Jack returned his waive.

As he neared the bridge he saw a man walking towards him. This man was dressed like a farm worker and was carrying a suitcase. The fact that he had the suitcase showed that he didn't live around here.

Jack knew all the farms and farm workers in this area. He had lived in this part of the county all of his life and went to school or worked with most of them. Since the start of the war he had got to know a lot more.

He was on call to over twenty farms in a ten mile radius and had met all the workers on these farms and was also getting to know the new land girls, as well.

Having crossed the bridge, he noticed, about two hundred yards ahead of him, two men. They disappeared, before he reached them, by turning down the road that led to Littleington. That was five in all; there were ten in the party so what had happened to the remaining five?

As he reached the junction with the road for Littleington, he changed down to bottom gear. He had a short 'S' bend to negotiate and then he would have the long and steep uphill to manage, to take him out of the Cuckmere valley. With his van heavily laden, especially with some extras, he had started carrying since joining the Auxiliary Forces. The van would need all the power he could muster, to get up Exceat Hill.

As he turned the last corner, before the hill, he came across the 'Tramp'. He was stood out in the road, with his hand up, indicating for Jack to stop. Other than run him down there was not much else he could do but stop.

"What the hell do you think you're doing?" shouted Jack, out of the driver's window.

"Give me a lift mister," said the 'Tramp'.

"I don't give lifts to tramps," said Jack, angrily.

"Only to the top of the hill, I'll walk from there, only I have come a long way and that hill will kill me." The 'Tramp' pleaded.

Jack was surprised at the sound of this mans voice, he was not from around here, he sounded more like one of these officers he had met recently, from the army, well educated men from private schools.

What was he doing as a tramp? By giving him a lift, maybe he could find out more about him, before giving his report to John.

"OK, get in. Just to the top of the hill though," ordered Jack.

The 'Tramp' got in and put the bag, he was carrying, on his lap.

Jack immediately noticed, now the man was closer to him, was that there wasn't the smell of an unwashed man but of the sea. This man had a clean bouquet about him. Although he was not clean shaven, there was only about a weeks' growth on his face. All his clothes appeared to be made with new material but made to look that they were well worn. This confirmed what he had suspected; these men were not what they appeared to be.

"Thank you," said the tramp. "My name's Simon, I'm trying to get to Dover and see my sister."

"You've a long way to go then," replied Jack as he started the van moving again.

Exceat hill was very steep and long, the extra weight he was now carrying made the van struggle, he feared that he may blow a gasket or the big ends, before he reached the top.

This reminded him that he must spend some time giving the van a really good service and replace the gaskets before any real damage is caused. He would find it very difficult to replace the van or get a replacement engine, if it went completely.

"Ever been around here before?" asked Jack

"No never. I came from Dover and moved to Norfolk some years ago," replied Simon.

Jack was going to say that he was also a long way from Norfolk but refrained from doing so, he was a tramp after all and they travel all over the place, rarely in a straight line.

Once the van had managed to reach the top of the hill Jack decided not to let the tramp off here, he would take him along to Friston, where he would have to turn off for Jevington. In the mean time he would be able to find out a little more about Simon.

"I'll take you along to Friston pond," said Jack. "That'll save you about a mile and a half walk".

"Thank you, you're most kind."

This mans accent was neither from Kent or Norfolk, thought Jack. He didn't have a foreign accent but he was not from where he said he was from, that he was sure of. This was no tramp.

As Jack drove along they spoke little. Half way along the road, as they reached South Hill, to the right of the road, a military camp came into view.

He knew what it was, as he had passed it many times and he had been informed about its role in the war, at one of their many briefings.

This was an emergency airfield, to be used by allied airmen if their aircraft were too damaged for them to get them back to their home airfield.

"This is a funny place to have an airfield," said Simon, although there were no signs up to show what type of establishment it was.

"Is that what it is?" said Jack. "We had always wondered what they had built there!"

Jack didn't look at Simon, had he have done so he would have known that Jack was lying. If he was a German, he may well have tried to kill Jack, to stop him telling the authorities about him.

When they had reached Friston Pond, Jack pulled up. Pointing ahead he said "That's the road to Eastbourne; I have to take this one, more tractors to repair."

It was as much an order as anything else. He now wanted to get this man away from him as quickly as possible.

"Thank you for the lift." Simon said, as he closed the van door.

Jack drove off, turned of to the left and went down the hill towards Jevington. The sign posts had been removed so Simon would not know where Jack was going to now. That was the reason Jack had pointed out the road to Eastbourne, as it was not signposted. Once he got to the bottom of the hill, Jack pulled up and took out his notebook and pencil. He needed to add some notes about his meeting with the Simon.

Now he had to find his brother.

Chapter 6
This message is urgent

Jack put away his pencil and tucked, the torn out page, into his shirt pocket, then started the van moving off again. He would have to stop off at Oxendean Farm and see if John was there or at least, if anyone knew where he was working today. Being this early in the morning, it was coming up to seven o'clock, he expected he would still be in the farm yard, preparing for the days jobs.

As he approached the track, that would lead him into the farm buildings, he noticed a familiar figure standing, with a carthorse, next to the dew pond, in the field to his right. It was John.

Jack stopped the van at the side of the road, got out and walked over to his brother.

"Morning John," Jack said as he approached him.

"God, what are you doing here?" asked John.

"Aren't you pleased to see me then?" Jack asked.

"I'm always pleased to see you but you're not due to visit this farm for a week, or two."

"No I had to see you."

"Don't tell me mums worried about me again." John said

"Rabbit" was all Jack said

John turned around and looked to see if there were any rabbits about, he hadn't seen any earlier. There was nothing there. He turned back and looked at his brother. Just as he was about to ask him what he was on about, Jack repeated the word.

"Rabbit"

It suddenly twigged, what Jack was saying.

"Hare" John replied.

"I've an urgent message that needs to get to the Sussex Patrol. I saw ten men being landed from a fishing boat, at Exceat. They weren't fishermen either." Jack said, earnestly.

"I'll see that they know about this straight away." John said.

Jack reached into his shirt pocket and handed John the page out of his notebook and asked him to give his regards to Wendy.

John watched Jack return to his van. Immediately he turned around and picked up the reins and started to lead Hercules back to his stables. As he walked along, he opened the paper that Jack had handed him and started to read what he had written.

Fishing Boat in Cuckmere River – 6am.
Ten men got off boat.
2 men dressed like travelling salesmen, with bicycles
6 men dressed like farm workers, one with motor bike
1 appeared to be a fisherman
1 man looked like a tramp

Men gathered around and it appeared that the tramp was their leader.
One of the farm workers gave him a salute?
I passed the salesmen going up the hill towards Seaford.
2 of the farm workers were heading down the road to West Dean
I gave the Tramp a lift to Friston Pond.
The Tramp said he was going to Dove to visit family. He knew that the camp at South Hill was an airfield?
The Tramp dressed right but the clothes were new. He didn't smell, called himself Simon.
He spoke English like a posh school boy.
He was walking towards Eastbourne.

This was very important. John would have to get this information to the Sussex Patrol as quickly as he could. By now he was entering the farm yard and heading towards Hercules's stable.

"I thought I said that you were to go to Butcher's Hole, today?" called Mr Trusler, the farm foreman.

"Sorry Mr Trusler, I'm not feeling well, I need to go home."

"You've got to be dead before you can just go home."

"Well if I don't go home, you may well find me dead in the field." John said, forcefully.

Before Mr Trusler could say anything else, John had taken Hercules to his stable and was making sure that he was settled in for the day. He didn't turn around to confront Mr Trusler, again. He just headed for his bicycle and rode down the twitten and headed off home, along the road leading back to the village.

Note: What John did with this message, is told in the authors book 'The Pheasant'.

With the message delivered, Jack had returned to his van and instead of going to Folkington Bishop's Farm, he turned the van around. He returned to Friston pond and headed back to Exceat Bridge. He didn't expect to see any of the men he observed earlier, on the road, but he did keep an eye out for them.

Once he had crossed the Exceat Bridge, he took his pocket watch out of his jacket pocket and checked the time. It was only about Seven Thirty if he was quick he would have time to stop off at his home, in Seaford, grab a bit of breakfast and pick up his packed lunch, that Mary would have ready for him. The farm he worked at was Bishop's Farm in Bishopstone. This was on the far side of Seaford, so as long as he didn't stay to long, he would be able to get to the meeting with Mr Savage and Frank.

Mary was surprised that Jack was so late, he had gone out very early and so she expected him home for his breakfast at about seven o'clock.

"Sorry I'm late. Frank had really buggered up the binder's blades." Jack lied. "I can't stop long. I've a meeting at the farm at eight."

"I've got your sandwiches ready and a bottle of tea, for your lunch." Mary said. "I'll have your breakfast on the table by the time you've cleaned those grubby hands."

Once he had eaten his breakfast he picked up his lunch, kissed Mary and ran out of the house. He just hoped that the roads were clear, or he would be late.

He wouldn't go to the farm but head for the nearest of their two hides, the one at New Barn. Jack arrived just as he saw Mr Savage walking over the field, from the farm house.

Good he wasn't late. He drew up his van, around the far side of the barn, out of the view from the nearest houses, some of who may have seen him arriving.

"Morning Sir," Jack greeted Mr Savage.

"Morning Jack," Mr Savage replied.

"What's this all about then?" he asked Jack.

"Frank said that he thought that we should talk this out in the hide." Jack said.

By this time the two of them had reached the back of the barn. Jack went around to the rear of the pile of coal and removed the three railway sleepers, which were propped up against the coal. This was the entrance to their hide.

Jack knocked at the door, which was hidden behind the sleepers. Within a moment, the door opened, inwardly and Frank was stood there, with a big smile on his face.

From the outside this was just a pile of coal, for use by the traction engine but it had been skilfully built to hide the corrugate Iron building that was beneath it.

The room they walked into was quite big. The floor had been lowered by about three feet from the ground level, surrounding it. This was to insure that it still retained its height but did not mean that the coal heap was too large and cause suspicion.

Frank had been busy since he arrived. He had lit a couple of lanterns and set out the table and three chairs. He had prepared the map board and placed it on the table and lent the top of the board against the side wall of the hide.

He had everything ready for the meeting. Time was tight so the quicker they could discuss this matter the quicker that the three of them could get back to the days work.

Once the three of them were seated, Mr Savage asked Jack to explain what he had seen and why he thought this meeting was so important.

"I was up on the hill, overlooking the Cuckmere estuary, repairing a binder for Chryston Farm. While I was taking a short rest, before testing it to ensure that it was working.

I turned and looked down into the valley and noticed a fishing boat, two hundred yards inland and approaching the river bank. What really got my attention wasn't the fact that I'd never seen a fishing boat up the river, but that there were a lot of men on the deck."

"How many?" Mr Savage asked.

"Quite a few. I got out my telescope and had a better look. It was then that I saw that other than two men, they were all dressed in normal, non fisherman's clothing. Not the normal wear for fishermen.

By this time the boat had drawn up against the river bank and two of the men jumped off the boat and, using ropes from the front and rear of the boat, held it against the bank, whilst the others got off the boat and unloaded two bicycles and a motor bike. Each man had a suitcase, with the exception of what looked like a 'tramp', he had, what looked like a sack."

"I still don't understand why you think they are important?" Mr Savage said.

"Just wait until he tells you the next bit," Frank interrupted.

"It was what happened when the only man left on the boat, took the boat away from the river bank and started off towards the sea. The 'Tramp' appeared to gather all the others around him and they talked for a minute or two and as they started to break up, one of the men, dressed as a farm worker, gave the 'Tramp' a salute, much like the ones we see at the cinema's of how the Nazis' salute." Jack reported.

"Oh." Was the only comment that came from Mr Savage?

"It was about this time that I arrived to see if Jack had finished the repair and to ensure that we could get back to the harvest, today. Jack passed me his telescope and I watched the men and saw them picking up their goods and walking off towards Exceat Bridge and joining the roads. I told Jack to report this to the Sussex Patrol and that I would arrange this meeting." Frank reported.

"Did you deliver this message?" Mr Savage asked.

"Yes. But not before I came across the 'Tramp'. I had just passed the turning to West Dean, and there he was standing out in the road, blocking my way.

I gave him a mouthful about stopping me like that. He asked for a lift up to the top of the hill. I said OK but ended up taking him as far as Friston Pond. As we were passing the emergency air strip, he said that 'this was a funny place for an air station'. As there are no signs about what was there, it confirmed my suspicions that these were German spies." Jack said.

"I added this to my report for the Sussex Patrol."

Peter Savage sat back for a little while, deep in thought. There were reports that the German's were preparing an invasion force. Where these men an advance party? Were they here to sabotage our important roads and railways? After a while he sat forward.

Right this is what we're going to do. We need to know where these men are going. Frank, you will need to get back to the binder and get that field cut.

I may have work for you tonight. Jack, I know that you have to get over to Folkington Bishop's Farm, but can you take a round about route and see if you can find out where these men have gone?" Mr Savage asked.

"I know where two of the 'travelling salesmen' were heading," said Jack.

"Where to?" Mr Savage asked.

"Towards Seaford, but my guess would be they are heading for Newhaven and the port." Jack stated.

"Right that is three we know about. It's the other seven we need found now." Mr Savage said, as much to himself as to the others.

"OK, I'm going to see someone I know, who may be able to help us out. I think they will be able to track down the two headed for Newhaven. You two get off and we'll meet back here later. I'll get Tom and Eddie over as well." With that Mr Savage got up.

"Jack. Be very careful what you say to anyone. You may need to enlist some help but you can't let them know who or what we are." Mr Savage said.

"Don't worry. Most of the people I know think I am a member of the Home Guard. I'll tell them that this is a special Home Guard training exercise. That should cover us for a few days." Jack said.

"Frank you say the same thing. Be careful, the two of you, if this gets out to far, some of the Home Guard units might start to ask questions."

All three of them left their hide, but firstly they ensured that they had put out the lanterns and, before they left the cover of the hide, made sure that they would not be seen getting out of the coal heap.

Frank headed off, back to Chryston Farm to collect his tractor. Jack walked back to his van and drove away from the Barn.

Chapter 7
I need a room for a few nights

The meeting finished, Peter Savage walked back across the field and returned to the farm house kitchen and called out for his wife. It was only a few minutes before she walked into the kitchen.

"Jill, I've got to go out for a while, I should be back by lunch time but I could be late."

"What's so important?" She asked.

"I can't tell you, just a problem that needs sorting out."

Peter walked into his office, closed and locked the door. He needed to get something out of his secret box, without being disturbed. He pulled his desk away from the wall and went around the side, so that he could reach behind it. Just under the desk top was a small catch, which he moved to the left.

This catch released a spring that pushed a secret draw out, towards his hand. He took hold of the draw and pulled it further out, but not all the way. He reached into the draw and took out a .38 service revolver and a box of ammunition. He quickly loaded the six chambers with bullets and placed a further six, into his jacket pocket. He replaced the box and then reached in and brought out a commando knife, in its sheaf. He then pushed the draw back in place and slid the catch back, to hold the draw in place.

With a practice movement he slid the desk back in place and ensured that he had left no trace of the fact that the desk had been moved.

Peter unlocked his office, walked out and headed for the front door.

"Do take care, Peter." Jill called out, from the kitchen.

"Don't I always?" Peter called back.

Peter climbed into his car and started it up. Before he drove off he ensured that the commando knife was attached to his belt, but was out of sight.

He had already placed the revolver in his right hand jacked pocket. Now he had to get over to Hill View Farm and to call on a fellow farmer, Mat Palmer. He headed towards the main coast road. Now he was off towards Newhaven.

After about a mile and a half he turned right, again, and drove through Denton village and out the other side. His destination was not far out of the village.

Hill View Farm stood up on the hills, overlooking Newhaven, so had a good view towards the port. The man he was going to see was an old friend. Both of them were from farming stock and their parents had been friends, before them. It was Mat that got Peter into the Auxiliary Forces in the first place.

It was no secret, between them, that they were both leaders of Auxiliary Forces units, in the area. They had kept secret, from each other, the other members of their respective units.

Peter was in luck, Mat was in the farm yard. He was talking to one of his men and a couple of land army girls.

Mat looked around, as Peter drew up and waived for him to go to the farm house.

He parked his car, nearer the house and walked around to the back of the farm house. He knew that Betty, Mats wife, would be in the kitchen making a cup of tea for Mat. It was nearly nine o'clock and Mat always had tea about then.

"Morning Betty" Peter said as he creped up behind her and put his right hand on her bottom.

"Peter Savage, you take your hand off my bum before I land you one." Betty said without even looking around.

"Mat told me to come in and see you ..."

"Yes but not to molest my wife I didn't." Came the voice of the 'owner' of the lady Peter was talking to.

Peter turned around and greeted his friend. He asked that they go into his office and talk. Mat asked if Betty would bring the tea in, when it's ready, but no biscuits for Peter.

Once they were seated, Mat asked what brought Peter over to his farm, especially during harvest.

"Look Mat, I know we're not supposed to talk to each other about our other work but this is important. One of my men observed ten men being landed from a fishing boat, at the River Cuckmere's estuary, early this morning. It was his impression that they were German's and with all the talk of an imminent invasion, I thought we should take this seriously." Peter said.

"Have you reported this?" Mat asked.

"Yes, they reported it to the Sussex Patrol, even before telling me the details." Peter said.

"What's it you need me to do then?"

Just then Betty came in carrying a tray with two mugs of tea and a packet of Rich Tea biscuits. She told Mat to share them with Peter and then left them to talk.

"Well we believe that two of these Germans are headed this way, for the harbour. I was told that they appear to be dressed like travelling salesmen, on bicycles and are carrying heavy looking suitcases. What I need you to do is to find them, track them down but do nothing else. Can you get your men keep an eye on them? Hopefully we should get some orders, in the next day or two. It may be nothing or it could be vital to know their where abouts." Peter ended.

"What if I find them, who do I report to?" Mat asked.

"For the time being, you had better let me know. We'll call them rabbits. If you have them, then 'you have found their burrows'. If not, you haven't." Peter said.

"One of my men suggested that, if we have to say anything, we could say that it is a Home Guard training exercise, we are involved in. After all those German Paratroopers that are reported to have landed in Kent, the other week, we should get away with it. Well for at least a couple of days, anyway." Peter said.

"Yes that should cover it, most people around here think my team are members of the Home Guard and we haven't done anything to make them believe otherwise. The men of the local Home Guard think we belong to a central, area unit." Pat said with a shrug.

They continued talking, while they finished their tea, mainly about the harvest and how hard it was to meet the Ministry's targets. Mat asked if Jack could be spared next week, to check his binder and help them put together a larger plough, one of his men had designed, to make the work easier. Peter agreed but couldn't say which day he would be free.

They both got up and returned to the kitchen, where Peter gave Betty a quick peck on the cheek and thanked her for the tea. He lied in saying that Mat wouldn't give him any of the Rich Teas. He left the kitchen before Mat could retaliate.

Once Peter had left, Mat told Betty that he may be a bit late in for dinner. He had some work to do, that Peter had delayed him doing. This was to get his own back on Peter, as Betty had always been close to both Peter and Mat. If Peter hadn't bumped into Jill, one day at Hailsham cattle market, Betty might have had to toss a coin as to which one of them she married.

Mat got on to his horse, which was already saddled and ready, as he intended to ride off, over the hills, when Peter had called. He had seen the person he wanted to meet, earlier, heading off up the hill, so he guest the direction to go, to catch up with him. The person he was looking for was David Smithers, the local Game Keeper and a member of his Unit.

Within fifteen minutes he had found David and asked that he came to the Inn, in half an hour. He had a job for both him and Charles, the inn keeper, another member of his unit.

Mat rode off and headed up to the top of the hill and took out his binoculars and scanned the area. He was looking to see if there were people around that he did not expect to see. He could see a couple of tanks and two Army Lorries, moving along one of the tacks that led towards Alfriston. These must be from the trials unit that were testing the new 'Churchill' tanks.

By the time that David had reached the inn, Mat was just arriving there as well. Mat tied his horse up to a fence post, at the field opposite the Inn and walked over to accompany David. They both went around to the back of the inn, as it was not yet time for it to open for the lunch time 'rush'.

Charles was just coming up the garden path, as they turned the corner of the building.

"I'm not open yet, not even for you two!" Charles called.

"You don't think we would drink here, during the day time, do you?" David replied.

"Is there somewhere we can talk?" Mat asked

"Yes, in my shed at the end of the garden. No one is brave enough to enter without my permission." Charles replied.

They all moved down the path and into the shed.

"What's this all about Mat?" David asked.

"Well we have a job to do, it's been reported that two German spies are heading this way and we need to find them and keep an eye on them, for a day or two. They were part of a party of about ten men that landed at Exceat, early this morning." Mat reported.

"How will we know them?" David asked.

"I was told that they are dressed much like travelling salesmen and are carrying, what looks like quite heavy suitcases."

"That's not much to work on." Charles said.

"Oh, they are also on bicycles." Mat put in.

"That is the best we've got. They were a long way from the person who saw them land, so we'll have to look at any foreigners in town." Mat said.

"Look David, I need you to go into town and see what you can find out and then report back to me. Charles, I need you to keep your eyes and ears open for any talk about strangers around."

"The cover story, if you need it, is that this is a special Home Guard training exercise. Remember the report we saw about the German Paratroopers who landed in Kent. This exercise is to find out our readiness for such an event along our coast, OK?" Mat said.

"But what if the local Home Guard hears about this?" David asked.

"Well in a couple of days it should have been sorted out. Things take a week or two to filter into that lot." Mat countered, with a big smile.

The other two agreed and they all went their separate ways.

Chapter 8
He's got on a train to Hastings

Jack thought that the best thing for him to do was to get others using their eyes, on his behalf. For that reason he decided that his first port of call would be Simon Goringe, the village policemen of Alfriston.

This village was about two miles up river, from Exceat Bridge. Other than Seaford, this was the largest conurbations in the area. It would be the first village that the Germans would encounter, after landing at Exceat.

He knew that he wouldn't be able to tell Simon the full story, but he would have to tell him enough so that he would act as his eyes and ears, in and around Alfriston. It was also important that he realised the importance of what he was being asked to do.

On arriving in the village he turned up Weavers Road and then turned right, down Star Road. This was just a short road, linking the back road to the main road, through the village.

There were only a few houses along this road and Simon's was the third one on the right. Jack pulled up, before he reached the High street.

He got out of his van and locked the driver's door, because, before he left the hide, in New Barn, he had taken a few weapons, and other things that he may need, over the next few days. He couldn't afford these to fall into the hands of ill prepared villagers.

He knocked on the door of the police cottage and it was soon answered by his old friend, PC Simon Goringe, although he was up and about, he was not fully dressed. He was wearing his boots, trousers and a vest. Either he had spilled something down the front of his shirt or, more likely, he wasn't fully dressed yet.

"What brings you to my neck of the wood then Jack?" Simon asked.

"Aren't you going to invite me in then Simon?" Jack said.

Simon showed him into the house and then into his small office to the left of the front door. On the way he asked Mary, his wife, to make them a cup of tea.

"Right, what's this all about? You only come to see me when you're in trouble." Simon asked.

"Well, I was up in a field on Seaford Head, early this morning. I saw a fishing boat landing a group of men near to Exceat Bridge." He let that sink in before he continued.

"I think that they may be German's."

"Are you sure?" Simon asked.

"No, I'm not sure but I have discussed this with Mr Savage and with all the rumours going about, and the fact that the other week a group of German paratroopers landed in Kent, we are pretty sure."

"How many men were there?" Simon said, taking up a pencil and pulling a sheet of paper towards him.

"Fred and I counted ten. We can account for three of them, but need to know where the other seven have holed up. Mr Savage wants me to let him know where all these men are." Jack said.

"Why does he want to know, this is a Police problem." Simon protested.

"Well, he thinks that this may be a special Home Guard training exercise, as a result of that thing in Kent. He's been told to report these sightings to the Home Guard, as well as the Police." Jack lied.

"It's our job to arrest these men, not the Home Guard." Simon said, with some authority.

"Yes, but the Home Guard needs the training. We can't have you plods stopping their fun, can we?" Jack said.

"I see your point, OK, I'll let him know if I find any, around the village." Simon reluctantly agreed.

"I need you to ask around and see if anyone has seen a stranger in the village. If so, where is he now? He's not to be arrested, just kept an eye on. Can you do that for me? If you find him, let Mr Savage know."

"What do I tell him? I don't trust Sally, in the Post Office, not to listen in when she puts me through, to anyone."

"Just tell him you've found one or two of his lost sheep. He'll understand." Jack said.

Just as he had completed his request, Mary came in with the two cups of tea, and placed them on the table, before the two men.

"Simon. You're on Police business. Get your self dressed. What do you think Jack will think of you?" Mary scolded her husband.

Simon realised that Mary was right. He should be dressed properly, even in his own house, if he's doing Police work. So left his office and ran upstairs to collect his shirt and tie. He put the shirt on, in his bedroom but tied his tie, as he walked back down the stairs.

"How are you keeping, Jack? Are Joan and the kids keeping well?" asked Mary.

"Yes thanks, we're both keeping well."

"How is Johnny? I haven't seen him for some time, growing up I expect." Jack enquired.

"Yes we are both well. Johnny is eleven now and is growing up very quickly. I just hope that this war's over before he's old enough to join up and fight." Mary said, reflectively.

"I don't think you have too much to worry about. It will be over by next year." Jack said.

Simon now rejoined the pair of them. It was obvious to Mary that the two men had been deep in conversation about something very important, so she slid out of Simon's office and returned to her kitchen to prepare his dinner.

While they were talking, the telephone in Simon's office rang. It was from the Police Headquarters, in Lewes. They were also informing Simon about the possible landing of a group of Germans. They told him that if he saw any of them around, he was to contact them immediately.

"I just heard that it's a Home Guard Training exercise." Simon reported.

"Well we weren't told anything about that." Simon put the phone back on its cradle.

"It seems that you're right, Jack. My bosses have asked me to do the same task. Do you still need me to contact Mr Savage?" Simon asked.

"Yes, before you contact Lewes." Jack insisted.

After Jack had drunk the tea he bade farewell to Simon and shouted his thanks for the tea, through the house to Mary. He left by the same door that he came in by and returned to his van. Young Johnny was standing beside the van.

"Not at school today, Johnny?" Jack asked.

"No, Mr Fintch. I missed the morning bus so mum said that I would have to do some school work at home. Not fair is it?" Johnny asked.

"May be that'll teach you not to get up so late." Jack said as he unlocked the driver's door.

"Can I come around with you today, please Mr Fintch?" Johnny asked.

"What and get both of us in trouble with your mother, I don't' think so." Jack said as he opened the door and got behind the steering wheel.

His next destination would be Berwick Station. If any of the men were intending to go further inland, the train would be an easy means of achieving that. The station was only about three miles from where he was now.

He started up the engine and continued down Star road, until he reached its junction with the High Street. Here he turned left and soon was at the Market Cross. He branched to the right and headed off towards Berwick Station.

It didn't take him long to reach the station. There wasn't much traffic on the roads, these days. With petrol rationed, people kept their travel down to just what needed to be done, not what they might like to do.

Jack had a larger ration than most, because of his job and also an extra ration for being a member of the Auxiliary Forces, although, if asked, he said it was because of his job.

The actual village of Berwick was, in fact about two miles from where the station was located. Originally the station was called 'Dicker Halt' but over time its name gradually changed to the nearest village, that of Berwick.

A few houses and businesses had initially grown up near the station, mainly for the workers, on the railway, but soon others saw the advantages of living near the station and so more houses were built and then there were more residence around the station than in the actual village of Berwick, itself.

Jack parked up, near the station office and again locked up the van. He had to really remind himself to lock the van. Normally he just closed the driver's door and walked off to see whoever it was he needed to talk to.

Carrying weapons meant that he needed to be more careful, so he would always ensured that he locked it, securely.

He walked into the booking office area and shouted out for the station master, Mr Henry Lake. There was no immediate answer to his call, so he started to walk out onto the platform, to see if he was out there.

"You need a platform ticket to go out there." A loud voice boomed from behind him.

Jack recognised the voice, it was Mr Lake. He had often heard this voice, when he and Vivian Lake had been playing in Mr Lake's garden and trampling over his vegetable patch.

"Mr Lake, I was just looking for you." Jack said as he turned around to face the Station Master.

"What can I do for you today?" He asked

"Have you seen any strangers around this morning?" Jack asked.

"Well there was this fisherman. Don't see many of them around here now. For that mind, I never have, at this station."

"Were there any other men, farm workers, travelling salesmen?" Jack tried to see if any others, from the boat, had come this way.

"Not on the station, no, but I did see the fisherman getting off a motor bike before walking up the road to the station. The man on the motor bike was dressed like a farm worker." He put in.

"Where was the fisherman going?" Jack asked.

"He bought a single ticket to Hastings, if I remember right. I don't sell many tickets for there." Henry said.

"Thank you for that. By the way have you heard from Vivian lately?" Jack asked after his old friend.

"No, the last I heard was that he was going up to Scotland for some special training. He really enjoys the Army, still when this war is over I hope he'll come back and work on the railway, with me." Henry said, as much to himself as to Jack.

"Thanks for that." Jack said

"Why did you want to know about the fisherman?" Mr Lake asked

"They're running a training exercise for the Home Guard. I was sent to find two of the 'enemy'." Jack replied

"I must be off, I've to get out to Folkington Bishop's Farm, by lunchtime or I'll be in trouble." Jack said as he turned and walked back to his van.

So two more of the ten men had been seen, that was five so far. He thought that the most likely town that the second German would be going to would be Hailsham, as it had a regular Farmers Market there and the man should find it fairly easy to get a job. Many farmers were short handed nowadays, so an extra pair of hands would always come in useful.

Hailsham had station and a railway line running through it. This would be a good place to bring in reinforcements, to repel the German invasion, along the coast from Eastbourne to Newhaven.

Jack headed back, the way he had come so he could join the main road, between Lewis and Polegate. Once he arrived at the cross roads, he turned left and head towards Polegate. As he drove down towards the bridge that crossed the River Cuckmere, he thought about the likely hood of finding any more of the Germans. If they really were here to assist the German's invasion, then they would have to be stopped.

After about a quarter of a mile, he drove across the bridge, over the River Cuckmere, and started up the hill, towards Wilmington.

Half way up, he noticed a farm worker stood, to his left, by a hedge that separated the road from the Wilmington Flying Club. The man seemed not to have noticed Jack's van chugging up the road towards him. Jack thought he saw the man looking through a pair of binoculars, into the Flying Club. Was this another of the Germans?

Jack remembered that the 'Tramp' was interested in the air strip, up on the South Hill. Now this man was looking at this private air strip. Could he be looking to take control of the Flying Club, when the invasion starts? In that way the Luftwaffe would have a ready made air strip, at their disposal. Consequently they wouldn't have to return to France or Germany for refuelling.

One of the interesting things about this flying club was that it not only had a club house, hanger, its own supply of fuel but they had built a control tower, above the club house building. This made it look very much like a normal airport or RAF station. Jack was surprised that the War Office had not taken it over or at least had troops stationed near by, just in case.

By now Jack was at the top of the hill and about to pass the side road, leading into the Flying Club. He glanced down the road, as he slowed, going passed the entrance. Down, near the Hangers, he noticed another man, also dressed as a farm worker.

There was no reason for a farm worker being there. All the local farm people knew that there was a fence all around the Flying Clubs grounds. To keep farm animals off the runway.

So now Jack could identify seven Germans. All of them appeared to be staying within easy reach of the coast and in places where they could be of use to the invading armies. It was important that he got this information to Mr Savage but he knew that getting the tractor, at Downs Farm, in Folkington, fixed was just as important, for the war effort

Jack felt that he had been very lucky, in being able to find so many of the Germans. Either he was good or they were being very cock sure of themselves and not being careful. Everyone knows the Germans are very arrogant, so he believed the later to be the case.

When he had been talking to Peter Savage, they had agreed that these men would need somewhere to stay, until the invasion started and they could then reveal themselves as who they really were. The only place, near to the Flying Club would be the Inn in Wilmington, so this was Jack's next port of call.

He had known Luke Evans for several years. He used his Inn, whenever he was working over this way. He served a good pint of ale and they usually exchanged gossip. Hopefully today would be no different.

He turned off the main road and up the side road that led to the village Inn. He parked the van and for the umpteenth time he ensured that the van was well secured.

Happy that no one was around to see him take these, unusual precautions, he walked into the Inn and ordered himself a half pint of ale.

"Not staying for lunch, today then Jack?" Luke asked.

"No I'm late getting to see Jack Abraham. One of his tractors is playing up." Jack replied.

"Can you spare me a moment, Luke? Over at the table." Jack said as he moved away from the bar and two of Luke's village customers.

Once they were seated, Jack explained to him about the Home Guard training exercise.

They had been set the task of finding ten men who had entered this neck of the woods, but they were not from around here. They were trying to pass themselves off as farm workers. Jack then went on to tell Luke that he believed that two of these men were just down the road, at the Flying Club. He said that he believed that they would be coming up to the Inn to get accommodation.

Luke had suspected that Jack had something to do with the Home Guard. Jack had never told him he was but there was something about him that gave Luke the idea that he was. The only problem with that thought was that he knew all the men in the local Home Guard platoons. Over the months, most of the local Home Guard platoons had used the hills and fields around his village for exercises. On each occasion, they had come into his Inn for a drink, before going back home. Jack had never been among any of the platoons.

Why had he not heard about this training exercise before now? The local platoon had been mustering in the local hall, last night. Then they came to the Inn for a drink before they went home. He hadn't heard any talk about this training exercise.

"When did the exercise start? The local Home Guard boys didn't say anything about it last night." Luke asked

"It started this morning. Not all the platoons are involved." Jack improvised.

"Jack what do you want me to do, arrest them?" Luke asked.

"No you mustn't do that. It's important that they don't know that we suspect them." Jack said

"If they come in and ask for a bed for a few nights, you make sure they get them. If I'm right, they'll be here before you close, after lunch. I'll call back later, after I've completed my work, just to check up. If I can't get back, let Simon Goringe know." Jack said.

"Why Simon, he's not in the Home Guard?" Luke said

"It's a joint training exercise, their working with us. If we find them all, the Police will step in and arrest them all." Jack said.

Luke appeared to be happy with that explanation so returned to the bar and his other two customers. Jack drank down the last mouthful of the ale and thanked Luke for listening. He then left the Inn and drove off to Folkington and Downs Farm.

Chapter 9
No Pheasants today

Charles Oliver had returned to the Inn and, with his wife Carol, they set about getting the barroom ready for the lunchtime customers. Being harvest time, he didn't expect many of the farm workers to call in at lunch time. They would call in, once the harvest had been gathered in, for the day.

Charles's main job was ensuring that the ale was on tap, that the glasses were ready and clean. Carol went around and made sure that the fire place was clean and tidy, with a stack of logs in the basket. She then made sure that the tables were clean and that the ashtrays had been emptied and cleaned properly by Mrs Davidson.

As she was finishing polishing the table nearest the window, at the front of the Inn, she looked out and noticed a man peddling his bicycle up the road, towards the Inn. To her surprise and delight, he rode towards the front door, got off his bike and placed it next to the porch. Unfastened a suitcase, from the carrier, over the rear wheel of his bicycle and headed towards the Inn's door.

"Looks like we have an early customer, or someone coming to try and sell us something." Carol turned and said to Charles.

"I don't mind a customer by I'm not buying anything from someone I don't know, though." Charles replied.

By the time that Carol had returned to be behind the bar, so that she could take orders for food, the door opened and in walked a tall man, over six foot. He had to duck his head as he came through the door. Being an old building the doors were only about five foot eight inches tall. In the times that this Inn was built, people were much shorter than they were today.

"Good morning." The man said as he walked towards the bar.

"Do you know of anywhere I could find a bed for a few days?" He asked.

Before Charles could say anything Carol said that they had a room, and asked how many days he would need it?

"I'll be in the area for about a week." He said.

"That'll be three shillings a night or four if you want breakfast as well." Carol said.

"Yes I'll have the breakfast."

"Your name please, we need it for our records." Carol smiled, as much because of the extra money this man was brining in to the Inn, as the fact that she was a pleasant person, by nature.

"Steffen, sorry Steven Cook." He stumbled out his name.

Carol didn't appear to notice, but Charles was well aware of what this man had said. If he was right, this was one of the Germans they were looking for and here he was, right in front of him.

Once Carol had booked Steven into the Inn's register, she took him up and showed him his room. She asked if he wanted lunch in the bar but he declined, as he had an appointment, in town, within the hour.

When Carol returned to the bar, she asked Charles if he had noticed that this man had said his name was Steffen. He replied that the man had said his name was Steven. Carol thought that she must have misheard him, so put it out of her mind.

While Charles had been getting his bar ready, David had now reached Newhaven and was crossing the bridge, into the High Street of this small port.

David had decided that he would, firstly talk to one of his contacts, in the town. One that he knew he could trust, the local butcher, Robert James. His family had been butchers here for over a century. They knew everyone around and about, so a stranger would soon be noticed by Robert.

When David walked into the shop, there were several people being served by Robert and his wife Tina. Robert and David had a long arrangement where by, if David had any spare game, he would bring it over for Robert to sell and they would share the profits.

Because of this, David moved over to the far end of the counter and Robert left Tina to serve the customers, while he and David talked business.

"What have you got for me today?" Robert asked

"Nothing I'm afraid but I do need something from you."

"What?" Robert asked.

"Have you seen any strangers in town, travelling salesmen?" David asked.

"I don't know. I've been very busy today. No one strange has come in to the shop today." Robert said, after a little thought.

"If you do see any, will you let Ken Proctor know? It's very important." David said.

Having promised to bring some rabbits over later next week, David left the shop and headed up the High Street. He had only walked a very short distance when, walking towards him, he noticed a man dressed like a travelling salesman. Was this one of the Germans he was looking for? He then noticed that this man was carrying a suitcase. This sealed it for him. The few salesmen he had ever seen carried briefcases and a bag, not suitcases. He could hardly stop the man and he would be silly to turn around and follow him.

But luck was on his side. When they were only about ten yards apart, the man turned into the White Heart Inn. David decided that he would follow him in. He would bill the pint, he was about to order, to Mr Palmer, after all he sent him over here. The man had walked over to the bar, placed his suitcase on the floor, beside his feet and was talking to Tom Kemp, the landlord. David followed the man to the bar and stood a few feet away, to his right. As Tom was the only person serving at the moment David would have to wait.

Once Tom had finished serving the German, he moved along the bar to David. While he was taking David's order, the German picked up his pint and suitcase and moved away from the bar and took a seat by the window, so he could look out at the people passing by.

"Tom, what did that man want?" He asked

"He ordered a pint and then asked if I had a room to let." Tom replied.

"And did you?" David asked

"Yes. He said that he was working in the town for the next week and needed somewhere local to stay." Tom said.

"Tom. If he moves or there is anything not quite right, I need you to let Ken Proctor know."

"Why?" asked Tom.

"There is a Home Guard training exercise going on. Ten men, from outside Sussex are going about and, with the Police, the Home Guard have to identify these men, without them knowing they have been recognised." David lied.

"I can't tell you why, but I think that man is one of those we are trying to identify." David said in a low voice.

"Do you want me to get him out of here then?" Tom asked.

"No, don't do that. We need to know where he is. When its time for Ken to come and arrest him, he'll need to find him easily." David told another white lie.

"Tom, I wouldn't tell Jenny what I've told you, keep it to yourself. Once I've finished your fine ale, I'll go and find Ken." David said, just as a group of men came up to the bar for their lunch time pints. Tom moved away from David and served his new customers.

Once David had downed the last drops of the ale, he got up, waived out to Tom and left the Inn, without taking a glance towards the stranger. He didn't want him to think that people were taking any notice of the stranger in the Inn. If the German knew anything about the English he would have known that he would have be spotted immediately. His mind was on other things, so whether or not people were taking notice of him he didn't bother about it. He was on a mission that meant far more to him than the thoughts of these men.

David came out of the Inn and continued in the direction he had originally been taking. After thirty yards he turned right and within a few yards he was outside Ken Proctors Police house.

David knocked on the door and it was soon opened by Ken, himself.

"David, what can I do for you? I haven't seen you for ages." Ken greeted David.

"I need a word, it's important." David said in a quiet voice.

Ken ushered him into the house and took him through into his backroom, which he used as his office. On the way he asked his wife, Lilly, if she could get them tea and bring it into the office.

"Well, what's so important then David?" Ken said after they were both seated.

"Ken, I don't know if you've already been told, but there is a Home Guard training exercise going on this weekend. It is said that someone spotted a group of Germans, getting off a fishing boat, in the River Cuckmere estuary, very early this morning." David reported.

"No I've heard nothing, mind you they always forget about me, out here." Ken replied. "I think they believe that I'm out there fishing, myself."

"Well I heard that two of the men were spotted heading this way. The story goes that they are headed for the Port." David said.

"How do you know all this David?" Ken asked

"You know I'm with a Home Guard central unit, don't you? Well it's our exercise. After what happened in Kent, the other week, with the German paratroopers landing, we didn't want to be caught out, here in Sussex." David said sternly.

"I've seen one of the men. He's booked into the White Heart Inn for a week. I spoke to Tom and he'll let you know if the man moves on or there is anything suspicious you should know about." David said.

Just then there was a slight knock on the office door and in walked Lilly with two cups of tea. She passed the time of day with David, asking how his wife, Hazel and the children were. Although she was Hazel's cousin, they didn't get much chance to see each other.

Once Lilly had left the office Ken tried to find out more about this man and how David knew so much about him. More importantly, he wanted to know why it was so important that this man was kept an eye on.

Just as David was about to tell him the telephone rang and Ken picked it up.

"Newhaven Police station, Can I help you?" Ken said.

"Oh. Hello John. So you've remembered that I exist then?" he replied to the caller.

"Yes I've just heard... No I can't say.... Yes one of them has been seen here... I hear it's just a Home Guard training exercise. Who says it real? I'll have to get back to you about that... Right I'll call you back after lunch, bye John." Ken concluded.

"What was that all about then Ken?"

"Well there appears to be some sort of panic in Lewes. Some say they are Germans and the big wigs think someone is pulling our legs." Ken reported.

When the two of them had drunk their tea David said that he had to get back to Denton. He got up and Ken walked him to the front door. Just as he was about to open the door, David put his hand on the door to stop it being opened and looked at Ken.

"Ken, if anything strange happens, with this and the other man, if you find him. You must telephone Mr Palmer and let him know. If you don't ask the question, I can't tell you a lie." David smiled at Ken and released his hand so Ken could open the door.

Ken had heard rumours, that David had been away on some special Home Guard training, but no one could find out if that was true or not and David said nothing about why he had been away. They had been friends for a long time so he knew that, when the time came, David would tell him what he had been up to.

It was now time for David to head back to the farm and report to Mr Palmer. He felt very pleased with what he had done this morning.

He hoped that Mr Palmer would be as pleased with what he had achieved as he was.

It took him about half an hour to get back to the farm and report to Mr Palmer. David had been able to locate the first of the Germans that were headed their way. He would now need to find a way in which they could keep an eye on him. Whether they would be able to find the second one, as easily, he doubted, but they must work hard at finding him.

David was just about to leave the farm house when Charles knocked at the kitchen door. He had come to report his progress and the fact that the second of the Germans was booked into his Inn, for the next week.

They all went back into Mr Palmer's office, so that they could talk without any word getting out about the Germans. Charles reported that he was sure that the man was a German as, when he booked in, he gave his name as Steffen and then quickly corrected himself and said that it was Steven Cook.

"Are you sure that is what he said?"

"Yes, Carol asked me if I had heard him, I said no."

They discussed these finding and came to the conclusion that these men were here for a specific purpose. They must be kept and eye on. It was no good Charles being involved in the following of either of these men. He was known to the second German.

Although David had been seen by the first of the Germans, it was just a brief encounter and more than likely, as neither of them had looked at each other, eye to eye, the German would not recognise David, if he saw him again.

"I'll get Andy to follow them. We must know what they are looking at and why." Mr Palmer said.

"Mr Palmer, It might be a good idea to have a second person to watch over them. Mrs Davidson has a son, Will. He would be good at following these men. Who notices kids running around?" Charles said.

"That's a good Idea, I know young William, he knows the area well and I'm sure that he's been poaching over our area, but I haven't caught him, yet." David reported.

"Right, get the two of them to report to me at one o'clock. We'll start this afternoon. Charles get back to your Inn and find out what the man in your place is up to and if he's gone out, where he was headed. I'll send William around, once I've spoken to him." Mr Palmer ordered.

Charles returned to his Inn, but, on the way he diverted so that he could call on Mrs Davidson's house. He hoped that Will would be around or at least that Mrs Davidson knew his were abouts.

As he approached the house, Will was coming up the other way, heading home for his lunch, Charles expected.

"Will, just the man I wanted to see." Charles said as he greeted the boy.

"I thought you were coming to see mum." William said

"No I need you to go up and see Mr Palmer, at the farm at one o'clock." Charles said.

"Why do you want me to do that?" Will asked.

"He has a job for you."

"But I should be at school!" William replied.

"You're not, as usual, are you Will?" Charles said.

"I wasn't feeling well."

"Not so bad that you couldn't go and catch a brace of rabbits, I see." Charles observed.

"You won't tell Mr Palmer, will you?"

"Not if you go and see him, as I asked, there'll be no reason for me to say anything." Charles said.

With that he turned around and walked back to his Inn. He hoped that the German, who called himself Steven Cook, was still at the Inn. It would make his job much easier if he could know in which direction he went, when he left the Inn.

Charles expected that he would settle in to his room, unpack his suitcase and then have lunch, in the bar, before he went off to Newhaven and, most likely meet up with the other German.

Mat walked out, into the farm yard and shouted for Andy. He was not sure it he would be around or not. If not he expected that another of the hands would respond and tell him where Andy was working. He was right, Angela, one of the new Land Army girls came out of the barn and said that Andy was working in 'Smithers field'. Mat sent Angela up to give Andy a message that he was to report to the Farm house at one o'clock.

At one o'clock, there was a knock on the kitchen door of the Farm House. Mrs Palmer answered the door and found Andy and young William Davidson, standing there. Andy told her that they had been told to report to Mr Palmer. She showed them through to Mr Palmers office, where he was waiting for them.

After Betty had left the room and closed the door, Mr Palmer invited the two of them to sit down, on the two chairs that were placed before his desk. He looked at the two of them and saw that neither of them was at all comfortable. Mat guessed that Andy was not happy that young William was at this meeting.

Andy would have suspected that this was about Auxiliary Forces business and Will was not a member. William, on the other hand was not sure why he was here. Mr Oliver wouldn't have had time to tell Mr Palmer about the two rabbits, so why was he here?

"William. What I'm going to ask you to do today is very important for the War. You can't tell anyone what I've asked you to do, not your mum, dad or any of your friends." Mat said.

"Why? I don't keep secrets from my mum." William protested.

"Well, you will keep this a secret because your life will depend on it, and for that matter, many lives will depend on you keeping it a secret. Do I make my self clear?" Mat asked.

There was a lull in the conversation for a couple of minutes, as Will thought out his response.

In the mean time, Andy was very concerned. He knew that Will's father was a member of the Home Guard and that Will always goes along with his father, for all their parades.

He didn't fancy a young boy knowing what he was in the British Resistance. One wrong word and, if the Germans did invade, the whole of their unit would be arrested and most likely shot.

"Mr Palmer, if I do what you ask, can I tell my mum, ever?"

"William, you can never tell anyone about what you have done today." Mr Palmer said earnestly.

"If you ever do, I'll kill you." Andy whispered into Will's left ear. Loud enough for William to hear but not so loud that Mr Palmer could understand what he had said.

William turned and faced Andy. He looked him in the eyes and saw that he meant everything he had just said. What was he getting into? What do these men want of him and why is it so important that he never talks about it?

He had never kept a secret from his mum. Mainly because she seemed to know whenever he had been up to something and would give him, that look. As a consequence he would always tell her, and suffer what ever punishment was coming his way.

"Alright, Mr Palmer, I'll do whatever you ask, but if my mum badgers me, I'll have to tell her that she'll have to talk to you." William said, with a smile.

"Now that's settled, I'll tell you what I need you both to do. William, Andy and I are in a special unit, of the Home Guard. That's why you can't say anything about what I'll be asking you to do. What we do is Top Secret, very special work. Do you understand?" Mat asked.

"My dad said that you were all objectors and wouldn't fight." William said.

"We know what is said about us but it is far from the truth. When the Germans have overrun your dads Home Guards, it is us who will take the battle to the Germans. Do you understand?" Mat asked.

"Not fully. But if it is important for us to win the war, I'll do it and say nothing." William answered.

"We're taking part in a special 'Top Secret' Home Guard exercise. It is said that ten 'Germans' have been landed around here. In fact they are regular soldiers, helping us out. We have to track them down. That's were you two come in. We have spotted these men and we need to keep them under observation, until they can be arrested, then the exercise will be over." Mat stated.

"We can't have young William involved. He's not one of us." Andy protested.

"We're not taking them on, Andy. Our job is to follow them and see what they are doing here. What is their target? I have found out that one of them is staying at the South Heighton Inn and the other is booked in at the White Heart Inn, in Newhaven."

"How do you know that?" William asked.

"I haven't been sitting here twiddling my thumbs." Mat said with a smile.

"Right, Andy, I need you to go over to the White Heart Inn, see Tom Kemp, and find out where the 'Travelling salesman', staying at his Inn, has gone. He'll tell you how he's dressed. Then you are to find him, follow him and at six o'clock, report back here." Mat said.

"And if I can't find him?"

"Still report back at six o'clock" Mat said.

"William, I need you to do the same thing, but your man may still be at the South Heighton Inn. See Mr Oliver and he'll tell you all about the second German. It's your job to find and follow him. I need you back here at six o'clock with a full report."

"But young William can't be expected to follow a Regular Soldier. What if they see him?" Andy asked.

"You will both have to be very careful. They have been told that they can knock you about a bit, if they suspect they have been identified." Mat said.

"We can't put Will in that sort of danger." Andy protested.

"Well David told me that William is very good at hiding and going about the area without anyone seeing him. He's sure that William helps himself to game, all over the hills here abouts." Mr Palmer said with a smile on his face.

"I don't know what Mr Smithers is talking about, he's never caught me." William protested.

"Look William, if you do what I want you to do, you can enter my land any time, but don't let Mr Smithers catch you, OK".

"Right the two of you, here is five shillings each, to cover any expenses you may have. I need you to account for every penny, do I make myself clear?" He said sternly.

Both of them accepted the money and confirmed that they would keep a record of how they spend the money.

"Look, William. What I'm asking you to do could be very dangerous. If these men do catch you they'll not hold back, if they think they may get captured. You will need to be very careful that they don't know they are being followed." Mr Palmer said.

"What if they do see me?" William asked.

"Just go about as if you have no interest in them, say good morning, if you have to, but don't get involved in a long conversation with them. You might start to ask questions, without realising it."

"Do we still follow them?" Andy asked.

"No. Just walk away and make your way back to the White Heart Inn, or here, if it's nearer. Then get a message to me and I'll send someone else to take over from you. William you had better go to the Police cottage and ask the policeman to ring me, tell him, to tell me, that you have lost the sheep." Mat smiled.

"Both of you had better get going now. Remember to be back here at six o'clock, tonight." Mr Palmer said as he stood up and led the way to the office door and escorted the pair of them through the house and out the way they had come.

Before Andy left the office, Mat pulled him back and closed the office door. He quickly told Andy that it was not an exercise but the real thing. The men they were following were German spies.

Now that meeting was over he then got into his car and headed off to talk to Peter Savage, at his farm. It was strange, up until Peter had come to see him, this morning. He hadn't really taken much notice of the people walking along the roads, as he drove by. Today he looked them all over. Who were they and how were they dressed?

For the first couple of miles he recognised most of the people along the road, and waved out to them. As he got further away, from his farm, he only recognised a few people. The nearer he got to Seaford, the more he noticed that he was not recognising any of the people about.

The one thing he did realise was that they all looked 'right'. They were dressed as they should be. The clothes looked as you would expect such a person would be wearing.

Before he got to the outskirts of Seaford, he turned up the road that led to Bishopstone. He now started to get together his thoughts of what he had to report to Peter. He was so deep in his thoughts that, once he had driven out of the village, he nearly missed the turning into Peter's farm. Luckily he was going slow enough that he could quickly swing his car into the side road, without causing an accident, or hitting the fence posts at the turning.

Mat stopped his car, in front of the Farm House and was greeted by Peter, who had heard his car coming up from the main road.

"I hadn't expected to see you again today, anything up?" Peter asked as he shook Mat's hand.

"I've a lot to tell you, can we go inside?" Mat replied.

They went into the farm house and Peter took Mat through to the kitchen, where Jill was just laying up the table, for lunch. Peter asked if there was enough for Mat to join them and she confirmed that there was, so she laid a third place at the kitchen table.

"Jill. How long before you serve up?" Peter asked his wife.

"About twenty minutes." She replied.

"We'll be in the office then." Peter said.

Peter and Mat walked out of the kitchen and headed for the office. Once seated, Mat started to give Peter his report.

"We know where the two men are. One is staying at the South Heighton Inn and the other is staying at the White Heart Inn, in Newhaven." Mat reported.

"Well done Mat! Where do we go from there?" Peter asked

"I've sent two men to follow them and report back to me, tonight. By tomorrow I'll have a couple more men to follow them. Hopefully that will ensure that they don't get too suspicious, if they see the same person near them all the time." Mat said.

"Does anyone else know?" Peter asked.

"Yes, Ken Proctor, the policeman at Newhaven and a young man that I have used, to follow one of the men. He's very trustworthy and his father is a member of the village Home Guard. They won't see him but he will know every move they make. You can trust both of these men not to say a word." Mat reported.

"I think one of my men told the young man that if he ever said anything about what we had asked him to do, he would shoot him. The only trouble is that even I believe him!" Mat said

By this time Jill had shouted out that she was about to put the plates of food on the table. The two of them returned to the kitchen and sat down. The three of them discussed how they were coping with the increased demands by the Ministry, for yet more and more food. She said that the WI was setting up jam making sessions.

After lunch was finished and the table cleared away, Peter and Mat retired back to Peter's office and Jill made them all cups of tea, taking the two cups for the men, into Peters office and then she took her tea into the lounge and sat there doing some knitting.

Chapter 10
What do we do now?

It had not taken Jack Fintch very long to reach Folkington Bishop's Farm, once he'd left Wilmington. As soon as he drove into the farm yard, George Semple came over to him and gave him a hard time for being so late. They had expected him, just after breakfast, not dinner time.

Jack said that he had got held up, repairing a binder, over at Seaford Head. This was not a complete lie but did stretch the truth quite a lot. He asked where the tractor was and was directed over to a shed, just behind the main barn. Jack knew that he may need a verity of tools, from his van, so decided that it would be best if he drove the van over, to be closer to the tractor.

The tractor that he was to work on was a Fordson N. He was use to these. They were always having trouble starting and this one was no exception. He had been called out to it five times, this year alone. Mind you it was over ten years old and had been heavily worked. For a long time, it was the only tractor on this farm. They now had a more powerful David Brown VAH-1 and its better engine allowed it to be used more efficiently over the hills.

Jack had found that the Fordson was prone to fowling up its plugs and, although he had shown George how to clean the plugs, it appeared that Mr Abraham didn't trust George with that job, so he always called Jack over to carry out this simple task.

He was paying for Jacks time, so he was not averse to doing an easy hours work, now and again.

When Jack had finished cleaning the plugs, adjusting the magneto and checking that it started without any trouble, he went and reported to the Farm Manager, Jack Abraham. He was quite a bit older than Jack but had worked all his life on the farm. He stood about six foot two inches tall and wore a close cut beard and was extremely fit and strong.

"Sorry I was late here this morning but there were some problems, I need to tell you about." Jack said.

Mr Abraham led the way into the farm office, just next to the large barn that dominated the farm yard.

"What's this all about then?" Mr Abraham asked.

Both Jack and Mr Abraham were on a training course, run at Coleshill House at Highworth, for the Auxiliary Forces. With both of them being 'Jack' it caused some confusion to the instructors, when trying to put their points over, to the one they wanted to address. The confusion had started when they had both arrived at the Highworth Post Office, at the same time.

When they both gave their names as 'Jack', the Post mistress was not sure which one, from her list, she had in front of her. She couldn't ask them for their full name, as that was against the security rules. No member of the Auxiliary Forces was to know the full names of any other member, who was not part of their small group.

The Post Mistress had to send Jack outside, so she could identify Mr Abraham. She then sent him outside and asked him to send Jack back in, so she could ensure that he was the other 'Jack' on her list of trainees. Once she was happy she had the right men, she telephoned Coleshill House, who arranged for transport to come and collect them.

Both Mr Abraham and Jack didn't tell their instructors that they knew each other. To have done so would have meant that one or both of them would not have been allowed to serve in the Auxiliary Forces.

"This morning, while I was working up on Seaford Head, I saw a fishing boat landing about ten men, up the river a bit, from the estuary. They were all dressed in civilian clothes and one of the men appeared to give another, of their group, a Nazi salute, which I thought was very strange. After that, they all either, walked, rode their bicycles or one of them rode a motor bike, to the road, where they all went their separate ways." Jack reported.

He let that sink in for a moment and then continued.

"I reported this to my leader and we agreed that it was more than possible that these were Germans. He sent me about to try and track them down. We knew that two went to Newhaven, one had gone to Eastbourne. I have also found that one brought a train ticket for Hastings, another was headed towards Hailsham and I saw another two looking over the Flying Club at Wilmington." Jack said.

"Who else knows?" Mr Abraham asked.

"I've sent a message to the Sussex Patrol about them landing at Exceat but we've not yet told them about where they have dispersed to." Jack said.

"What do you think our unit should do?"

"My leader thinks we should be ready to stop them carrying out, what ever it is that they are planning. He believes they're here in advance of the invasion." Jack said.

"OK, my men will be put on alert and I'll issue them with the necessary weapons, we might need to fight these Germans." Mr Abraham said.

"We are using the Home Guard as a cover for what we are doing. If you have to tell anyone, say that it is part of a special Home Guard training exercise." Jack said.

"I can't see how we'll be getting that involved. Your unit seems to have most of it covered." Mr Abraham said.

With that said, Jack told Mr Abraham how much the bill was for the repair of his tractor, ten shillings. He could pay Mr Palmer at the end of the month.

"You know, you would save yourself a lot of money if you let George clean the plugs on that old Fordson." Jack told Mr Abraham.

"I did, that's why we called you in, in June. If you remember the plugs were really buggered up, that was George's handy work." Mr Abraham said, with a smile.

With that matter sorted out, they shook hands and Jack got into his van and drove out of the farm yard.

He decided that he would go back, via Jevington and up to Friston. He could then drive back along the coast road, through Seaford and on to the farm. To do this, he could go back onto the main road, drive towards Polegate and then take the road up to Wonnock and Jevington or he could go the scenic route.

He chose to just turn right, as he left the farm yard. Drive into Folkington village and up passed the church. From there he could take the track that led up to the hills. This would bring him in behind Jevington. He chose this route, as it was shorter and would save him fuel. The only downside was that the track was made of flints and they could have very sharp edges. If he ran over such a stone, they could make ribbons of his tyres. He thought 'what the hell'.

Jack was in luck, there were no sharp flints along the track or he just didn't drive over any. As the track brought him within sight of Jevington, he turned left, down another track that would lead him back to the road, which ran through the village.

It had been a very long day, for him, so he decided that he would call in and see if his brother was at home. He would then be able to confirm that he had delivered the message to the Sussex Patrol. If he wasn't at home he was hopeful that he could get a cup of tea from Wendy.

Jack knocked on the door of John's cottage and waited for a reply, but there didn't appear to be anyone at home. He knew that Wendy had a part time job at Monks Rest, a small hotel opposite the cottage. So he walked over the road and around the back of the hotel. He met up with a young lady and asked if Wendy was working today.

She said that she wasn't but she'd done breakfast and went home. She did see her walking up towards the church, about a quarter of an hour ago. Jack thanked her.

He realised that he didn't have enough time to go and find Wendy, so he got back into his van and headed off, out of the village, towards Friston. This road took him passed the farm, where John worked, but he didn't intend to call in and find him.

He was sure that he would have done his duty. As he drove along, he looked about and on the right side of the road, far across the other side of the field he could see a man ploughing, with a heavy horse. From the look of the animal, it was the one he had seen John with earlier.

It didn't take Jack long before he was at the top of the hill and approaching Friston Pond. Here he turned right and headed towards Exceat. Just after he had started driving over South Hill and passed the emergency air strips parameter fence, he caught a movement in his left wing mirror.

He took a good look back and could see two men climbing over the fence. They appeared to be looking around, as if to see if Jack had noticed them.

These men look as if they were dressed like those who got off the fishing boat, earlier. These two had the look of farm workers.

61

They soon turned away from watching Jack driving away from them.

Satisfied that the driver had not seen them climbing over the fence. The two of them then turned and started to walk back towards Friston Pond. If Jack was right, they would be heading for The Tiger Inn, where he guessed they had already obtained accommodation.

That was nine of the ten men accounted for. He felt very pleased with himself and the good job he had done today. If it hadn't been for him, these men would be wandering around the area, doing whatever it was they had been sent to do, without anyone's knowledge.

It took him about fifteen minutes to reach the farm and a further five minutes to find Mr Savage. He was showing one of the Land Army girls how to fit the ball of string and then thread it, on a binder.

Because what they had to discuss was not for the ears of this young girl, Mr Savage led the way back to the farm house and through to his office. Once they were comfortable, Jack gave him his report, detailing where and when he had identified each of the men.

Peter took notes and at the end he was very pleased. He told Jack that the two in Newhaven were being watched and their every move was being recorded.

Just as he had finished speaking, his telephone rang.

"Peter Savage, can I help you?"

"It's Simon Goringe. We've found your missing sheep. It's at the Star." Simon reported.

"Thanks, Simon. I'll send one of my men to retrieve it tomorrow." Peter said and hung up.

"Well that's number ten. The last one's in Alfriston, staying at the Star Inn." Peter said with a smile.

"Look Jack, you get on home. Be ready if I call you. I think things could get very busy for us over the next few days. There'll be no weekend off for any of use now, thanks to you. Now off you go, I've to get this report out."

Jack stood up and left the office. He closed the door behind him and quickly Peter got up and locked the office door. He couldn't afford for anyone to walk in on him, for the next half an hour.

At one of the many briefing, that the Sussex Patrol had given him, he was told that if ever the Germans landed, he was to contact a person code named 'The Pheasant' and make his reports to him. This person was to take command of all the Auxiliary Units in the event of the German invasion. As such it was his duty to report what he had found out, about this apparent landing of German saboteurs, to him.

Peter had not passed this information on to the members of his unit. It was because of this that they had sent the initial report to the Sussex Patrol. He had to assume that they had passed their report on to the Pheasant.

The first thing he had to do was draft out his message to the Pheasant.

To The Pheasant
All men identified.
One gone to Hastings – Fisherman.
One believe in Hailsham.
Leader headed for Eastbourne.
Location of others known and can be dealt with.
Bishopstone Unit.

Happy with what he was to send, Peter uncovered his radio transmitter, switched it on and tuned it in to the required frequency. Peter was one of only a very few of the Auxiliary Forces leaders who had been permitted to have his own transmitter.

Partly because his farm was a long way from places where they could sight a radio operator and be able to keep their identity secret from each other.

Peter put on his headphones and picked up the microphone. He flicked the switch to transmit. He gave his call sign and flicked the switch off and waited for a reply. There was an almost instantaneous reply. The lady at the other end was ready for his message. He read out his drafted message and she confirmed receipt and then she went off the air.

He had hoped that he could speak to her for a little longer but she was very business like and kept their contact to a minimum. She had told him to be stood by at eight o'clock, this evening and again at six o'clock tomorrow morning, to receive orders.

Chapter 11
Find the Tramp

Sam Carter got up as usual, at about eight twenty in the morning. His wife was already up and in the process of getting his breakfast ready. She always had it on the table by eight thirty. In that way Sam could be out of the house by eight forty five and walking through the gates of the Star Brewery, for nine o'clock.

He had ten minutes to get a quick wash and get dressed. Sam was an important member of staff so he dressed in a suit and he also would put on a bowler hat, when he left his cottage, for work. The most important meal of the day, as far as he was concerned, was breakfast.

This set him up for the day, particularly a Friday, as this was the busiest day of the week. There would be a lot of deliveries to be made and he needed to ensure that everything was ready when the draymen came to collect the barrels of beer.

Being the type of man he was, he finished his breakfast, drank down the last vestiges of the mug of tea, Sally had made for him, within the fifteen minutes he had set himself. Sam said good bye to Sally and headed towards the front door.

He reached up to the row of pegs and took his bowler hat off its allotted peg. After stopping and facing the mirror, he placed the bowler on his head and adjusted it to sit how he liked it to be. Now he was ready to face the world.

Sam stepped out of his cottage, closed the door and, after three steps, he was on the foot path, that ran passed his cottage. He then, immediately turned right to walk down Watts Lane. At the end of the Lane he, again, turned right, into Crown Street. Then, more or less immediately, he would cross the road and soon turned into Star Road. Within twenty strides he would have reached the Star Brewery main gates.

But today was different, as he approached the junction with Crown Street; he looked down at the low wall that ran beside the foot path. This wall separated the narrow strip of land between the last of the cottages, in the Lane, from the foot path. What he was looking for, as he did each time he passed this way, was to see if a message had been left for him at the 'dead letter box'.

He was never sure if he was pleased to find that there was a message for him, or not. If there was, then his day might get quite exciting, if there wasn't any message, then he just had his normal work to do. Today he could see that the brick, which marked the 'dead letter box', was sticking slightly out from being flush with the rest of the bricks in the wall.

As he drew level with this brick, Sam bent down, as if to tie his shoe lace. He glanced around to make sure that he was not being observed. Sam didn't think he was, so with his left hand on his shoe, he used his right hand to remove the brick, place it down on the path, between his shoe and the wall. He reached into the hole in the wall, with his fingers and felt for the message that had been left.

His fingers felt the paper that had been stuffed into the hole and had been rammed home, when the brick was replaced.

He withdrew the paper and tucked it into his sock. With a practiced move the brick was replaced. And, because there was nothing stopping it, the brick finished flush with the other bricks in the wall. Now that he had retrieved the message he could stand up and carry on his walk to the Brewery.

As he drew closer to the Star Brewery, he was meeting others who worked there. Being The Master Brewer, he was always addressed by the workers and management as Mr Carter or Master Brewer. He walked through the main gates and received a salute from the gate guard.

Sam quickly walked over to the delivery's warehouse, to ensure that they were ready for the draymen and that there were sufficient barrels for today's deliveries. He was assured that there were.

Now he needed to see what this message was all about. So he headed towards the main brewing building, where his office was located. Normally he would do his rounds of the Brewery, before going to his office but that could wait for quarter of an hour. Once in his office he took off his hat and placed it on its peg, on the back of his office door. He hung a notice on the outside of the door, saying that he was not to be disturbed.

Then he closed the door and turned the key in the lock, to ensure that he was not disturbed.

It's funny how a notice 'Do Not Disturb' never applied to the person who wanted to see the person behind the door, where such a notice was hung!

Sam sat on his chair and reached down to his right sock and felt down the side, to retrieve the piece of paper that he placed there earlier. It had not worked its way down too far, so it was easy to retrieve. He opened the folded paper and read it:-

From The Pheasant.

10 Germans landed at Exceat.
1 German agent is in your area, dressed as a tramp. You are to find him and ensure that you know where he is at all times.

'Good, action at last', thought Sam. Sam Carter was the leader of the Eastbourne Auxiliary Forces Unit. In fact his unit was the first to be set up in any part of the country. At his last meeting with the Sussex Patrol officer he had been briefed about 'The Pheasant'.

This person was the overall commander of all the Auxiliary Forces in the South of England and if he gave any orders, they were to be carried out. The radio operators would ensure that the messages have come from Him, before they pass them on to you. As such, you were not to question the message.

The radio operators were also a secret group. It was their job to collect messages from the Auxiliary Units, via the 'dead letter boxes' and pass the information on to the appropriate people. These people could be other local Auxiliary Unit's radio operators, The Military Command or the Sussex Patrol. They were also there to pass messages on to the Auxiliary Units.

Right, now he would have to mobilise his unit. Firstly he would need to get them out, around the town and find this German 'Tramp'. Once found, he would need to ensure that they could follow him, without him noticing. His men had all been trained to carry out this type of work, so he didn't think it would take them to long to find him.

The first member of his unit, he would need to get hold of, was Terry Cooper. He knew that Friday's weren't too busy for him. He was mostly busy on Tuesdays and Wednesdays. Terry was the senior Cooper for the Brewery. He had two assistants, so he could leave them to do any urgent work that may be required, in his absence.

The next person he needed would be 'Uncle' Tom Kelly. One of the Brewery's longest serving draymen. The other members of his unit worked outside the Brewery, so he would need to send for them.

Sam unlocked his office door, removed the notice. He took his hat off the peg and returned the notice to its hook, behind the door. With his bowler hat on he walked out of the office and into the main yard of the brewery.

As he reached the yard, Sam saw 'Uncle' Tom bringing his horses and wagon into the yard, to collect his first delivery of the day.

"'Uncle' Tom, I need to see you in my office. Let Henry sort out your delivery." Sam boomed across the yard.

"OK" answered 'Uncle' Tom.

With the first one sorted out, he walked to the end of the yard and into the building where the empty barrels were stored and repaired. He needed to get hold of Terry.

"Terry, I need to see you in my Office." Sam shouted, as he entered the Cooper's workshop.

The rest of the coopers looked at Sam and then at Terry. What had he done wrong now? They asked themselves. Mr Carter rarely ever came over to this part of the brewery. When he did, someone was in trouble. Terry, on the other hand guessed that it was Auxiliary Forces business, so just shrugged his shoulder, when his colleagues asked what he had done.

As Sam and Terry walked back towards The Master Brewer's office, Sam saw Andrew, the messenger boy. He called him over. He needed to get a message to the other two members of his unit. He saw utilising one of the messengers for Auxiliary Forces work, as getting him to do his bit for the war effort.

"Andrew, I need you to cycle over to the golf course and find Mr Young, the grounds man. Tell him to get here as quickly as he can and report to me in my office. Oh and on the way, Andrew, call into the Police station and ask Sergeant Davies to come and see me, as well." Mr Carter ordered.

"What if they won't come?" Andrew asked.

"Don't worry, they'll come." Mr Carter reassured him.

While this was going on, Terry continued towards Sam's office. But before Sam went to his office, he went over to the main gate and spoke to Michael Nevis, the gate guard. He told him that he was expecting two guests and they were to be shown to his office, immediately. He gave Michael their names and then walked back to his office.

Terry was waiting, outside the office door, when Sam eventually arrived.

"Come in Terry. 'Uncle' Tom will be here in a moment. Then we'll start." Sam said.

Within a few moments there was a knock on his office door. He called out that the person should come in. It was 'Uncle' Tom.

Once 'Uncle' Tom and Terry were seated, Sam closed and locked his office door and then took his seat, behind the desk.

"I've received a message from 'The Pheasant'." Sam said.

"I thought he was just imaginary." Terry said.

"No he's real enough. He has a job for us. I don't know if it is a training exercise or not but we'll treat it as real. Lieutenant Hamilton had said that he would be contacting us and he may choose to have a training exercise but this order may very well be for real. As you remember, Lieutenant Hamilton briefed us, last week, that there are thoughts that the Germans are massing, in France, for an invasion, so we had better be ready." Sam reported.

"What's this job then?" 'Uncle' Tom asked.

"Well it appears that there is a Tramp, heading for this town and that he is in fact a German spy. Our job is to find him and keep an eye on him." Sam said

"How the hell are we to do that? We don't know what he looks like or where he'll be." 'Uncle' Tom said.

"I know, but we must find him. Tom, you go on your rounds and ask the publicans to keep an eye out for a tramp. Tell them if they let you know if they see our 'tramp', there's a keg in it for them."

"Terry, you head for the Martello Tower and walk along the promenade." Sam said.

"Is that as far as you want me to go?" Tom asked.

"No, go on the Pier, he may be looking that over, as a landing place. Then walk on, passed the Redoubt and as far as Princes Park. If you haven't found him by then, walk all the way back and check the sea front out again. Then report back to me." Sam said.

"Don't we get any help?" Tom asked.

"Yes, I've already sent for the other two but I wanted to get you two out, looking, as soon as possible. Now off you go and remember to report in as soon as you find him." Sam ordered.

As the two of them were leaving the office, Sergeant Luke Davies was just being escorted into see the Master Brewer. Luke was stationed in the Old Town police station, so this gave him a certain amount of autonomy.

"Been bad boys, I see. Has the Head Master given you both a good caning?" Luke asked.

"No, he's saving the cane for you." Tom said, as both he and Terry disappeared.

"What's this all about then? I've just had the Inspector over and he's ordered me to get all the men out, looking for a Tramp!" Luke asked.

"Why?" Sam asked

"There is a report that some men landed at Exceat and one, dressed as a tramp, was headed for this town." Luke reported.

"Well that is what I wanted you for. I've had an order to find this same tramp." Sam said.

"I'm sorry but I can't help, today. I'm the only one left in the station, until we find this man." Luke reported.

"What are your orders, once you find him?" Sam asked.

"We were to find him and then report it to the main station in the town. What we do then I don't know." Luke said.

"Well I do, this unit has to keep a track on him and be sure where he is at all times." Sam said.

"Why is this tramp so important then?" Luke asked.

"As you know, the Gerry's are getting ready to invade us and it's believed that this group, of ten men, are here to ensure that their landing goes to plan. Why he's in Eastbourne we don't know but here he most certainly is."

"Luke, if your men find him before we do, will you make sure you let me know the tramps whereabouts." Sam asked.

"No worry, I'll let you know." Luke said and left the office, he did not have much time to hang around. He had left one of his constables looking after the station and he needed him out and about, looking for this tramp.

Sam was just making plans for his days work when there was, yet another knock on his office door.   "Come in." Sam shouted.

"You sent for me Sam." Will greeted Sam with his usual big smile.

It had taken him longer to get here as he was the green keeper at the local golf club, about a mile away from the Brewery.

"Thanks for coming Will. Look we have an important task to carry out. There appears to have been a German landing in Exceat. About ten men, as far as I can find out, all dressed in civilian clothes. One of the men is reported to have been heading here. He's dressed as a tramp." Sam said.

"Where do I come in?" Will asked.

"I need you to get up onto Beachy Head and see if you can find him or if anyone has seen him. Then report back to me. If you do see him, don't let him know you're watching him. We need him to carry on with whatever he's doing. When the time is right, he'll be dealt with, but not before." Sam said

"Will. Once we have him, I'll need the unit to watch him 24 hours a day, until we are told what to do with him." Sam stated.

"OK, I'll see what I can find out. If he's still up there, I'll stay and watch him." Will said

"How will we know you've found him, then?" Sam asked.

"Well if I'm not back here by dinner time, you'll know I'm watching him." Will said.

"Alright, you be off. Report back as soon as you know anything." Sam said.

Will left the office and headed back to the Brewery's main gate. He had arrived, at the Brewery, on his bicycle and parked it behind the main gate office.

On his way out, he stopped and asked if it was alright if he left it there for a while. He had to carry out a task for the Master Brewer and then report back to him.

The Main Gate Guard said that it would be alright, as it was for the Master Brewer. He had no intention of riding it all the way up onto Beachy Head.

Will left the Brewery and walked back up Star Road into Crown Street. He knew that there was a bus that ran along this road, in the next ten minutes. This bus would take him up onto Beachy Head. That would be much quicker than walking.

'Uncle' Tom's wagon was loaded by the time he had returned from Mr Carter's office. He checked that everything was secure. He may have trained Harry well, over the last two years, but he knew that, on the one occasion when he didn't check the load, the load would shift and before he could do anything about it they would have an accident. As he was responsible for the loading of the wagon, he couldn't then blame Harry.

Tom climbed up into his seat and took the horses reins. He called them to move off and gave a slight flick with the reins. Now they were on their way for the deliveries, to the far end of the town. On leaving the Brewery main gates, they headed towards St Mary's Hospital, then over the railway bridge. When they reached the junction with Seaside Road he turned left for Langley.

All the time, Tom was watching everyone they passed. He also looked down each of the side roads they passed.

"Who are you looking for Mr Kelly?" Harry asked, after watching him for about half a mile.

"Just a man." Was all he said.

"Well maybe I can help you find him?" Harry suggested.

"Harry I'm looking for a man. He's dressed as a tramp. Don't ask me why but it's important." Tom said, looking Harry directly in the eye.

They carried on until they reached the first of their deliveries. While Harry and the Publican's pot man unloaded the barrels, destined for this pub, Tom took the Publican, John, to one side and asked if he had seen a tramp around in the last 24 hours. He said that he hadn't, if he had he would have sent him away with a fly in his ear. Tom asked that if he did, to let Mr Carter, at the Brewery, know. He agreed to that. Especially after he was told that if it was the man they were looking for, he would get a keg of beer.

Tom carried on with his deliveries, gradually moving back towards the Brewery. At each stop he asked the same question and offered the same reward, but he had no luck.

Both Sam and Tom knew that, with the offer of a keg of beer, the publicans would get word out that they were looking for a tramp. It had been stressed that it was just his location they wanted. They didn't want him disturbed. Each publican offered various rewards for any information, but in each case, the person who found this man would not have to buy any beer, in their pub for at least a week.

Terry made it to the sea front, in about fifteen minutes. He looked up towards Beachy Head but there were no suspicious characters in view. So he turned and started his long walk along the sea front. He reached the Martello Tower and looked around but there was no sign of any tramps. He walked over to a soldier, who was stood by a tent, under the Tower.

"Hi Bombardier have you seen a tramp around here?" Terry asked.

"Funny you ask, when we came on duty there was one standing over there, looking up at the top of the Tower. He appeared to be looking at our anti-aircraft gun." The Bombardier answered.

"Did you notice where he went?" Terry asked

"Yes, he walked off down towards the Pier."

"You're the second person to ask about him this morning." The Bombardier said.

"Who else has asked?" Terry enquired.

"A policeman"

"Well thank you very much, you have been very helpful. If you see the tramp, again, send one of you men to the police station and let them know where he was headed." Terry said.

"OK Sir, I'll do that." He said and threw up a salute, to Terry. Terry smiled back, then walked off and headed down the promenade, to the pier.

It was a nice day, although the wind was getting up. Still it was better being out here than working in the Cooper's Workshop, at the Brewery.

By the time Terry had reached the pier, Will was getting off the bus by the pub, on the top of Beachy Head. He quickly headed for the pub. This would be the best place to make some initial enquiries about the tramp. If he was what people thought he was, then he would have headed this way.

Beachy Head gives you a very good view over the whole area. On a clear day you could see as far as Fairlight, passed Hasting, to the East.

To the West you could see as far as Brighton, but not the actual town, as that was behind some of the hills along the coast line. It also gave you a good view, inland for about fifteen miles.

"Good day." Will said as he entered the public bar room. Addressing the woman stood behind the bar.

"I'm looking for a man. I think he may be a tramp." Will said, as he approached the bar.

"We haven't seen any tramps here today." The lady replied.

"I think he's stolen some equipment from my sheds, at the golf club." Will reported, hopeful that that would jog her memory. But he got no response.

"What about yesterday? I don't know if the things went missing last night or the night before." Will said.

"Frank. Have you seen a tramp around here?" The lady shouted, to a man in the back room.

"Yes, I saw one this morning, at about eight o'clock. He was standing on the top, looking around. What caught my eye was that he appeared to be using a pair of binoculars." Frank said, as he returned to the Bar.

"Did you see him leave?" Will asked.

"No, I was too busy getting the bar cleaned up and restocked for today." Frank said.

"Thank you. If he comes this way again, will you tell the Eastbourne police?" Will asked.

"Aye, we'll do that." Frank confirmed.

Will didn't have time to stop and have a half pint of beer. He had a lot of work to do at the Golf Course. He knew that first he would have to report to Sam Carter about what he had found out.

Will started to walk towards Eastbourne Old Town, as he was not sure when the next bus would pass this way. If he heard one coming, he would flag it down.

The bus drivers were not so particular about picking people up, away from the nominated bus stops, out in the country side, as they were in the towns.

He hadn't gone far when he heard the sound of a vehicle, coming along the road, behind him.

Will turned around and saw that it was the car of the Captain of the Golf Club. He didn't know if he should flag him down, for a lift back to town or to let him pass by.

The decision was taken out of his hands. The car pulled up, about ten yards passed where Will was stood. Major Swanson opened the driver's door and got out and turned towards Will.

"Young Will, what the hell are you doing up here? You have the bunkers to rake today." He asked.

"I'm up here on Home Guard duties, Sir." Will lied as he wasn't in the Home Guard but the Major had been told that he was a member, to cover his disappearance, on occasions.

"Would you like a lift back to the Golf Club?" the Major asked.

"I would love a lift, but I've to call in to the Old Town Police Station before I come back to the Club, Sir." Will replied.

"That's OK. I'm going that way, anyway. Hop in." The Major said.

Will opened the passenger door, got in and closed it again. During the journey back to the Old Town, the Major tried to get Will to revel what he had been up to Beachy Head for but he was not going to tell him. He successfully avoided answering any of his questions, much to the annoyance of the Major.

The Major stopped the car, outside the Police Station and Will thanked him for the lift. He quickly headed into the Police Station and called out for Sergeant Davies.

"Wait a moment. I'm just getting a mug of tea." A voice came from behind a large cupboard, to the right of the counter.

"It's me, Will. I've something to report to Mr Carter." Will called out.

Luke returned, from behind the cupboard, clutching two mug of tea. He placed one of them in front of Will.

"It was two spoons of sugar?" Luke said.

"Thanks." Will responded.

"What have you been up to?" Luke asked.

"I've been up to Beachy Head and spoke to Frank. He said that at about eight o'clock, this morning, he saw a tramp standing on the top of the hill. He appeared to be looking around the area, with a pair of binoculars." Will reported.

"Oh. He must have been checking out the area, before he came into town." Luke said, as much to himself as to Will.

"Luke, I haven't got time to go into the Brewery and report to Mr Carter. I've got to get my bike, from the main gate, then hurry back to work. Major Swanson gave me a lift, from Beachy Head and I promised I'd get back to work soon." Will said.

"Yes. I've got to go passed Star Road soon. I've to report to the main Police Station in an hour, so I'll call in on my way." Luke said.

Once Will had finished his tea, he thanked Luke and went on his way to collect his bike and make his way back to the Golf Club.

Terry had arrived at the town's pier and wondered if he could have a quick look around but it was sealed off with coils of barbed wire. They had been told that if the Germans invaded, the pier would be blown up, so that the Germans couldn't use it as a landing point. It appeared that the preparations were now completed.

Terry continued on along the coast line. He passed the Queen's Hotel, which overlooked the pier and walked on down the road until he reached the Redoubt. He could see that there were more anti-aircraft guns located on the roof of its main tower. Some soldiers were sitting around the wall that ran all around the tower.

They were too far away for him to talk to and shouting might carry to the Tramp, if he was nearby. He decided to carry on walking along the road.

Terry knew that once he had gone passed the fishing huts, that were next along the beach, he would be at Princes Park and his long walk would have been for nothing. Still, he had to complete his search for this tramp. He would never forgive himself if it was found that he hadn't done his duty.

Half way to the park, Terry decided to leave the foot path and walk up onto the beach head and walk between the fishermen's huts. He had no idea why he had taken this route but, he was soon glad that he had.

As he was walking past one of the huts, he looked between two of the fishermen's boats, which were drawn up on the beach. Under the hull of the first boat, a man sat, who looked completely out of place. He wasn't a fisherman, Terry was sure of that. He didn't know why but he decided to speak t the man.

"Are you alright?" He asked.

The startled man looked around and looked visibly shocked at being discovered hiding there. Simon had thought that he had found the idle place to hide out, but he had been easily discovered.

"I'm alright, thank you." The 'tramp' replied.

"Would you like a smoke?" Terry asked, taking out his tin of tobacco and his cigarette papers from his pocked.

"No thanks." The 'Tramp' said, declining his offer.

"Don't mind if I stop for a smoke, do you?" Terry asked.

"No, help yourself." He said.

Terry stood against the second of the boats and started to roll himself a cigarette. All the time he looked away from the tramp's face. He had been taught that the less actual eye contact you make the better. If the person you were with, was of some interest to you.

"I love it down here, by the boats. It's so peaceful." Terry said but he got no reply from the tramp.

After five minutes of trying to make small talk with the tramp, Terry stubbed out his cigarette against the hull of the boat and bid farewell to the tramp, walked off the beach and back to the road.

He remembered that he had seen a telephone box, down one of the side roads that he had past, about a hundred yards back up the road. Terry headed for that. He was itching to look back and see if the tramp was watching him but knew that it would be wrong. If the tramp saw him looking he would get suspicious.

When Terry reached the red telephone box, he pulled the door open and went inside. He knew the telephone number of the Brewery's switchboard. He picked up the hand set and waited for the operator to answer.

"Number please." The operator asked.

"Four five seven two, please" Terry said.

"That will be two pence. Please put the money in the slot." Terry put the money into the slot.

"I will connect you now. When they answer, please press button A." She said. "If you don't get a reply, press button B, to get your money back."

Terry waited for the connection to go through. He heard a voice come on the line and so pressed button A, as directed.

"Can you put me through to Mr Carter, please?" Terry asked the Brewery's switchboard operator.

Chapter 12
Four five seven two

"Master Brewer, can I help you?" Sam Carter said as he answered his office telephone.

"Mr Carter, I've found the missing barrel." Terry said.

For a moment Sam didn't realise what he was being told, then he recognised Terry's voice.

They hadn't set up any passwords or codes so he was taken back that Terry had come up with his own. He then clicked that Terry had realised that the switchboard operator may have recognised his voice and neither of them needed anyone to know their business.

"Where is this barrel?" Sam asked.

"It's between the Redoubt and the park." Terry reported.

"Are you sure that it's our barrel?" Sam enquired.

"Yes, I went up to it, stood and had a smoke, before I came to ring you." Terry said.

"Right, you stay near there and I'll send someone to take care of the barrel for a while until I can arrange for it to be collected." Sam said.

Just as he was putting the phone down, Luke knocked on the door and, without waiting, walked into the office.

"Sam, Will asked me to give you his report. The publican at Beachy Head said that he saw a tramp up there this morning, at about eight o'clock. Then he thinks he headed for the town." Luke reported before Sam could answer.

"Well Terry has found him. He just telephoned me." Sam said

"Where is he?" Luke asked.

"Luke this is not a Police matter." Sam said.

"I'm sorry Sam but it is. We were tasked to find this man before you got your message." Luke insisted.

"OK but he must not be arrested or know that we know who he is. Do you understand?" Sam ordered.

"Yes. The Inspector had said that their orders were to find and follow him but not to arrest him." Luke reported.

"Right, Terry is by the Redoubt. He can show your men where he is. Terry stood talking to him for about five minutes, so he can't get too close, again." Sam said.

"Thank you. I'm on my way to report to my Inspector, so I'll have to go. I'll report back later." Luke said, as he turned and walked out of the office.

It took Luke only about ten minutes to reach the main town police station, on his police bicycle. As soon as he arrived he asked to see Inspector Roberts, as a matter of urgency. He was quickly shown into his office.

"Sergeant Davies, what do you want, that's so urgent?" Inspector Roberts asked.

"I know were the tramp is, Sir." Luke reported.

"How do you know, we haven't had time to do a proper search?" The inspector protested.

"I have friends, whom I trust. One of them found him and will show us where he's hiding." Luke said.

"I'll get a car. We'll use the bells to get us there quicker." Inspector Roberts said, as he stood up and reached for his cap.

"No Sir. No bells or we'll scare him away. We need to watch him not arrest him, remember what you said this morning, to my men?" Luke said.

This brought the adrenalin rush that was causing through the Inspector, to do rash things, to back down. He quickly realised that the Sergeant was correct.

Inspector Roberts could get just as much credit in finding this man, by sending the Sergeant to locate him, as he could if he went himself.

He instructed Luke to get one of the junior constables and take him to watch over the tramp. He would ring the front desk and get a car brought around to the front of the Police station.

They would be instructed to take Luke where ever it was that they needed to be. In the mean time he would report this to the Chief Inspector.

"By the way, where is this tramp?" Inspector Roberts asked.

"Bye a fishing boat, near the Redoubt." Luke answered.

Luke left the Inspector's office and headed off to find someone to watch over the 'tramp'. He had decided to use one of the detective constables. Being in plain clothes they would be a better bet than some new recruit, in uniform.

He walked into the detective's office and spoke to the Sergeant and asked to borrow one of his men. He detailed off Jacob Oliver to go with Luke. The two of them headed for the main entrance of the Police Station. Just as they reached the bottom step a police car pulled up.

Luke got into the passenger seat and Jacob Oliver climbed into the seat behind Luke's. Luke told the driver to head for the sea front. As he started moving the driver switched on the bell, so as to make people move out of his way.

"No bell." Luke ordered.

"Not so fast either. I want you to drive like a 'Sunday Driver' not a racing driver." Luke said

"I was told it was urgent, Sarg." The drive said.

"Urgent, yes. Fast, no." Luke replied.

Once they reached the sea front, Luke told him to turn left and head for the Redoubt, but as they neared their destination, he told the driver to slow right down and to be ready to stop, when he said so.

As they neared the Redoubt, Luke looked at the driver in a way that told him to do just as he had been told. He drove slowly around the left hand bend. Luke told him to pull up, into the first side street he came to.

Once the car had come to a stop, both he and Jacob got out of the car. Luke told the driver to wait for him to return. Jacob and Luke then walked off and crossed the main road.

78

They continued further along the road, the way they had been travelling. After about twenty yards, they come up to Terry, who was looking away from them.

He had not even heard the car approaching, which had been Luke's intention. If Terry didn't hear them, the 'Tramp' wouldn't have heard them either.

"Terry, this is Jacob, Jacob, Terry." Luke introduced the two men.

"Terry found the man you are to watch."

"Terry, Jacob is going to watch our man. He'll be relieved later. Will you show him where our man is and he'll find the best place, to be able to watch him." Luke said.

"But I thought we..." Terry started to say.

"This is a Police matter now young man." Luke said sternly.

"Now go and show Jacob where he's hiding." Luke ordered.

"Terry, I'll take you back to work, once you've finished." Luke said, more softly this time.

Terry and Jacob walked off, down the road. Luke could see Terry stop, and point in the direction of the fishing boats. They didn't walk onto the beach, but parted company. Jacob walked on and appeared to enter the fisherman's club house. It was then that Luke remembered that Jacob came from this side of the town and would have good contacts down here. That would help.

It only took a few minutes for Terry to walk back and rejoin Luke. They then crossed the road and Luke took Terry back to the Police car. He told the driver to take Mr Cooper back to the Star Brewery and then he could take him back to the Main Police Station, so that he could report to Inspector Roberts. Again he reminded the driver not to use the bells, but he could drive at a normal speed.

It had been a busy morning, but a successful one for Sam. He now needed to get his report back to 'The Pheasant'. He had to be careful what he wrote. He didn't know who the radio operator was.

His only contact with them was via the 'dead letter drop' at the junction of Watts Lane and Crown Road. For the first time he would have to use the signal that told the radio operator that there was an urgent message to be sent. He sat down and wrote his message.

From the Star.
To The Pheasant.
Located missing man.
Now being watched 24 hours as day.

He folded the paper and tucked into the sock of his left leg. He reached into the third draw of his desk and fumbled to the back of the draw. Here he wanted to find one of the red hankies that he needed to hang on the shrub above the 'dead letter box'. Once he had this, he put it into his pocket and headed out of the office.

Sam always returned home for lunch, at this time, so his departure wouldn't be thought of as unusual.

He walked up Star Road and turned right on reaching Crown Street. He quickly crossed the road and after a few paces he was turning into Watts Lane.

He looked around, as he turned the corner, then, once he reached the loose brick, he bent down to tie his shoe lace, again. Sure that no one was about he slipped the brick out of the wall, slid the note into the hole and replaced the brick.

He stood up and looked around. There was no one in sight so he took the red hankie out of his pocket and tied one corner of it to a branch of the shrub the other side of the wall. Satisfied that it could be seen but was far enough away to prevent youngsters from noticing it and stealing it, he went on his way home.

Sally had his lunch on the table, ready for him. He went to the basin and washed his hands. Then he joined his wife at the table. They talked about general things but he never talked about the Auxiliary Forces work he did.

After he had finished his lunch and they had drunk their tea, Sally returned to the kitchen to do the washing up and Sam went up to the bedroom and opened his wardrobe. He reached up and removed a shoe box on the top shelf, to the right hand side. He then got onto tip toes and reached further back for a small case and pulled this out and placed it on his bed.

This was his little secret. Sally could not reach up onto the top shelf and particularly not reach the back of it. As such what ever he put there was safe.

He opened the case and flipped the lid backwards, onto the bed. Now he could get what he needed. The first think he removed was the Service Revolver and the .38 ammunition that went with it.

Sam checked to ensure that it was still loaded, it was. He placed the revolver in his right hand jacket pocket and six rounds of spare ammunition into the left hand pocket. Next he took out the commando knife, together with its sheaf.

He had adapted the sheaf so that he could strap it onto his left arm, between his elbow and wrist, so that the handle of the knife was easily available for him to grip and remove the knife from its sheaf. Having armed himself he closed the case, replaced it onto the top shelf and place the shoe box in front of it, so it was well hidden.

Now he was ready, Sam returned downstairs, and gave Sally a quick kiss on her forehead and left to return to the Brewery.

As he approached the 'dead letter box' he noticed that his red hankie had gone, but a green one had taken its place. This meant that his message had been sent and that there was a reply. Sam reached up and pulled the hankie from the branch and dropped it onto the foot path.

With the hankie on the floor, he knelt down to pick it up. As he did so he pulled out the brick, retrieved the new message and smoothly returned the brick into the wall.

As he walked off he decided that as the message had come back so quickly, it must be important so he read it as he walked.

From The Pheasant
Good.   Stand your team too. Further orders at 16:00 hrs

Chapter 13
Let them know

Friday night was the night where most of the men went out to the local public houses for a drink or two. Even during harvest, once their work was done and the sun had dipped over the horizon, the workers would meet up at the pubs. They would only go home, once they had had sufficient ale.

This Friday was an exception, for the men of the Auxiliary Forces, some were already out on duty, following or watching the Germans who had arrived that morning. The others were going to their base, to await orders.

They had told their families that because of the expected German invasion, they may be out all night, on Home Guard duties, they had to be ready. None of the families complained, they knew that they were lucky to have their men here, at home. A lot of their friends had their men away, many serving overseas.

The leaders of the various Auxiliary Units were waiting for the orders, from 'The Pheasant', to come through. As they were not in actual contact with this person, they had to wait for him to communicate with them. He had said that the message would be sent out at 16:00 hours but for most of them, they would need the special signals operator, who they did not know, to deliver the message to the 'dead letter box'. As a result they would not go to collect it until about 16:20 hours. In that way they would not run into the person delivering the message. Secrecy was paramount, to both sets of people.

The message, when it arrived, was short:-

From the Pheasant

All Germans found.
Ensure that they are followed tomorrow.
More orders at 08:00 hours Saturday

The leaders took the message to their bases and discussed what action, they should take. Those with Germans in their area worked out which members of their unit would be following the Germans. Those with no Germans knew that they would most likely be called up, once the decision was made as to what action was to be taken against the Germans.

It had also been a busy day for Simon Johns, the German's team leader. Having found the fishing boats, drawn up on the beach, in Eastbourne, he had decided to make one of them his base.

The one he had chosen was a boat with a hole in its hull. This boat was going nowhere and from the looks of it, no one had yet tried to repair the hole.

When he thought it was safe, he threw his bag up onto the deck and then climbed up, behind it. He had not noticed that his every move was being watched, from the fisherman's club house, by Detective Jacob Oliver. Simon thought that only the man, who had stopped to have a smoke, even knew of his existence. As such he felt quite secure here.

Once aboard, he made his way down into the hold of the boat. Here he found some sacks, piled up in one corner. This would give him something to sit or lay on.

His next task was to get out his radio and test that he could send and receive messages. He could not afford to have the aerial up on deck, so he treaded it around the roof of the hold, going between the various pipes and rafters so as to give him a good length of wire so as to get the best reception possible.

He tuned into his contacts frequency, in France. They said that they could receive him well. He then turned into the Fishing boats frequency and called up Tobias. He confirmed that he could receive him and that he was sitting off Beachy Head, about two miles out.

Once he was happy that his radio worked, he took out some of his rations and sat and ate his first meal, on English soil.

When six o'clock in the evening came, he switched on his radio again and this time tuned into the frequency that had been set up for his team to contact each other.

Today they had been told just to find somewhere to stay and to get to know the area they would be working in.

Tomorrow they would start to locate the places they were told to find and then set about ensuring that they could take control of these places, once the invasion started.

He called up each of his men, in turn. He knew that all of them would be listening in but he wanted to ensure that he had contact with each and every one of them. It took him about half an hour to contact them all. He now set about making himself a place to sleep. After all he was a 'Tramp' and an inn was not the place for the likes of him. There were none of the 'privileges of rank' for him now. Not over the next few days, anyway.

Day two – Saturday 14th September 1940

Chapter 14
Let them know

Saturday 14th September 1940 was a very busy morning for all the Auxiliary Units, in the area. They all received the same message.

From The Pheasant.

All the sheep must be aware that they have been found and that they will be rounded up Sunday Morning. Ram to be Sheppard back to field.

Report back by noon.

Mat Palmer called on David, as soon as he could. He needed him to find out exactly where the two Germans were. He was to contact Andy and William, then get back to him. He would meet him at the White Heart Inn at nine o'clock.

David got on to his bicycle and rode down to the South Heighton Inn and asked Charles where his German was. He was told that the German had gone out about half an hour ago and headed for Newhaven, with Will on his tail.

Finding both Will and Andy, in Newhaven may not be an easy job. The town had many narrow lanes, twists and turns. The docks were not the easiest places for a non seaman to get around, unnoticed. Although Andy may stand out, mainly because of his height, young William could go about without, even his mother, noticing him.

David's first thought was to go to the White Heart Inn. It was fairly easy for him to get to and it was possible that the two Germans would meet up there, before going about their business.

Unfortunately they were not there, when he arrived. Tom said that they had been there but had left about ten minutes ago.

He said that a young boy appeared to be following the one that was not staying at his Inn and another man was following his German. David asked if the Germans knew that they were being followed. Tom said he didn't think so. He only noticed the others because they were not regulars about town, especially at that time in the morning.

David thanked him and went off in the direction that Tom had indicated that he thought the German's were heading. David rode off and as he turned one of the corners he nearly ran over Constable Proctor.

"What do you think this is the Isle of Man TT race?" Ken protested.

"Sorry Ken." David said, as he drew to a halt.

"Have you seen either Andy or young Will, on your travels?" David asked.

85

"Yes. Andy appeared to be following those men you asked about. Young Will, I saw him running over the sports field and heading up towards the fort." Ken reported.

"Where were the German's heading?" David asked.

"They appeared to be taking the road that would lead up to the fort." Ken said.

"Thanks, Ken." David said as he rode off in the direction of the fort.

In a few minutes he was in sight of Andy and he could see two men about fifty yards ahead of him. These must be the two German's. David continued up the road and drew along side Andy.

"Andy, don't get too close but you are to act so that they know that you're following them." David said.

"Why the hell do that, I thought that they weren't supposed to know we knew about them?" Andy huffed.

"Orders have changed. I'm meeting Mr Palmer at the White Heart at nine o'clock. I need to be able to tell him that the Germans know you and Will are following them." David said

"OK. If they do what they did yesterday, they'll reach the fence, walk along it for a hundred yards, then walk back down the hill and rejoin this road. They then walked back to the Inn." Andy reported.

"See you for a pint later." David said.

On his way back to the Inn, David again bumped into Ken Proctor. This time he asked that he come to the White Heart at nine o'clock and be in his uniform. David also told Ken what Mr Palmer wanted him to say, when he was sure that the Germans were in the bar room. Ken didn't understand. If this was only a Home Guard exercise, why don't we just arrest them and the exercise would be over? David said that orders had changed and they were going to have a bit of fun with these outsiders before they arrested them.

Once he arrived at the Inn, David walked his bike around to the rear of the Inn and went in, via the kitchen. Hazel was not too pleased to have customers walking through her kitchen, even if he was an old friend of Tom's and her brother-in-law.

Being a sea port, the Inns in the town were allowed to be open from early morning, through lunchtime and in the afternoon. Closing between six and eight o'clock, when they would open for the evening trade.

This was to allow for the seafarers, fishermen and those who worked on the docks to come for a drink, at any time during the day, mainly dependant on the tides or the cargo's they were loading or unloading.

David found Tom and spoke to him in a quiet corner of the Bar. There was no one in, at the moment but that could change at any time. He explained to him that they needed to put on a bit of an act, for the two Germans, when they returned from their 'walk'. Tom understood and agreed to go along with what ever was being said.

At nine o'clock, Mr Palmer walked into the bar. David was stood at the centre of the bar, taking to his brother Gerald, who worked in the docks. There was no one else in the bar, even Tom wasn't present.

David had enlisted the help of his brother, Gerald. He explained that they were on a Home Guard exercise and were after a couple of Regular Soldiers, who were acting as German spies. They needed to know their reaction to what Ken was to say, in their presence, a bit later. Gerald had agreed to help out.

"Hello David. How are things going?" Mat asked

"Fine. Ken's coming along and I've briefed both Tom and Gerald what we need to do. All we need now are the Germans." David said.

Gerald left the two men talking about what they were going to do and say. He went and sat at a seat, by the window, and looked out. Apparently he was watching the town folk going about their business.

"David." Gerald called from his window seat.

"Those men are headed this way." Gerald said.

It was not long before the two 'travelling salesmen' walked into the bar. With Gerald seated at the only seat by the window, they couldn't take up the seats they wanted. They needed to see who were following them.

After ordering a half pint of ale each, they took the next table next to Gerald. This gave them a reasonable view of the road they had just walked down. If they were being followed, then the two of them should appear shortly.

Andy and Will were now walking together and heading for the High Street. As they reached the street the local Police Constable walked up to them and they spoke for a short while. During the conversation, the younger one pointed towards the Inn and the Policeman looked in that direction. Once he had finished talking to them, they walked away and he headed for the Barroom door.

"Not a Police raid at this time of day, surely Ken?" Tom said as Ken Proctor walked into the bar.

"No, still your family must have been used to raids, when they sold contraband brandy?" Ken replied, as he walked up to the bar and joined Mat, David and Tom.

"Why are you about then?" Mat asked.

"Well…" Ken said as he looked around the bar room.

"There's going to be an operation going on tomorrow morning." Ken said, with a louder voice than would normally be prudent.

"There's a report going about town that there are a couple of German spies in the town and we have to arrest them at first light." Ken said.

With that said, the four of them gathered together, in a closer huddle and their voices were much lower, so as not to have the Germans understanding what they were saying. They just hoped that their message had got through. After a couple of minutes, the two Germans got up from their table and the one staying at the Inn asked if it was alright if he took his colleague up to his room, as they had some business to complete. Tom said that it was alright.

Once they had disappeared up the stairs, to the right of the bar, Gerald got up from his seat and walked over to join his brother.

"Ken, when you said that two German spies were to be arrested, they looked at each other and the one who is staying here said something, very quietly to the other, in German. I couldn't get what it was he said but it appears that they were going to contact his officer." Gerald said.

"Well done Gerald. Right everyone. Go about your business, we'll deal with this now. Ken, don't report what's gone on here today, will you? If you have to, give it a day or two before you do." Mat asked.

"I haven't understood what's been going on anyway." Ken replied, with a broad smile on his face.

"Tom, give everyone a drink. I must go and report this." Mat said and left a crown on the bar.

"David, I thought you said that those men were Regular British Soldiers? They may have spoken English but their German was native." Gerald said.

"Keep that to yourself, Gerald. Those men are special." David said with a wink.

"Oh." Gerald replied and picked up his free pint of ale.

On receiving his unit's message, Peter Savage sent Frank to Alfriston. He was to contact Simon, the village policeman.

They needed to know where the German was. Once they'd found him they were to make him aware that he was under suspicion of being a German spy and that all the German's, who landed on Friday morning, were to be arrested on Sunday morning. How they did it, Peter could not suggest but they would have to play it by ear.

Frank was in luck. Simon was just about to go into the Star Inn, when he arrived, in the village. He followed Simon into the Inn and walked up to the bar, behind him. He quietly asked if he knew where they could find the German.

Simon didn't turn around but said that he was the one sitting by the window, to the left of the doorway.

Frank accepted a half pint of ale from the landlord and then he ushered Simon to a table next to the one at which the German was seated.

"Constable Goring, I've just come from Eastbourne." Frank said in a voice that was neither loud nor soft but had an air of authority.

"That Foreigner, you reported. He's to be arrested tomorrow, at dawn." Frank said.

"I can't do that by myself." Simon protested.

"Don't worry, first thing tomorrow they're sending a car full, to help you out. They'll take him away to a cell, at the main Police station, in Eastbourne." Frank said.

Now that he appeared to have got his message across, Frank and Simon spoke in lower voices and finished off their ale. Just as he was about to get up, Simon reached out and took Frank's arm.

"Frank, I was speaking to a friend of mine, last night. Norman Leatherhead, he's a policeman in Hailsham and patrols the area of the Cattle Market. He said that a stranger, dressed in farm workers clothing walked into the Market, on Friday and asked for a job. They gave him one. He's sweeping the market, to get it ready for Market Day."

"Can you contact him and ask him to be in the Market at ten thirty?" Frank asked.

"That won't be a problem, I'll just finish my pint, here, and then I'll phone the station and get a message to him." Simon said.

He released his hand from Frank's arm and they both stood up and Simon walked Frank to the door. He then returned to the bar and spent the next five minuets talking to the barmaid.

While Frank had been about his task, Jack was on his way over to East Dean and The Tiger Inn. It was his job to make sure that the two men he had seen, by the emergency airstrip, were aware that they had been seen.

"Hi Lance, a half of your best ale please." Jack said

"Hi Jack. You appear to be around this area a lot this week." Lance said, as he pulled Jack his half.

"This time of year, the harvest, they just don't take care of their equipment, so I've to go along and repair it. Still it keeps me busy." Jack said, as he reached out for the glass.

In the mirror, behind the bar, Jack had seen that the two men he noticed yesterday were seated, behind him, to his left.

"I saw two men climbing over the fence to that field, just passed Friston Pond, yesterday." Jack said in a voice loud enough to carry to the two men behind him.

"What were they doing?" Lance asked.

"I don't know but there's a rumour, going around, that there are some German spies in the area." Jack said.

"There had not better be any in this village." Lance said, angrily.

"I hear that they'll all be rounded up tomorrow morning, so we'll be able to sleep well in our beds again." Jack stated.

Once Jack had finished his drink, he thanked Lance, put his glass back on the bar and handed over six pence. Now it was time to get back over to Wilmington, before he had to report back to Mr Savage.

Frank arrived at Hailsham Market just before ten thirty and as he approached the main gate, he saw the back of a policeman turning into the Market.

89

Good, Simon's message must have got through. Frank rode his bike through the market gates, got off it and lent his bike against the wall of the small café, used by the workers and, on market day, all the visitors to the market.

"Norman." Frank called at the departing policeman.

The policeman turned around, to see who was calling after him. It was not a voice he recognised, so was interested in whom it might be. The man who had called to him walked up and held out his hand, to shake his.

"Simon sent me. I'm Frank." Frank smiled as he introduced himself.

"I'm Norman, how can I help you. Simon didn't say what you wanted but that it was important." Norman said.

"You told Simon that there was a new man working in the Market."

"Yes but how is another worker in the Market so important?" Norman asked.

"I'm in the Home Guard and we have a training exercise going on. They have put some Regular Soldiers into the area, dressed as farm hands. We have to find them as they are supposed to be German spies. I need your help, to give a message to this new man." Frank said

"That's easy, that's him over there, in the cattle pens." Norman said. "You can tell him yourself."

"No the message needs to come from you. I'll tell you what you are to say, as we walk over there." Frank said.

As they walked over towards the pens, Frank told Norman what he had to say. He made him promise that he would tell no one about this. It must not appear in any of his reports. Norman was not at all happy with this request. He was a stickler for procedures but he would do it this once, as a favour to Simon.

"Not very busy around here now a days then Norman?" Frank said loud enough for the German to hear.

"No, just the same old pick pockets on Market Day and a few drunken farmers, if they have a good sale." Norman reported.

"Still you get Sunday's off." Frank said, as the two of them reached the pens and stood, leaning against them, as they appeared to watch the men cleaning out the pens.

"No. Not this week." Norman said

"Oh, what's on this Sunday then?" Frank asked.

"They say there's a German spy in the area. We're to round him up tomorrow morning." Norman said.

The two of them stood watching the men for a few minutes longer and then turned around and walked back to the café. Frank invited Norman in for a tea, which he accepted.

While they drank their tea, they watched, out of the café window, to see if the man Frank suspected of being the German spy, did anything. He soon left the pens and walk over to one of the buildings, were the workers kept their spare clothing. He was gone for about fifteen minutes and then he returned to the pens and carried on with his work.

Frank thanked Norman for his help and then got back on his bike and rode off, back to the farm and report to Mr Palmer.

By this time Jack had driven quite quickly through the country roads, far faster than he would usually do, but he was on a tight schedule. He had to be back at the farm before noon.

He called in at the Wilmington village pub but the publican didn't know where the men had gone, this morning. Jack took a gamble and headed for the Flying Club.

It was here that he had seen them and it would be here that they would need to be if or when the invasion started.

He turned his van into the roadway that led him into the Flying Club car park. Once he had parked his van, he took out his tool box, locked up the van and walked over to the larger of the hangers. He had never been here before but decided that he was more likely to find people in the largest hanger than the smaller one.

There was a door stood open, on the side of the hanger that faced Jack, so he headed for that.

It was a large impressive building but it had no windows on this side. As he neared the door, a farm worker walked out and approached him.

"What are you doing here, this is private?" The man asked.

"I got a call to come and look over the tractor. They're having trouble starting it." Jack replied.

"It must be somewhere else, this tractor is working well." The man replied.

Jack knew that he couldn't push his luck, if these were German troops. They could well be specially trained men, for this mission. Like him, they would have been trained to kill, if the need arose.

If he was not careful, he could be their first kill, on this side of the English Channel. He decided to play it cool, get into a conversation with this man and, hopefully he would be able to get his message across, if the moment was right.

"Do you have a light?" Jack asked, taking out his packet of Craven A cigarettes.

"Yes. Oh have one of mine." The man said, taking out his own packet of cigarettes and offered one to Jack.

Jack took one look at the packet and noticed that they were not cigarettes that could be brought in this area.

In fact he didn't think they were even English cigarettes. They looked much more like the American packets he had seen, but this packet had the name of 'Amateur' printed on it.

At first he thought it may have been a miss spelling but then he glanced down and saw the word 'Sigaretten' and realised that this was not an English or American packet of cigarettes.

"No thanks, I prefer my own." Jack said, as he   offered one of his cigarettes to the German. The man took one of Jacks and got out his lighter and gave Jack a light.

91

They spent a few minutes talking about the view from here and watched, as a pair of spitfires flew up the Cuckmere Valley and banked off towards Lewes.

"They say the Germans are massing in France, ready for an invasion." Jack said.

"I wouldn't take much notice of that." The man said.

"Oh, I heard that they say a group of Germans, landed at Exceat yesterday. Talk is that they may be here, ready for the invasion." Jack said, still watching the Spitfire's flying away.

The German said nothing. Just kept pulling away at his cigarette and blowing smoke rings. Jack thought that this would be the right moment to give him the message, he was here to deliver.

"Still the Constable, in Alfriston, said that they know where they are and that, first thing tomorrow morning, they'll all be rounded up." Jack said as he stubbed out his cigarette on the ground, with his right boot.

"Thanks for the chat. See you." Jack said and then bent down, picked up his tool box and headed back towards his van.

It was now that he felt most vulnerable. He had just told this man that he was to be arrested, tomorrow and then turned his back on a trained killer. He must be mad, but Jack now needed to get away from him and his mate.

There was no time to enter into a further conversation with this man. Leave while he is taking in what Jack had just told him. As he walked away, he listened out to hear if the German was going to follow him or, more likely, take out his pistol, cock it, and shoot him.

Jack was prepared for a shoot out. He had his fully loaded Service Revolver in a shoulder holster, hanging down under his left arm. He had hidden its existence from anyone he had spoken to today, by having his jacket buttons fastened but, as he walked away, he undid them. Now he felt that he was ready to defend himself.

As he got into his van, he breathed a sigh of relief. If he was right, behind the hanger door, stood the second German. He would have been standing guard, on his companion, but not with just a pistol, he would have either a rifle or a machine gun. If he thought Jack was going to do something to compromise their mission, he would use it. All Jack wanted to do now was to get safely back to the farm and give his report to Mr Palmer.

When the Sussex Patrol received the message, from the Pheasant, they were visiting the Beauport Park secret hide. This was one of the special hides. Very much like the one in the woods at Jevington. It was designed to hold at least twenty men. It had beds, food and an arsenal of weapons and ammunition, to resupply any of the units that had needed to leave their own hides, before they could empty it of its weapons and explosives.

Being just outside Hastings, They were the nearest unit to where the German fisherman was. Lieutenant Hamilton decided that he would take action. There was no time to activate the Fairlight unit.

He detailed off Sapper Fred Kindle to accompany him. They would use their army vehicle to get down to the Old Town and the fishing huts. Here they should be able to track him down. He told Signalman Bob James to come with them to operate the radio.

It took them a quarter of an hour to reach the Old Town. Fred parked the lorry on the Stade and then they walked towards the fishermen's huts. Peter carried his Thompson machine gun and Fred carried his .303 Lee Enfield rifle.

The Thompson was not in general issue to the British Army. The Auxiliary Forces were one of the few units that had, so far been issued with these weapons.

Being attached to these units, a few had been issued to the Patrol leaders.

"Good morning Lieutenant." The old man said, sat on a lobster pot.

"Good morning." Peter said.

"Has there been a stranger around here, in the last day or two?" Peter asked.

The old man looked a little weary. Peter was a stranger, himself, so he didn't know if he could answer this. He had seen a stranger, but he was a fisherman. Being a close nit community, the fishermen of the Old Town kept things very much in house. Outsiders were not welcome.

"No, no strangers about here." He replied.

"Pity, There's a big reward for his arrest. A German spy, they say." Peter said and turned around and started to walk away.

"How much is the reward?" The old man asked.

"Fifty pounds" Peter said, as he halted and turned to face the old man.

The old man beckoned Peter back to him and whispered in his ear that he knew where the man Peter was looking for was. With that he held out his hand for the reward.

"Once he is in my custody and I'm sure I've the right man. Then you'll get your reward." Peter said.

The old man got up and told Peter to leave his young man there and he would show him where the stranger was. Peter told Fred to stay there, but be alert, it could be a trap. He then walked after the old man.

They walked past two more Net sheds and then turned towards the beach, where the local fishing fleet pulled their boats up, out of the sea, when not needed for fishing. Hastings did not have a harbour, where the fishing boats could shelter. They were brought up onto the beach, away from the ravages of the sea.

In the next line of buildings were huts, where the fishermen kept their equipment and, when they returned from fishing trips, their catch. Some of which was sent up to London but the rest, they sold to the local community, from their sheds.

As they approached the third of these huts, the old man stopped. That hut, pointing to the next shed, with a green door, has not been used for a couple of years.

Since the 'Youngster' sunk in the big storm in 39. But, he said that they had noticed a man going in and out of it yesterday and this morning.

Peter thanked the old man and returned, with him, to his net shed.

"Fred. Come with me." He ordered.

"I hope you have a full magazine on that rifle?" Peter said.

"Of course I have." He replied.

"Right, put one up the spout, you may need it in a minute."

Fred did as he was ordered and followed his officer towards the huts, behind the Net sheds. As they came towards the one with the green door, Peter stopped.

"The man we are looking for is said to be holed up in that hut. I'm going around to the sea side of the hut and will enter from there. I want you to stand by that green door and when you hear me, you're to come through that door and be ready to use that rifle of yours, but remember what I look like." Peter said, with a smile.

That said, he walked onto the beach, between two of the fisherman's huts. Once he had cleared the end of the hut he turned towards the hut, which was his target.

As he came closer to the rear door, he noticed that it was open. His problem was that he was stood in the daylight and would be walking into a darkened room, as he had seen no windows along the side of the hut.

Peter took a deep breath, un-slung his Thompson machine gun and readied it for use. He realised that if he cocked it, just outside the hut door.

If the man inside was, indeed a German soldier, he would recognise the sound of a weapon being readied and would be prepared for Peter's entrance. He was well versed in the action of his weapon and so made sure that he had his hands in such a way that he could cock the weapon and fire it in a split second.

Being sure that he was ready, Peter walked into the hut and looked around. Just as his eyes were getting used to the light conditions, in the hut, he noticed a man sat at a table, at the far end of the hut. Near to the 'green door'.

"Good Morning Sir." Peter said.

"Hi." The man replied.

"I understand you're new around here." Peter said, keeping his Thompson's barrel pointed towards the floor, as he advanced.

"Yes, I got here yesterday." The man replied.

"Can I see your papers, please?" Peter said, holding out his left hand.

The man put his hand into his jacket pocket and pulled out some papers and handed them over to Peter.

"Why the check?" The man asked.

"We understand there's a German spy in the area. We're checking on people who don't come from this area. We hope to make an arrest tomorrow morning." Peter said, while he continued to examine the man's papers. His papers gave his name as Simon Johnson.

Peter thought it unusual for one of this mans papers to give an address in St Leonards and the driving licence to give an address in Rye, but he said nothing. Peter handed them back to him and called out for Fred to come in.

The German was shocked to find that he was now faced with two soldiers, holding weapons and pointing them in his direction. He didn't know what to do. His first instinct was to put his hands up and surrender but there again the officer had not looked as if he suspected him to be the German spy.

"We'll let the local police know about this man. We don't want them arresting the wrong man, do we?" He said to Fred, with a broad smile.

Peter thanked the man for his time and ushered Fred out of the hut, via the Green Door. Hopefully they had given him the message and he would now contact his officer and get orders. If the English knew about them, then their whole mission would be a failure.

As they walked away, back towards their army vehicle, Fred asked if he was the German they were looking for? Peter replied that he was sure that he was. After a little time he had decided what they would do. When he got back to their vehicle he told Bob that he was being dropped off at the Station and that he was to watch out for the German Fisherman leaving the town.

In Eastbourne, Sam Carter received the message, as he was headed for work, on Saturday morning. Instead of heading for the Brewery, Sam, instead walked up the road and entered the local Police Station. Here he called to see Sergeant Davies.

Luke took Sam into his side office and they talked about the message and how they could play this. It appeared that the Pheasant wanted the 'Tramp' back in Exceat. Was he herding the Germans into a trap?

After ten minutes Sam sent Luke to contact the policeman who was watching the tramp. It was his job, then to make contact with the tramp and get him to move on.

Chapter 15
The killing fields

At four o'clock on Saturday afternoon, Mat Palmer received a message. He was told that one of the men he was watching was to be killed silently. If possible it was to be carried out in the sight of the second man. The second man was to be allowed to continue until just before he reached Exceat Bridge. He, on the other hand, was to be arrested within the sight of the 'Tramp'.

At five past four, Peter Savage received his orders. The man in Alfriston was to be arrested, if possible, as he left the Star Inn. If this was not possible then he should be killed. Under no circumstance was he to be allowed to reach the boat. Half of his men were also to lay in wait for the man from Hailsham.

He was expected to be coming along the road, from Berwick station and heading towards Alfriston. Peter was to be aware that the fisherman may also come along that way. The other half his team are to go up onto Seaford Head, with the Bren gun, and lay down fire towards the Fishing boat, as it starts to head for the open sea. No one was to be killed, on the boat, but they were to believe that they were the target. He was also told that these men were not to be surprised if the boat was fired on, from the other side of the river. Any of the Germans, arrested by their unit were to be taken and handed over to the Alfriston Policeman.

Sam Carter walked up to the dead letter drop, at four fifteen, as he had been instructed to do, last night. There were his orders. His unit was to split in half. The first half was to track the 'Tramp' and ensure that he headed back to Exceat.

The second half was to get themselves over to East Dean and follow the two men from The Tiger Inn. Just before they started down Exceat Hill, into the Cuckmere valley, these two were to be arrested. Any Germans arrested were to be taken back to Eastbourne and handed into the police station.

Because they had already been following the 'Tramp', out of the town, Other than himself, his men were already near to both the 'Tramp' and the two at The Tiger Inn.

Sam had ordered his team to base themselves in Friston Church, overnight. With one of them keeping a close watch on the overnight location of the 'Tramp'.

Graham Fowler, the unit leader for the Exceat Auxiliary Forces Unit was ordered to have all but one of his men, laid up in the estuary, by first light. They were to be hidden, but needed to be able to open fire on the fishing boat, when it started to head out to sea. Again they were told not to kill anyone on the boat but the people were to think they were the targets.

One of his men, for the estuary party, was to be the Units sniper. It would be his job to stop anyone, other than the 'Tramp' getting on to the fishing boat.

Graham had already been told that one of his men was to ensure that the West Dean barn was ready to receive any bodies of the Germans. His man was not to interfere with the people bringing them in. In fact he should be out of sight, but be aware if any villagers approach the barn. Graham detailed off Ian Badger for this task, as the barn belonged to the farmer he worked for. Further orders would follow.

Jack Abraham was the last to receive his orders. He was to get his men onto the road between Wilmington and Littleington, no later than six thirty, Sunday morning. It would be their task to arrest the two men who would be leaving the Inn in Wilmington.

It was not known how many Germans would be coming their way. There were two more, one from Hailsham and an outside possibility that the 'Fisherman' from Hastings, could use that route. The reason for this is that if they took a different route, they could very well escape the ambushes that had been laid for them.

Their likely alternative route would be along this road. If so, it was their responsibility to arrest them. For this reason his men were to stay hidden until they heard the shooting coming from Exceat.

Jack realised that sound can travel a long way, at that time in the morning and as such he ordered his men to fit the silencers to their Thompsons. They would not greatly affect the accuracy or range they could be shooting at, if the Germans decided to resist arrest.

The most important thing was that the sound of the any shooting wouldn't be heard more than a quarter of a mile away and hopefully the Germans wouldn't be travelling that close together. He was ordered to take any Germans, who were arrested, to the Hailsham Police station.

Along with the orders to arrest the majority of the German's, all units were told that if the Germans tried to resist arrest, they were authorised to kill them. Any bodies of the German's were to be taken to the large barn, by the church, in West Dean village. They were to be laid out for identification, later. As high tide was due at about nine o'clock, they should assume that the Germans would be aiming to arrive at Exceat Bridge close to nine o'clock. As such they should all be in place no later than six o'clock Sunday morning.

Peter and Graham were also told that only the 'Tramp' was to get on the fishing boat. If any of the others got through their net, they were to be killed. It was imperative that they did not leave, on the boat.

What none of the Auxiliary Forces Units were aware of was that there would be a lot of military activity along the main coast road. They would have to put their training to good use and keep out of sight of the British and Canadian soldiers.

In the same way as they had been trained to evade the German's. It was stressed that they needed to go about their tasks in such a way as to ensure that they left no evidence, for the police to find.

If anyone got in their way, or if they could identify any of their men, be they civilians or soldiers, then they were authorised to be killed and to make it look like the Germans carried out the killings.

Once they were back in their area and they had debriefed their men, they were to send in a full report of what ever happened to each of the Germans that came into their sphere of influence.

Mat and his Auxiliary Forces Unit met up at their hide at eight o'clock on Saturday evening. They were there to discuss how they were to carry out the operation that had been sent to them, to perform. The first thing was to hand out the various tasks and agree on their timings.

They would all need to set out in plenty of time, to ensure that they arrived at their positions, well before the German's arrived.

Charles was the unit's main sniper and as such he would take on the first kill. David and Andy would later try to arrest the second German but be prepared to kill him if the arrest was not possible. Mat would follow on behind, with the van, to collect the Germans, dead or alive.

Later he and David would deliver any bodies to the West Dean barn and then, if they had arrested any, take them to Newhaven Police station. Once that was done, they could all go home and mark this up as a successful operation. Mat would then have to report in with the password, indicating success.

Mat issued out all the weapons and ammunition that they thought they would need. As well as their specialist weapons, they would all carry their service revolvers. Even thought Mat wasn't going to be involved in the actual killing or arrests, he had to be prepared, in case they ran into the rest of the Germans, who might put up a fight.

Having got everything ready, they all dispersed and went their separate ways. Tomorrow morning would be an early start for them all, so they would need to get to bed early and set their alarms. If any one of them was late, the whole operation could collapse.

Chapter 16
Don't be late

This had been one of the most uncomfortable night's sleep, Simon Johns had ever had. He had slept fittingly and so had not woken up refreshed. The final straw was when he was woken up by a group of men moving one of the fishing boats down to the shore and launching it, for its fishing trip. He kept his head down. He could not afford to be seen. Not now he had established himself a base.

After he had eaten his breakfast, he set about cleaning his weapons and checking that they were in working order. Being an Officer he was allowed to carry his own hand gun. His was a 9mm Beretta Model 38. He liked this one as it had the option of being automatic or a single shot weapon. He had three 10 shot magazines for this pistol, each loaded with just nine bullets, so as not to compress the springs.

His second weapon was a Maschinepistole 40, better know as a Schmeisser. With this weapon he had four magazines, each could hold thirty two rounds but, again, he only loaded thirty rounds in each. Although both weapons had about the same effective range, the Schmeisser had a greater rate of fire and when things got hot, he may well need that sort of fire power.

He finished cleaning his weapons and ensuring that the magazines, for both weapons, were not only loaded but functioned as required. The last thing you need, in the height of battle, is for your weapon not to fire because of a magazine malfunction.

It was then that he was distracted again, from planning out his days activities. He heard the sound of, what appeared to be two men, walking between his and the next boat.

"Sergeant I've looked all around, I can't find that tramp. I'm sure he's not around here." The first man said, from outside Simon's hide out.

"Well, you'd better find him. Search all the boats, if you have too but he must be found. The Inspector says that he, and the rest of his men are to be arrested first thing tomorrow morning and I don't want to be the man who has to tell him we can't find some filthy tramp." The second man said.

What's going on? None of his team had said anything about being seen when he spoke to them last night. In fact they had all said it had been easier than they had expected. No one questioned their papers or the stories they had given. How could they have found out about them?

Simon heard the men walking away from his hide out. It was nearly time for him to contact his men, for a morning report. It was eleven o'clock. He switched on the radio and plugged in the headphones. He could not afford for any sound to be heard outside the boat.

He had just got it tuned in when he heard one of his men calling him, on the radio. It startled him. They had been told not to contact him except in an emergency.

"This is Richard, I was in an inn and heard a policeman say that they knew about us and we would all be arrested tomorrow morning."

"This is Lange. I just heard the same thing, while I was working at the Cattle Market."

"This is Erich. We overheard a man tell the publican that he had heard that there were German spies in the area, but they were to be rounded up tomorrow."

"This is Hans. I was just questioned by two soldiers and they said they were looking for some German spies."

"This is Jan. I talked to an auto engineer. He said that the local policeman had told him that a group of German spies were to be rounded up tomorrow morning."

"Alright, I'll get back to you at twelve o'clock." Simon said and switched frequency.

"This is tramp. Urgent message." Simon said as he called up his base.

"Go tramp, send." Came the reply

"All the team report that the English know about us and that we are all to be arrested Sunday morning, Orders?"

"Wait."

After half an hour he receive a message that told him that he must get his team out, the same way they had arrived. Simon contacted Tobias, on the fishing boat, to come and get them but he said that the earliest would be at high tide Sunday morning, at nine o'clock.

At twelve o'clock Simon contacted all his team and told them to make sure they were out of their accommodation very early and make their way so that they arrived at Exceat Bridge at nine o'clock. No earlier than eight fifty or they may be noticed.

If the Policeman was searching all the fishing boats, along this beach, Simon decided that he needed to get away from here. He had chanced his arm, long enough, but he couldn't move his radio until he had made the calls to his team at noon. It took him five minutes to gather up all his possessions. Wound up the aerial, for his radio and put everything into his bag. He had already tidied up the space he had occupied to ensure that it was as he found it.

Now he was ready, he climbed up to the deck and looked around to see that no one was around. Happy that it was clear, he lowered his bag and then followed himself. He stopped, before he moved any further. He needed to ensure that that Policeman was not around and for that matter, any fishermen.

He could see or hear no one, so he got up and walked onto the beach. He found a pole, about two metres long and picked it up. He could use this to steady himself as he walked on the pebbles. He was very uneasy, not about what was under foot but about the fact that they appeared to know where he had been hiding. He so much wanted to look back and see if he was being followed, but thought better of it.

Simon had planed to walk along the beach and then head up to Beachy Head.

Up there he could hide out during the day and in the evening make his way to Crowlink Farm, at Friston. In this way he would only be a half an hours walk to Exceat Bridge, in the morning.

After he had walked for about a quarter of a mile, having passed by the Redoubt, he decided that it would be better if he got back onto the promenade and walked along that until he reached the far end of the seafront.

There appeared to be several soldiers working on the Pier, as he passed by, but they took no notice of him. There were a few older people who shouted out to him that he would be better off in the Army, fighting the Hun. He just waived his fist at them and walked on.

It took him about half an hour to reach the paths that would take him up, onto Beachy Head. It was here that he decided to stop and have something to eat, before he climbed the hill.

Simon felt rested and the time had allowed him to take in what had been happening to both him and his men. Had they been betrayed by their own side? Was this just a diversion to lead the English away from where they were actually going to land? It was then that he remembered the man who had given him a lift, in that old van. He was just a farm worker, he was not bright enough to see through his disguise and, anyway, he was on his own.

As he started to walk up the hill he began to think about what they were doing. They were running away and his Generals had agreed to this. If they were sure that the invasion was going ahead, then they wouldn't have called them back. It would have been better to order them to hide out, in the country side and then go back to their designated places, once the landings started. No there was something very wrong here.

He reached the top of the hill and looked back, down towards Eastbourne town and the coastal road. There didn't seem to be very much activity and so he believed that he had got away from his pursuers and was now safe to reach Exceat and Tobias's fishing boat, tomorrow morning.

He walked along the top of the cliffs and soon found some gorse bushes that he could shelter him from the wind, while he waited for the right time to head off to his night time accommodation.

After a couple of hours Simon felt that it was now time for him to get to Crowlink Farm as soon as he could. Once there he could set up his radio, just in case any if his men needed to contact him, before they met up again tomorrow morning.

It took him longer than he thought it would. It didn't look very far on the map but because of the folds in the landscape it had been a two hour trudge.

Chapter 17
I never liked the smell of fish

Hans Schmid had spent a disturbed night. After the visit from the British officer and the soldier, he felt very vulnerable. Hauptmann Krause had said that he was to make his way to where they had been dropped off, no later than nine o'clock Sunday morning.

He left the shelter of the fisherman's hut and walked along the sea front towards Hastings town centre. He was soon moving from the Old Town into the new part of Hastings. Around him were proper shops, not seaside stalls. It didn't take him long to reach the Memorial and the short walk up Havelock Road to the railway station. Once in the station he looked up the train times, for Sunday morning.

He was dismayed to find that the first train, on Sunday morning, which would be stopping at Berwick Station, didn't leave Hastings until nine thirty. That was far too late for him to be able to reach the boat.

There were two options open to him, catch a train Saturday night and hide up somewhere or catch an early train, to Eastbourne, and then run over the hills to Exceat. He felt that he was fit enough but it would also be tight, as the first train on Sunday morning would arrive in Eastbourne eight o'clock. That would give him just an hour to reach the boat. He didn't believe that he would make it.

Really the decision was taken from him. Just as he was about to leave the station he saw some soldiers approaching the station entrance. He was not sure if they were coming after him or just catching the train themselves.

It was a good job that he had brought his suitcase with him. With the soldiers around the fishermen's huts, he hadn't wanted to be separated from his weapons and explosives. This proved a wise move, if he hadn't brought them with him, he would have had to go back and collect it, before catching a train out of this town.

His best bet was to get out of town. He turned, walked over to the ticket office and asked when the next train to Berwick Station was due.

The clerk told him that there was one due in, in ten minutes but he would have to change at Eastbourne. He could wait for the train that was due in twenty minutes. This one was the train for Brighton and that went directly passed Berwick Station, not calling at Eastbourne. Hans decided to catch the later train. He purchased a return ticket so that, if asked, the ticket collector could say that he intended to return, the next day.

As he turned to walk towards the ticket collector, by the entrance to the walkway to the platforms, he found himself face to face with a British soldier. It startled him, for a moment but he soon recovered and stepped aside to let the soldier and his companions exchange their travel warrants for train tickets.

What he had not noticed was a loan soldier, seated just inside the station entrance, who was watching his every move.

Once Hans had purchased his tickets, this soldier got up and joined the end of the queuing soldiers. When he arrived at the front of the queue he asked the clerk where the fisherman was going. The clerk tried to say that he couldn't tell him but Bob James drew his Service Revolver and laid it on the counter, with the barrel pointing towards the clerk.

He got the message and told Bob that he had purchased a return ticket to Berwick Station. Bob thanked the man, turned and left the station.

Once Hans had handed his tickets to the ticket collector and had the outward ticket punched, he walked up the slope and along the walkway until he reached the steps that would lead him down onto the required platform. There were a couple of sets of seats along the platform. Hans took one, furthest from the stairs and sat there waiting for his train.

In five minutes the train destined for Eastbourne arrived and after the group of soldiers had climbed aboard, the Guard signalled for the train to move off.

A further five minutes passed and he watched as a goods train came out of the tunnel, to his left and slowly chucked past the station, on a rail that was separate from any of the platforms. The steam train was belching smoke from its funnel and it appeared to be pulling a heavy load. Hans thought of the steam trains, back in Germany, were far bigger and more powerful, than this small engine.

As the carriages appeared he could see that each one was carrying either a tank, covered in tarpaulin or and artillery piece. Every sixth carriage was a passenger carriage and, from what he could make out, those aboard were all soldiers.

It appeared that the English had more hardware than the Generals, back home, had been telling the troops. May be this would not be the walk over that they expected.

As the guards van passed by, a train was coming in the other direction and was on the line that would bring it next to Hans platform. Within a minute it had drawn up beside him and a porter was calling out that this was the Brighton train, calling at St Leonards, Bexhill, Cooden, Pevensey Bay, West Ham, Polegate, Berwick Station, Glynde, Lewes … By this time Hans was already on the train, he reached up and placed his suitcase on the overhead luggage rack and then took his seat. He sat facing the direction the train was travelling. He hated to sit with his back to the engine.

It was not long before the train started to move off. In a few moments the carriage was darkened by the fact that the train had entered the tunnel he had watched the last train exit from.

Someone had left the window ajar, as a result the smoke, from the engine started to enter the carriage. Hans was quick to reach up and close the window, much to the delight of the two young ladies that were sat opposite him.

Light soon returned as the train exited this tunnel and drew into St Leonards, Warrior Square station. It was more a pause then a stop, as soon as it drew up it started to move off again.

The train had hardly started to get up any speed when they were, again, flung into darkness. This was a longer tunnel than the first and it seems an age before the light returned.

He looked out of the window and enjoyed the views of the sea, as they travelled along. The next station was Bexhill. He had heard of this town. It was the town where motor racing first started. Once they started off again it was a pleasant journey, the train was travelling along the coast, so on his left he had the view of the sea and to his right the country side was flat and looked rather marshy.

They passed by the next three stations, Cooden, Pevensey and West Ham.

"I hope this train does stop at Berwick Station." Hans addressed the two ladies.

"You need to hang your head out of the window, before you reach the station." The younger of the two said.

"I don't know exactly where the station is, I'm meeting a friend there." Hans said.

"I'll tell you when we reach the right place to signal the Guard." The elder one said.

Just after they had left West Ham station the train seemed to branch to the right and head away from the large town, that Hans thought was most likely Eastbourne, and head inland. In five minutes the train pulled up at a station. This one was signed as 'Polegate'. It waited for a few minutes for a few passengers to get on and until the signal said that it could proceed.

After a short time the elder of the ladies told Hans that he needed to get ready to depart. He took down his suitcase and opened the window and stuck his head out and looked back towards the Guards van. The Guard soon looked out of his window and waived to Hans that he had seen him and that the train would stop at Berwick.

Hans brought his head back into the carriage and sat down again and waited for the train to slow to a stop. He quickly got up, picked up his suitcase and opened the door to the carriage. He stepped down onto the platform and before he closed the door, he thanked the young ladies for their help, closed the door and headed for the gate, where the Station Master was stood, waiting to collect his ticket.

"Didn't like Hastings that much then?" Henry Lake said.

"No, I couldn't get on a boat so decided to head home. Maybe I'll join the navy." Hans replied as he walked by and on to the road.

He didn't know how far he would get, before it became too dark for him to find himself a place to sleep, for the night.

After about a mile, he noticed a farm, up ahead. It appeared to have several outbuildings and a large barn. He decided that this would make a good place to kip down.

As he approached the farm, he noticed there were no lights on in the main house or around any of the outbuildings. He may be in luck. The farmer and his family might have gone out for the night, leaving the farm unattended.

He walked up the short track that led from the road up to the farm yard. As he came near to the barn, he heard a couple of dogs starting to bark, but they sounded like that they were in a kennel, at the rear of the farm house.

It was a large barn with great doors that reached from the ground up passed the rafters. A strange building but this had to be his home for tonight. There was a small door, cut into the left hand giant door. Hans walked up to the door and pressed down the catch and the door was released and opened inwards. He walked in and closed the door behind him. He was suddenly in total darkness.

Hans placed his suitcase on the floor and knelt down beside it. He opened the catches and lifted up the lid. He knew what he was looking for, it was his torch. It was soon in his hand and he brought it out, closed the lid, stood up and switched on the light.

This really was a big barn. He walked around and found a spot that would do him well for tonight. It was behind a wall of straw bails, out of sight of the main doors and there appeared to be another small door, just a few feet away from where he hoped to sleep tonight.

Having discovered a place to sleep he returned and picked up his suitcase and walked back to his hide. Now he could get things ready for tomorrow morning. He found his Schmeisser and a couple of magazines. He checked them over, to ensure that they were ready for use. When he repacked his suitcase, he intended to make sure that this was on the top, with a magazine already fitted, but the weapon would not be cocked, until he needed it. His Luger, on the other hand was to remain outside the suitcase. This he would carry with him, in his right hand coat pocket. He didn't expect to run into trouble but he had to be prepared.

Although it was early, he had had a long day and he knew that tomorrow would need to start early and could well be a long one. He moved the suitcase around so that he could use it as his pillow and got himself comfortable, closed his eyes and was soon asleep.

The farmer and his family arrived back at the farm at about ten o'clock. The large barn doors were flung open and the farmer drove his car into the barn.

The headlights lit up the barn and startled Hans. He sat up, with his Luger in his hand. He listened, in case they were looking for him but it was soon obvious that all they were doing was parking the car in the barn, for the night.

Once the barn doors were closed and he could hear the farmer closing his front door, he lay back down and was soon asleep again. Like anyone sleeping in a strange place, all the night time sounds would ensure that he could not settle down very well. Every strange sound brought him awake, even if only for a second or two. Occasionally he would look at his watch but the time just dragged on. Eventually he got use to the sounds and fell to sleep.

Chapter 18
How big is this operation?

Having followed the 'Tramp' up to Crowlink Farm and seen him settled in to one of the barns, for the night, Terry and Will retreated to Friston Church.   They knew that it would be open and it would give them the protection from the elements they needed tonight.

Terry called up Sam, on his portable radio. The reception was not that good as they were at its limits of range but he did get through and suggested that Luke and Tom join them, in the church for tonight. That way they would be on hand when the Germans started to move off to Exceat, in the morning.

Sam agreed. He borrowed a van from the Brewery and then he went to collect Tom and Luke. Once back at the brewery they went to their hide. This was a large disused barrel at the back of the cooper's shed. Terry had skilfully carried out alterations so that outwardly it was what it appeared to be. Closer examination could show the secret door and inside it was very much like an office but the walls were covered with maps and there were cupboards containing weapons, ammunition and explosives.

Once inside they decided which weapons each of them would need for tomorrow. Not forgetting ones that Terry and Will may need.   Once they had packed up the van and closed up their hide, they set off. It only took them about a quarter of an hour to reach Friston Church. It was on the top of a hill and set back a little, off the road, next to a large pond.

With them all together Sam went through the plan for tomorrow morning. Will and Luke would watch and follow the two Germans, from The Tiger Inn.

Tom and Terry would concentrate on the 'Tramp'. He instructed them that once he started to go down Exceat hill, they were not to follow him but were to hide up and be ready to support Will and Luke, when they brought along the other two Germans.

They didn't want to stop the 'Tramp' reaching the fishing boat. He must get on the boat, but no one else.

It was important that the other two Germans didn't, in fact proceed down Exceat Hill. They were to be arrested, if at all possible. If they put up a fight then they were to be killed.

Will and Luke were to follow the other two, from the moment they left The Tiger Inn until they reached the top of Exceat hill. As they got close to the crest of the hill, it was important that the two of them were up close, so that they could assist Tom and Terry with the arrest of these two German spies. They must not be allowed to escape.

"What if the three of them join up at Friston pond or along the road? How will we deal with that?" Terry asked.

"Well you will have to get ahead of them and ambush them at the top of Exceat Hill, but make sure that the 'Tramp' gets away." Sam instructed.

"What if he and one of the others get down the hill?" Luke asked.

111

"Don't worry. There's another unit, down in the valley. It is their job to ensure that only the 'Tramp' reaches the boat." Sam informed them.

"Just how big is this operation?" 'Old' Tom asked.

"As far as I know there are five units involved. Each unit has the responsibility for a separate part. None of us are to meet up, otherwise that will compromise our individual units security. So if you do get close enough to spot one of the other unit's members, remember that he will be able to see you and so your life will be in danger." Sam said.

"Come out and get your weapons, I have them in the van." Sam said.

"By the way, you do all have your revolvers with you?" Sam asked.

They all replied that they had, Will said that he had a browning with its silencer, instead of his revolver.

By this time they had all reached the rear of the brewery van. Sam opened the door and climbed up into it. He leaned over a barrel, that was secured to the side of the van. When he stood up he was holding two Thompson machine guns. He handed one each to Will and Tom.

He returned to the barrel and came back with another two Thompson's and handed one each to Luke and Terry.

Sam's third and final dip into the barrel brought up a bag that held a dozen, fully loaded, magazines. He handed them three each.

Sam got down from the van, closed the door and locked it. He told them that he would be back here at eight o'clock the next morning. He reminded them that there would be a communion service, in the church, at eight o'clock so they were to ensure that they were well away from the church by then. As soon as they could, after eight 'clock he wanted each of the teams to call in to him and let him know where they were and how the operation was going.

The men returned to the church and decide how they were going to ensure that they all got a rest and also ensured that they did not miss their targets. It was starting to get dark and as they could not put the lights on, in the church, they may as well try to bed down. One of them would take watch. The person on watch would look out of one of the widows, so that they could see the road junction, outside the church and pond. After an hour, they would wake another of their number and continue on, throughout the night until six o'clock.

Day three – Sunday 15th September 1940

Chapter 19
Going home

The 'Tramp' awoke at first light. He checked his watch and it showed five forty five in the morning. He got up and opened up his bag to find something to eat. He didn't know when he would be able to eat again, so needed to fuel himself up, ready for the day ahead.

Once he had eaten he packed everything up and closed his bag, before looking around. He couldn't see or hear anyone about, in the barn. Simon knew that he didn't have far to travel, to reach Exceat Bridge. He could rest up here until about seven forty five. He thought that would give him plenty of time to reach the bridge and make his rendezvous with Tobias.

What did strike him was that in the distance he could hear, what sounded like tanks moving about the countryside around him. He hadn't seen any, as he walked up to Crowlink farm, last night, so where had they come from?

He decided that he had better investigate this or he could find himself walking into a lot of trouble. As it was starting to get light, he saw that there was a big ladder leaning up against a stack of straw bales, at one end of the barn. At the top he could see that there was a small window, which he believed he would be able to see out off.

He hid his bag under some loose straw, so that it could not be seen, ensured that his Berretta pistol was tucked into his belt and then walked over to the base of the ladder. Before he started up the ladder he listened to hear if there was anyone about, in the farm yard, but could hear nothing. This was a long ladder and he didn't want to be halfway up it and have someone come walking into the barn.

Happy that no one was about, he started to climb the ladder. This was a high stack so it was luckily that he was very fit and so was able to get to the top run very quickly.

He stepped off the ladder, onto the bales, and walked over towards the window, he had seen from below.

The trouble was that he was only six foot tall and the window was eight foot from the top of the bales. The best way to reach the window would be to move a couple of bales and place them under the window. That way he would be able to step on them and see out.

Having moved the bales he stepped up onto the top bale and peered out of the window. He was amazed at what he could see. As far as he could see, with the exception of the emergency landing strip, were hundreds of tanks. They appeared to be lined up, facing the coast and, after looking through his binoculars, some in the distance appeared to be facing down into the Cuckmere valley.

Simon had to think quickly. Did he report this immediately or did he save it until he was out to sea, on the fishing boat? If he did report it now, could the English trace his radio signal and come and arrest him now.

If so then his whole mission would have been a total failure. On the other hand if he left it until they were away from this land, he would be able to send a much fuller report, which may help the Generals in their final planning of the invasion. He decided on the later option.

Should he make his move now? In this way he would be able to walk past the soldiers, while they are still involved in getting their tanks in the correct positions. If he waited until later and made a 'run' for it, he might raise suspicions, with the very same soldiers, once they were resting and taking more notice of who or what was around them.

Simon decided that he would be better to move now. It was possible that some of his men were in the same predicament and have decided to arrive early. If so he needed to be there to ensure that they hide up until the fishing boat arrives, to take them all home.

If he waited near to the junction, with the road coming from Littleington, he should be meeting up with most of his team and could direct them where to hide up.

What he hadn't realised was just how far up he had climbed, it wasn't until he stood at the top of the ladder that it came rushing back to him. He had suffered vertigo, as a youngster, but thought that he had overcome his fear of heights, due to his army training.

Getting back onto the top steps of the ladder was a nerve racking experience for him. Each time he looked around for the step to place his foot on, he could see the long drop to the bottom. He would close his eyes and try to feel with his foot, for the step but then worried that he would miss it and fall.

He decided that the best thing he could do was just focus on the ladder and the first few steps. Not look pasted these, in this way he would not see the ground, far below.

Simon took a deep breath, opened his eyes and looked only at the ladder. He watched as he left foot reached around the upright of the ladder and focused on his shoe, as it felt for the third run of the ladder. As he was able to transfer part of his weight onto the third run, he let out a sigh. 'Oh my god' he thought.

Having successfully found the third run of the ladder he then let his left leg take his full weight, as he then moved his right leg onto the same run of the ladder. All the time he was gripping the side rails of the ladder, to such an extent that his knuckles were becoming white.

Having got both of his feet, safely on the same run of the ladder he rested for a moment, to get him self together. Next he took another large breath and started, slowly down the ladder, run by run. He didn't care if someone came into the barn. At this moment his full concentration was on getting safely down.

Being back on the ground, Simon stopped and took a grip of him self. He needed to have all his faculties working and be able to focus on getting him self and his team away from here, on to the boat, all in one piece.

After gathering up his bag, he walked to the small door, beside the main entrance to the barn. Simon peered through the cracks in the wood and saw that there was no one about.

He opened the door, walked out and then closed it behind him. He had to leave everything as he had found it. He couldn't chance anyone raising the alarm, before nine o'clock this morning.

It had been his intention to walk over the hill, by pass Gayle's Farm and meet up with the road, just before it dropped down into the valley.

He now realised that he would be spotted, by the soldiers, more for the fact that he shouldn't be there, rather than him being a tramp. As a tramp, it was expected that he would be walking along the road, not over the fields.

He just had to hope that the people in the farm house were not awake, just yet. He moved very silently, as he walked away from the barn and the farm house. Once he was a short distance up the lane, he looked back but couldn't see anyone about. He now felt safe. He would reach Friston church soon and could then start to walk along the main road, everything, then, would be right again.

Chapter 20
I only hope the bike starts!

Hans Lange had slept in one of the Markets outbuildings, since he arrived. It was very smelly but far enough away for few, if anyone, to come about.

Being his second night there, he hoped that he would have slept better than he had the first night, but that was not the case. The thoughts that he might very well be arrested any moment meant that he had hardly slept a wink.

A Luger pistol had been his bed companion, throughout the night. His other weapon was a Mauser Karabiner Kar 98K with a telescopic site. He carried four magazines, for this rifle and in each was loaded with five rounds. Hans was the team's sniper.

It was he that Jack had seen, on Friday morning, with a funny looking shotgun carrying case. In fact it was a purpose built carrying case for this weapon and this mission.

The reason that he was assigned the motor bike was so that he could get about the area quickly and use his skills for any specific designated target. The problem, today, was that he was over half a mile away from his bike. This was causing him some concern.

The journey time from where he had hidden his motor bike, to Exceat Bridge would be less than three quarter of an hour, but if the bike wouldn't start, then he would have to walk about twelve miles. The journey time, if he walked, would be about three hours.

He looked at his watch, it was five minutes passed six and the light was starting to creep into the sky. Hans decided that it was time that he left his hideout and made his way to collect the motor bike.

Hans knew, before he broke cover, he needed to have his side arm available to him, whenever he needed it. For this reason he had packed a holster for his pistol, before he left on the mission.

He took the holster out of his suitcase and took his trouser's belt off, slid it through the lope of the holster and then replaced the belt around his trousers.

Now that he was ready, Hans ensured that he had left nothing behind and then opened the door and carefully looked about to see that he was the only person in the Market. Happy that he was on his own, he walked out of the shed and closed the door behind him. His rifle bag was safely hanging across his back and that his Luger was easily available for him to reach, if the need be.

He picked up his suitcase and walked across the Market and headed for the main gate. There was a small door, in the main gate. He had noticed that it was not locked, at night. At this time of a Sunday morning he didn't expect there to be anyone outside, so he just opened the door and stepped out of the Market.

Hans thought 'So far so good.' He didn't think that he had been spotted, so he turned right and walked up towards the high street.

At the first junction he turned right into Marshfoot lane. It was at the end of this lane that he would find his motor bike, hidden in one of Old Marshfoot Farm's small barns.

On his first day, he had met up with the Farmer who had offered to allow him to keep his motor bike in one of his sheds, until he found himself a proper place to stay.

As he approached the farm, one of the dogs started to bark. He knew that it was no good trying to silence the dog, so he just walked on. If the farmer or his wife looked out he would just have to bluff his way out. He was lucky that no one showed at any of the windows, they must have been in a deep sleep.

He walked up to the dog and offered it the back of his hand, to smell. The dog appeared to be reluctant to smell his hand but did so anyway. It soon took its nose away. The smell was horrid. Hans walked on and found his bike in the small barn he had taken it to.

There was a place where he could fasten his suitcase but his rifle would have to stay slung across his back. He wheeled the bike out of the barn and he closed the door.

Now was the moment he was dreading, would the dam thing start? He pulled the bike back, onto its stand and then opened up the petrol tap. Had this been a German motor bike, he was sure that it would start first time but this was British.

He pumped some petrol into the carburettor and then pulled the compression handle. Now was the moment of truth, he straddled the bike and flicked out the kick start peddle, so that he could put his right foot onto the peddle.

With one practiced movement he pushed down hard, with his foot and at the right moment he released the compression. There was a large cloud of smoke erupting from the exhaust, at the rear, but the engine was turning and he had a working machine.

He turned down the revs and eased the bike off its stand. Now he was ready to go. He was not interested if he was seen now. The power of this motor bike would have him well away from, not only the farm but the town as well, in a few minutes.

His left foot kicked the gear leaver into first gear and his right hand released the clutch. The bike moved forward at a controlled speed as he headed back to the lane and towards the town centre. The noise of the motor bike would be heard but as this was a captured British Army motor bike, from Dunkirk, it was thought that the locals would be familiar with the sounds of such bikes. He was right! Those who did hear the sound just rolled over and muttered about the 'bloody army disturbing their Sunday lie in', or the like.

When he reached the end of the lane he rode straight over the junction and down the road that would lead him out of the town, via the railway bridge. In a minute he had crossed the bridge and was on his way.

It was not long before he was riding past 'Greens Rope Factory', this brought back memories from when he was growing up in Berghausen. Just a few miles away from his village was a large rope maker – Manfred Hunk, in Asslar.

If the wind was in the wrong direction, these same smells would drift across his village.   But today was not time to reminisce, if he wanted to see his home town again, he needed to get to Exceat Bridge by nine o'clock.

Hans had a choice, did he head for Polegate and ride back along the road towards the Cuckmere Valley or did he head in the opposite direction, towards Horse Bridge and, basically follow the River Cuckmere, on its way to the sea. He chose this route, mainly because it was the route that he had taken, after he landed at Exceat, on Friday.

After he had passed Horsebridge, he headed past the pottery factories and then turned left towards Dicker. His next destination would be Berwick Station. He didn't know if he should wait there and pick up Steffen, when he arrived back from Hastings. He though not. He didn't even know if Steffen would be headed back this way and so he could get himself stuck, if he left it to late to reach the fishing boat.

He had spent some time, the evening before, studying the maps they had been given. He needed to find some alternative routes, in case the one he had planned to use was impassable. Up until now he had not encountered anyone on the roads. He felt at ease as he passed Berwick Station, now he was home and dry.

After about a mile he had to choose weather to branch left or right, at the road junction. If he went to the right, it would take him to Berwick village and a dead end. Going left would take him towards Alfriston; this is the way he needed to go. After a hundred and fifty yards at the cross roads, the road going from left to right was from Polegate and headed to Lewes.

The road opposite was the road he needed to travelled along and would lead him to Alfriston.

Being nothing about, he crossed the road and headed towards Alfriston.   Hans was not going into Alfriston; instead he turned off left and head towards Lullington and Littleington. It was this, much narrower road that would bring him directly to Exceat and to the Bridge.   He didn't realise that the small bridge, that crossed the river Cuckmere, was not only narrow but was a humped back bridge.

He took the bridge far to fast and as a result, he found that both his wheels had left the ground. He was flying through the air and, ahead of him, there was a corner coming up, very quickly. If he didn't get control of the bike, he could well find himself flying into the hedge, in front of him.

119

He had been in many battle field situations but he had never been so frightened for his life, as he was right now. He took a deep breathe and summoned up all his knowledge of riding a motor bike. It was no time to just close his eyes and pray. He would need to have all his whit's about him, when one or both of the wheels hit the road.

He was in some luck, the rear wheel touched down first. Now he had to use his skills with the accelerator to ensure that he could lower the front forks and wheel down, under control. He did this and immediately pushed down the break peddle and pulled on the front breaks.

At the same time he squeezed his legs together, gripping the petrol tank, in the hope that he could prevent himself from being thrown off.

When the bike came to a stop, Hans relaxed his knees and took a very deep breath. He felt that he had been very lucky to have survived this. He knew that he would have to concentrate for the rest of the journey, even though it was only about three miles to the bridge.

The engine hadn't stopped and was ticking over, as he sat there getting himself together. It was now time to get on and finish the journey. Before he reached the Exceat Bridge, he would have to find a place to hide the bike and also, to hide himself.

He was going to arrive, at his destination, before eight o'clock and could not be seen just hanging about, even this early on a Sunday morning.

He had pulled up just by the junction where the road branched, right to Lullington and to the left, towards Milton Court. He took the right turn and rode off, more carefully this time, to ensure that he was not taken by surprise again. After a short while he passed a large Sussex Barn, to his left and then followed the left hand bend that, would take him up to the main road, leading from Wilmington to West Dean and Exceat.

At the junction he turned right and decided that he could ride a bit faster now, as the road was wider and the light was getting brighter. Soon he would have left this dam country, hopefully for good.

Chapter 21
He felt uneasy

What woke Hans was the sound of a motor bike roaring along the road, past the farm. He recognised the sound of this bike, it sounded just like the one that Unteroffizier Lange had been given for their mission.

Hans swore to himself. If he had been on the road, he could have got a lift on the back of his bike and saved himself a long walk to the coast. This was a good time to get up and leave the barn. He had a way to go and the quicker he started the less chance he had of being found.

Having ensured that everything was in place, as he wanted it, he closed up his case. He had decided that he wouldn't carry any of his weapons, on his body. He had placed them both in his suitcase, earlier. He then walked over to the small door, in the barns main door. He quietly opened it and walked outside, closed the door behind him and, as silently as he could, he crossed the yard and walked down the grass verge, by the side of the track. On reaching the road he turned right and started his long walk home.

Hans knew that Hartmann was staying in Alfriston, but he had no intention of going into that village, to find him. He would head for Littleington and back along the road he had travelled down, Friday morning. He had used his experience to look around, as he rode on Lange's motor bike. You never know when you might need to travel this way again, he had thought.

After half an hour he took the turning, off the road that led into Alfriston village. He had followed the route that Hans Lange had taken earlier and crossed the humped back bridge. As he crossed the bridge, he stopped and sat on the wall and looked about. It really was a beautiful place, especially this early on a Sunday Morning. He rested for about five minutes and set off again.

After about a quarter of an hour he had reached the main road and turned right, towards the first of the two villages he would need to walk through, before he reached the woods. It now seemed like a very good day, the sun was shining and he enjoyed listening to the dawn chorus breaking what would have other wise been a very silent walk.

At the same time that Hans was sitting on the low wall, on the bridge over the river, Hartmann was just getting dressed. He had ensured that he was up, no later than seven o'clock, as he wanted to leave the inn before anyone was up and about.

He had asked about breakfast, for Sunday morning, last night and was told that it would not be until nine o'clock at the earliest. No one would be up before seven thirty. It was their only day they could have a lie-in.

Hartmann ensure that he had everything, especially his Luger. He had loaded a magazine, the night before and placed it on the Luger and put one round up the spout. He didn't want to be caught out, not just as he was to get out of this dreadful place.

Once he was sure he was ready, he opened up his room's door and, with his suitcase in his hand he walked along the corridor and down the stairs. Although he walked as quietly as he could, he was aware that the owner's accommodation was at the back of the Inn and far away from where he was.

Once in the bar room, he made for the front door, opened it and walked out into the street. He looked around but could see no one about. Over the last twenty four hours he had walked about the area and so he knew the best way for him to get out of the village and head for Exceat Bridge.

He would head for Frog Firle and when he reached the large Sussex barn, he would leave the road and head for the river. Here he could walk along the foot path that ran along the river bank. This would bring him right up to the Bridge at Exceat, without having to get onto any of the roads, in the area.

Once outside the Star Inn, he turned to the left and walked off, out of the village. There was no one around at this time on a Sunday Morning, so he felt good about life. It should only take him about twenty minutes to reach the Sussex Barn, and then he would be safe and sound.

He was enjoying his walk. No one was around so he could enjoy the sights and sounds of this lovely part of the world. When he was less than five hundred metres from the barn, there, ahead of him, about two hundred metres ahead, he saw a farm worker, walking towards him.

Richard felt uneasy as he had not anticipated there being anyone on the road at this time. Still he took a deep breath and gathered himself together. He felt his jacket pocket, to reassure himself that his Luger was still there. It was so he felt secure.

He walked on, for it was then not far to the barn and the river. Although, in Germany he would have walked on by, today he decided that he would exchange pleasantries with the man.

Chapter 22
A nice county walk

Jan and Simon had a good nights sleep. The beds in the Wilmington Inn were comfortable and, being away from the main road, they were not disturbed by what little traffic there was. They weren't that happy to be leaving, both because these beds were far more comfortable than those at their barracks and secondly because their mission hadn't been completed. Their part of the mission was well prepared and they were looking forward to securing the air field, when the invasion started.

To be ordered home, at such a late hour wasn't welcome. They wanted to earn the Iron Crosses they had been promised, if the mission was a success. Their families would have been so proud of them.

Jan had got up at seven o'clock, early for him on a Sunday morning, but they had to be out of here in half an hour. He pulled on his trousers, socks and shoes and walked along the corridor and gently knocked on Simon's door. There was no answer initially, so he knocked a bit louder and then he heard a stifled scream of a young girl. What had Simon been doing?

The door opened and the Inn Keepers sixteen year old daughter ran past him, draped in her dress as she disappeared down the corridor. Simon was starting to get out of his bed, as Jan entered.

"What the hell do you think you're doing?" Jan asked.

"Well I thought that as it was our last night, I may as well have an English girl, before I left." Simon said, with a smile all over his face.

"You'd better hope that Hauptmann Krause doesn't hear about this or you'll be in trouble." Jan said.

"Well the only person who would tell him is you. If you do, I'll shoot you." Simon snarled.

"We had better get out of here as quick as we can, now." Jan said, as he left the room and walked back to his own room, to get fully dressed and ready to leave.

Simon picked up his shirt and put it on and then found his coat and scarf and threw them on his bed. He bent down, by his bed, reached underneath, pulled his suitcase out and lifted it onto his bed.

He had decided that if it was true that the English Police were about to arrest them, he had better be armed. He knew that the English Police didn't carry weapons and as such this would give him a chance to escape their clutches.

He realised that he couldn't walk about the country lanes carrying his Schmeisser, but he could carry his Luger, in its holster, fastened to his trouser belt. He fitted the holster and ensured that the Luger had a loaded magazine fitted. He then placed the Luger into the holster and fastened the flap, so the gun did not accidently fall out.

After he had gathered up all his belongings and thrown them into the suitcase he looked around to see if he had left anything. He bent down, to look under his bed and noticed a pair of girls pants.

He reached out and picked them up, threw them in his case and closed it. He would have something to remember her by, now.

In the meantime Jan had got dressed and gathered up all his belongings and carefully packed them away in his suitcase. He didn't think to keep either of his weapons out. In fact he packed them at the bottom of his suitcase and covered them with his clothes.

Jan picked up his suitcase and walked out of his room and headed towards Simon's room. As he approached, the door opened and out walked Simon, with his suitcase in his hand.

"Lets go, I don't want to be late, the Hauptmann won't wait for us." Simon said.

They walked down the stairs and headed out of the side door. Simon looked around and hoped that he would see the face of Helen, looking out of one of the windows, but he saw no one.

Once they had gone around the building and reached the road, they hurried off, to their right. They were not sure how far they had to walk or how long it would take them to reach Exceat Bridge.

Still as long as they kept the hills to their left, they would be going in the right direction.

The road was not that wide and had high banks and hedges on both sides, so they couldn't see much around them, as they walked along. As such they contented themselves in talking about why they had been called back to France. Were they delaying the invasion, again or was it being cancelled? Neither of them had any idea.

They had got everything prepared, at the airfield. Charges were set, if they needed to destroy the main buildings or the aviation fuel, stored there. They had found places where they could defend the airfield from any advancing troops. They expected paratroops to arrive, once the invasion started and as such they could send them in the places to defend it.

By this time, the two of them had just past the path that led down to Milton Court Farm. The next place they arrived at was Lullington and its very small church. Well it is more just the chancel of a long demolished, original church.

They were soon passing the road that led back over the River Cuckmere and onto Alfriston. This was the road that both Hans Lange and Hans Schmid had used to join the road they were walking along, earlier. It might have been nicer if they could all have met up here and travelled together to the Bridge.

The next village they would arrive at would be Littleington. From there they would only be about half an hour from Exceat Bridge. Simon checked his watch and saw that it was nearly eight o'clock, so they had plenty of time, there was no real rush.

Chapter 23
Where are you bloody Germans going?

The church bells started to ring, not far from Erich's window. He reached over to the small table, by his bed, and picked up his watch. It showed six fifty on Sunday morning. Last night he had asked the innkeeper what was the earliest time they could have breakfast. He had told him that, as his wife would be attending Holy Communion, breakfast would be at nine o'clock.

He could hear Karl stirring in the room next to his, so he knocked on the dividing wall. This received an instant response.

"I know. I'm just getting up."

Erich got out of his bed and got dressed. They had agreed that they had to be out of here, no later than seven thirty. Erich, like his officer, carried a Beretta model 38 pistol. This one had been given to him, by his father, when he had been accepted for officer training, last month. The Hauptmann had advised him not to take this pistol on their mission. It could be a hindrance to him, until he was proficient in its use. The selecting of the wrong one of its two triggers to use, could cause both him and those around him danger. If he accidently pulled the rear most trigger, he could empty the magazine in one second. Whereas the forward trigger would release just one round at a time.

Being young and an up and coming officer, himself, he thought that he knew best. He picked up his pistol and placed it in his jacket pocket, after first checking to ensure that the magazine was fully loaded. He left the other three magazines in his suitcase, together with the Schmeisser and its four fully charged magazines. He did not envisage needing to use any of his weapons but had his pistol, just in case it was needed.

Karl had been in the middle of a dream, when the church bells started to toll. He was standing in Downing Street, together with the team.

They had all just been presented with the Iron Cross by Adolf Hitler. Now it was his turn, Hitler stepped in front of Karl and held in his hand the Iron Cross for Karl, just as he reached out to present it to him, he woke up.

Karl may have been the most junior member of the team but he was very professional about everything he did. He paid especial attention to the upkeep of his weapons. Before he had embarked on this mission he had taken great care to strip down both his Luger pistol and his Schmeisser and their respective magazines.

This morning he just had time to strip down the Luger and gave it a light oiling, with a cloth he carried for this purpose. He then put it back together again and ensured that this magazine was loaded correctly, one less round than it was designed to take.

Karl looked at his watch. He didn't have time to do the same to the Schmeisser. He had no need to check its magazines as he hadn't taken them out of his suitcase, since they arrived in England, so they should still be ready for use.

They were still wrapped in the cloth that he placed them in, when he packed them, before they left France, for this mission.

Before he placed his Luger into his coats right hand pocket, he ensured that not only did it hold a loaded magazine, but he also cocked it so that there was one round ready to fire. He then pushed the safety catch to 'safe'. Once this was in place he put the spare magazine into the left hand coat pocket.

He then rearranged the contents of his suitcase so that he could place the Schmeisser on top of all his clothes and two magazines along side it, then he closed his suitcase. He was ready now.

It was getting near the time for them both to depart. Karl put his coat on and knocked on the dividing wall so that Erich knew he was ready to leave his room. He quickly looked around the room, to ensure that he hadn't left anything and then picked up his suitcase, opened his bedroom door and stepped into the corridor.

As Karl stepped out of his room Erich did the same, both of them walked down the corridor and Erich led the way down the staircase into the barroom.

They had not expected to see the innkeeper standing behind the bar, but there he was, as if he was waiting for them. They knew that he couldn't be there to ensure that they didn't leave without paying their bill, as they had already paid for a week's board.

"Where are you bloody Germans going at this time in the morning?" he growled.

At the same time he brought his shot gun into view, from under the bar.

Erich froze. He didn't know what to do. Karl, on the other hand, not only knew what to do but, because he was carrying his suitcase in his left hand, his right hand was free to reach into his coat pocket and retrieve his Luger.

Karl moved slightly to his left so as to have Erich's body between him and the Innkeepers shot gun. This was not cowardice, but he needed to be able to bring his Luger out into the open, without the Innkeeper seeing what he was doing. It was now that he felt justified in ensuring that he had a round in the barrel of his pistol and the safety catch on. All he had to do, when he was ready, was to release the safety catch and he could fire the pistol.

While he was getting himself prepared to take on this man, Erich had started to ramble, in German, which confirmed to the Innkeepers that he had two German spies in front of him. He started to bring the barrel of his shot gun up and the butt of the gun up towards his shoulder, so that he could get off a good shot and kill them both.

It was now that Karl acted. He dropped his suitcase down onto the floor, which made a loud bang and startled both of the others, in the room. He reached out his now free left hand and gave Erich a hard shove to the left. As Erich was not expecting this, his balance was not prepared and he fell sideways onto the floor.

Karl was counting on the Innkeeper following the movement of Erich and would not only be watching him but would swing the end of his gun's barrel in his direction. It was this edge he needed and as Erich fell to the floor the Innkeeper did just what Karl had wanted him to do.

The Innkeepers fate was now secured, Karl raised his Luger, flicked off the safety catch and, once he was sure that he had a good aim, he pulled the trigger.

In the mean time the Innkeeper had been following the exploits of Erich, as he crashed onto the bar room floor. Why he did it he did not know but he just glanced to his left and caught a slight movement by the second of the Germans.

He realised that he was in danger and started to bring his gun to bear on this, more dangerous foe, but he was too late. Before he could do anything the Luger was fired and he knew nothing more.

Karl had shot the Innkeeper between the eyes and this had knocked him backwards. By the time any muscle spasms had reached his trigger finger, he was already falling behind the bar and his shot gun's twin barrels were pointing up to the ceiling. With a deafening raw the shot gun exploded and shot the pellets, from both barrels, up into the ceiling.

Erich had not realised what was happening or what needed to be done. All he knew was that he was lying on the floor, the room was full of gun smoke and he had been showered with plaster, from the ceiling.

"Are you staying or shall we go home?" Karl shouted at Erich, as he picked up his suitcase and headed for the door.

Erich scrambled to his feet, grabbed his suitcase and followed Karl towards the door. By the time he got there, Karl had already started up the slope, which would take them towards the main road and away from here.

Soon they had left the village green, after walking past a row of cottages that lined the green, on the same side as The Tiger Inn.

No one in the village appeared to have reacted to the shots that had been fired. Karl and Erich more or less ran towards the main road and then turned left to walk up the hill to Friston Church, where they intended to rest and take stock.

What neither of them realised, was that they were being watched, from the other side of the village green. Will Young had been stood beside one of the large houses, on the opposite side of the village green, to The Tiger Inn. It had been quite boring, just standing there and keeping watch on the Inn, but once the church bells had started to ring, some of the villagers had started to leave their homes and head for the church. This had mean that he had to duck behind some bushes, so that he was not noticed.

Karl was not happy with his companion. From what he had just seen, he was a complete liability. He didn't know why he had been partnered up with him. He was now happy that their mission was being cancelled, he couldn't rely on Erich.

He, after all, was a proper soldier and had been chosen for this mission, in part, because he was a good soldier and secondly because he spoke English, like a native.

As far as he understood, the only reason Erich was on the mission was because he spoke English, a soldier he most certainly was not. Well he wasn't going to stop Karl reaching the Fishing boat, on time.

There was nothing going to hold him back. He strode out. Erich asked that he slowed down but Karl ignored him and pressed on.

"If you want to get caught near here then that is up to you. I'm getting to Exceat as quick as I can." Karl said, and continued on up the hill.

After ten minutes they had reached the top of the hill and after a hundred yards they arrived at the church. Karl walked over to the horse trough.

He cupped his hands together, scooped up some water and threw this up into his face to give him a wake up. The shock of the cold water certainly did that.

Erich arrived about two minutes later than Karl. By which time Karl felt rested and ready to go again. Erich was not happy with that and so pulled rank on him and ordered him to allow him to rest for a few minutes, before they started off again.

While Karl had been waiting for Erich to join him he had watched as a convoy of Army Lorries drove past. They came along the road, from Exceat and appeared to be heading for Eastbourne. He counted about twenty vehicles in all. Three were pulling anti aircraft guns, one looked like a petrol tanker but the rest carried soldiers.

When he was ready, Erich got up and they started off again. As they were about to rejoin the road, a second convoy of Army Lorries came up the road, this time from the direction of Eastbourne, and these were headed off towards Seaford. They thought that this was unusual. They didn't expect the English to be moving about so much, this early on a Sunday morning.

After the vehicles had past they started to follow them. Karl suggested that, as they were tight on time, that they should trot along the road, where it was level. Walk fast down any down hill slopes but walk up any hills. Erich agreed to this and so they set off at a trot.

It was not long before they were trotting past the emergency air strip, on South Hill.

When they reached the entrance gate to the air strip and were surprised to find two Air Force men, stood guard at the gate. They had intended to have a rest, when they reached this gate but decided that it would not be wise so carried on along the road.

When they reached the first and only downhill stretch, along Scabs Island, they decided that it was best if they carried on trotting, as time was running away from them. They knew that if they were late, the boat wouldn't wait for them. The tide was the boats master. The boats captain would not wait for mere men.

As they went along, they were surprised to find that there were about a hundred tanks, drawn up on the fields, to their left, beside the road. They were all facing towards the coast and the soldiers were preparing to camouflage them, so as not to be seen by the enemy.

They had heard some tanks driving about on the hills, when they had been looking over the air strip, the previous day, but the sounds had come from the other side of the road. What were they doing? Was this an exercise or were they readying themselves for the German invasion?

As they reached Newbarn Bottom they heard the raw of three Spitfires flying along the coast and a further three Hurricane's flying over head. What was going on? Was this why we were being recalled?

Each time they turned a corner Erich said that the drop down to the River was just around the next corner but it wasn't. This made Karl very mad, as each time Erich had started to slow down, thinking that they had more time than, in fact, they had, to reach the Bridge.

When, eventually, they reached the crest of the last hill and could see the steep drop down into the Cuckmere River valley, Karl checked his watch. It was eight forty five. They had just fifteen minutes to reach the Bridge. They looked at each other.

"Race you." Karl said as he gave Erich a smile and moved away from him, at a pace.

Chapter 24
If only the Bridge had been open

Fritz had lain awake since six o'clock. He always woke up well before he needed to, if he had to get up earlier than his norm. It was as if he was afraid that his inner alarm would let him down, so he over compensated for any error that might occur.

At seven o'clock he got up, had a wash and shave, the got himself dressed. He looked at himself in the mirror and made sure that he could still be taken for a travelling salesman. He felt that he did, so was happy with his appearance.

He reached up, above the wardrobe, and pulled at his suitcase handle and brought it down, so that he could pack up all his things. The only things, in the suitcase, were the explosives, detonators, his two weapons and their respective magazines.

It had been his intention to plant some of the explosives, today, while the town was quiet and there were fewer people about. This was now not possible as they were being withdrawn. Still if they were sent back, he knew where the best places were, that would do most harm to the English.

He placed the suitcase onto his bed and opened it up. He decided that he would carry his Luger. Even on a Sunday morning, there could be people around who might be trying to stop him getting home.

The Schmeisser was not something he could conceal about himself, while on the bike. This he would also pack at the top of the suitcase so that, if needed and if he had the time, he could just pop open the suitcase and reach in and grab it. Just in case this eventuality might occur, he fitted a full magazine to it and ensured that the safety catch was on 'safe'.

Now he opened the wardrobe and took down the clothes that he had hung there on Friday, when he moved into the room.

He had wanted anyone that might go into his room to believe that he was here for the full week he had paid for.

After packing up his clothes and his washing things, he then placed his Schmeisser on top of it all and closed the lid of the suitcase and closed the catches so that it did not spring open.

Satisfied that he had packed everything, he put on his jacked, slid the Luger into the inside pocket, picked up his suitcase and left his room. The stair case was just opposite his room and he walked down the stairs. When he reached the Bar, he noticed that the publican was working behind the bar so thought he had better give him a reason for going out so early.

"Why the shopkeeper, in Peacehaven, wanted to see me early on a Sunday morning I don't know, but business is business." Fritz said as he waived towards Tom.

"Be careful, when you come back down that hill. If you go to fast, you'll end up in the river." Tom joked.

"I will." Fritz said as he walked out of the door.

He had been allowed to keep his bike at the rear of the Inn, so he went around and took it out of the small shed that he had left it, since Friday night.

Steffen had slept better than Fritz. He had brought a small travelling alarm clock with him. So he had slept until it started to ring, at about five minutes to seven o'clock. He decided to rest for a few minutes more. He was not getting up until seven o'clock, just because the alarm went of early, he was staying in bed.

At the due time he got up, walked over to the basin and tipped some of the cold water into it and then had a quick wash. Today he was not going to bother with a shave. That could wait until he was back in France.

Once cleaned, he got dressed and packed everything up into his suitcase. He didn't bother to keep his weapons out as he saw no reason to carry them today.

At seven fifteen, just as he was putting on his jacket, he looked out of the window and saw that the publican was walking off down the road and appeared to be carrying a sack over his shoulder. What was he up to, this early, he thought but dismissed any further thoughts, on the matter.

Steffen had arranged to meet up with Fritz, at the junction of the road that came through his village and the one coming from Newhaven to Seaford. They could then ride along together, safety in numbers.

It was now seven forty and time for him to leave. They had agreed to meet up at eight o'clock and as Steffen had less distance to travel he could afford to leave a little later than Fritz.

He left his room and walked down the stairs and out of the Inn. He went around to the back of the Inn and collected his bike and rode off towards his meeting place.

Fritz had also left his Inn and was now approaching the swing bridge that crossed the River Ouse. He was too late. The bridge was starting to swing to let a ship, coming down the river, to pass and head out to sea.

Even if he peddled as fast as he could, he wouldn't make it in time to cross. He cursed to himself, if he had been a couple of minutes earlier he would be over it before it had started to open.

Fritz reached the bridge and waited behind the barrier, as the small coaster moved down the river, past the open bridge and headed along the docks and towards the harbour entrance and out to sea.

Once the ship had past the confines of the bridge, the bridge started to swing back, so that the traffic could pass over it again. Being a Sunday morning, the only traffic, at this time, was Fritz and his bicycle. Once the bridge was locked in place the Bridge Keeper came over and raised the barrier, in front of Fritz and then walked, alongside Fritz, to the other side of the bridge were he opened up the other barrier. He waived Fritz on his way and then returned to his control box, for, what he thought, was a well earned cup of tea.

Fritz peddled off, a bit faster than he wanted to, as they had a fair distance to travel, this morning and he didn't really want to use up all his energy, this early. He knew that the bridge being open, had delayed him a good five minutes and Steffen would be waiting for him, at the junction.

As he neared the junction he could see Steffen sitting on his bike and was waiving out to him, he waived back and peddled on.

Chapter 25
First one down

Dave and Andy were up at about five thirty and had agreed to meet up at six o'clock, on the road to Seaford. Each of them had a bicycle and had suitable bags to be able to carry their weapons, unseen by any passers by. They didn't expect to come across anyone at that time on a Sunday morning but you never know.

Andy was the first one to arrive at their meeting place, the entrance to Foxhole Farm. He looked around as the daylight started to creep into the sky. He had only been there about five minutes, when Dave came careering down the lane, to meet the main road. Andy didn't think that Dave would stop in time, as he could see that he was pulling hard on his breaks, but eventually he slid to a stop, just as he reached the road.

"I must get these breaks fixed." David said

"You've been saying that for years." Andy replied.

"I hope you can stop before we reach the Cuckmere River."

"So do I" Dave replied.

With that, the two of them set off towards Seaford. They were glad that the wind was not blowing today. Part of their route would take them along the sea front, at Seaford and as it was very close to the sea, if the wind blows hard, the sea and shingle would be thrown over the road.

Within twenty minutes they had got through Seaford and were on the open road, towards Exceat Bridge. They started down the hill, with David holding his break down fairly hard. He had decided that it would be better to arrive slowly, than crash at the bottom and then he may be not able to complete the mission.

Andy went ahead. He could rely on his breaks to stop him. Once he reached the bottom, he waited for David to join him.

Once David arrived, they got off their bikes and took it in turn to climb over the fence, to the left of the road. Once David was over, Andy passed both bikes over to him and then their bags. He then climbed over to join David.

Andy looked around and found a spot that he could hide up the bikes. Just back up the hill there were some bushes that stood about six feet tall and ran for about thirty yards, beside the road. Laying the bikes down this side of the bushes would ensure that they couldn't be seen from anyone coming down the hill, even in a lorry. He pushed the bikes up the field and put them in their hiding place and then returned to join David.

In the mean time, David had scouted around to find the best place for them to hide up and where best to affect their ambush. They needed to be in a place where they could see the German coming down the hill but also allow them to be able to carry out their arrest, in the view of someone standing at the bridge. It was not easy. If he was able to look up the hill, he wouldn't be able to carry out the arrest, as requested.

If he stood at the spot where it was right for the arrest, he wouldn't be able to see the German approaching him, or it might be too late to be sure that whoever was approaching, was, in fact, their target.

When Andy arrived back, they discussed this problem. Whoever had thought up this task had not envisaged this problem. In their training they had been taught that they would have to think on their feet.

The only important thing, with any operation, was to succeed in its execution. They needed to minimise the risks to themselves but the mission came before their own lives.

Dave had said that it was all right for the instructors, but it was their lives that were at stake. To which the instructor said in that case they would have to improvise, do the mission and then get away.

They decided that Andy would lay by the fence and watch up the hill. When he saw the German, he would wave out to David and then, just before the German arrived, jump over the fence and wave him down.

He had decided that he would conceal the fact that he was carrying a Thompson, unless he saw the German going for his weapon. He did this by slinging the Thompson over his back, but within easy reach, if needed.

Providing that he stopped, Andy would arrest him and walk him down the hill to David.

If however he failed to stop, David would be stood in the road, further down the hill, with his Thompson ready and aimed at the German, prepared to open fire. If the German gave no indication that he was going to stop, David would open fire. With Andy coming up from behind, ready to assist David, the German was in a trap, the decision as to him living or dying was his.

In the mean time Charles was already up and had eaten a cheese sandwich and drunk his first cup of tea. It was nearly seven o'clock so he had better get himself out and along to the place he had selected to carry out his killing. The spot he had chosen was at the junction, where the road from Denton met up with the Newhaven to Seaford road. He would cross the road, walk over the field and lay up in some bushes about fifty yards from the junction.

He reached his hiding place at about seven thirty. No one knew at what time either of the Germans would arrive but the unit were all in agreement that this junction would be the most likely place the two Germans would meet up, before going on to Exceat Bridge.

Charles took out his Lee Enfield snipers rifle, attached the telescopic site and then fitted the silencer. He managed to get into the bushes and make a space where he could get comfortable and have a good sight of where he expected his target to appear. He broke off a few branches to ensure that he could move about, if the target moved, before he took his shot.

Once he was happy about his shooting position he then concentrated in being able to see the other German, as he arrived from Newhaven. Charles was hoping that the man from his Inn would arrive first, as it was him that he really wanted to kill.

As much out of revenge, for the German thinking that he had one over on Charles. But he had to be prepared for the fact that the other German would arrive first. Then he would have a decision to make as to the one he killed.

After a while, he decided that he would take out the one who was stationary. That would ensure that he achieved his kill. Moving targets were harder to hit, unless you used a shot gun.

He felt that being this close, he was confident enough to know that he would hit his target.

They had talked about what to do with the second German? If he turned back, towards Newhaven, then Charles was told to kill him as well. They could not let him return to the port and set of any explosives he may have already planted. If he continued towards Seaford, he was to let him go.

It was for this reason that Charles had prepared the bush so that he could move his rifle to the other side of the bush and would have a space to see his target, as he moved away, towards Newhaven.

By seven fifty, Charles was getting a bit board with nothing going on around him. He could hear the birds singing but not a tune he liked much. He was looking through his telescope and envisaging where his target would be stood and how he would take the shot.

The sure kill would be to his head but, even at this distance that could be risky. If the man stood very still, then it would be the best shot, but the odds were that at the critical moment he would move and so the bullet would sail passed his head. His best shot would be in the chest, even if he did move the bullet was likely to hit a vital organ of some kind.

He realised that he had not fired a shot, with this weapon, for a couple of months.

He needed to be sure that he was still as good a shot as he through he was. He looked around and saw that there was a fence post, just inside the field, this side of the road, in a direct line to where his target was expected to be stood.

Charles pulled the bold back and then slid it forward, again, moving a bullet from the magazine, into the barrel and locked the bolt. The bullets he had been issued with were the special sniper issues. They were made too a much higher specification than regular bullets. This ensured a greater degree of accuracy, as each bullet had the identical load.

In this way the sniper didn't have worry about the bullets, in his calculations of the distance and wind factors. He looked through the telescope and lined up the cross hairs onto a knot, six inches from the top of the post. He took a deep breath and held it as he steadied the rifle and then squeezed the trigger.

When the slight smoke cleared, being blown away by the breeze crossing the field, he could see that the knot was in tack but about an inch to its right was a new hole in the post. An inch, at this distance is nothing to worry about, considering the size of the target he would be aiming at. He would take this into account when he took his shot, as he wanted to hit his heart, if possible. A straight kill was what was called for today. Charles reloaded his rifle and was now more than ready.

At about seven fifty five he heard and saw Mat's van coming down the road, out of Denton, but it stopped about two hundred yards short of the road junction.

Charles used his rifle's telescope to ensure that it was Mat, in the driving seat. Mat must have sensed Charles watching him as he raised his hand and waived to him. This brought a smile to Charles face. They were all ready, now. All they need were the Germans.

Charles looked at his watch, it was nearly seven forty five and still there was no sign of either of the Germans. He wondered if this was all a big mistake.

Soon it would be too late for the Germans to make it to Exceat, before high tide. He wiped his eyes with his hanky and as the slight mist evaporated, he saw a man approaching the junction, on a bike. He recognised him as the German who had been staying at his Inn. Good, his target had arrived.

He lined up his sights and looked at the face of his adversary. Yes it was the man he wanted, so much, to kill. Steffen drew to a stop and sat there, astride his bike. Apparently he was waiting for Fritz to arrive. Charles guessed that, when he saw the second German approaching, he would waive out to him. This was to be his signal to open fire.

Five minutes went by and still no sign of the second German. Charles turned his head to his left and looked through the branches, to see if he could see the man. Just as he got focused, he saw a movement, so returned his head back to his target, looked back through the telescope and focused on him.

The wave, he had been waiting for came more or less as soon as he eyed his target.

Charles slightly lowered the sight and ensured that the cross hairs were just an inch or two to the left of Steffen's shirt buttons.

He squeezed the trigger and felt the kick in his shoulder, as the bullet sped on its way. The wind dispersed the smoke very quickly and Charles had a full view of the German falling backwards, off his bike and landing on the grass verge.

Before Charles could do anything, the second of the Germans arrived, jumped off his bike and ran over to his colleague. In a matter of seconds the man got up, ran to his bicycle and ran off towards Seaford, jumping back on his bike after a few yards.

Charles watched as the German cycled off as fast as his bike could take him. He watched as Fritz looked back to see if he, himself, was another target to the gunman. Having seen no one, he returned to the task in hand, getting away from here as fast as he could. Steffen would have to fend for himself.

Charles stayed where he was for five minutes, he continued to watch to see if the German, lying on the verge, was moving but he appeared not to move. He was just about to move when he heard Mat's van start up and start to move down the hill, towards the apparent dead German. Charles broke cover and walked over the field and, after he was sure that the German was not moving, he climbed over the fence and crossed the road and stood by the body.

Mat arrived soon after Charles. Stopped the van and got out. He walked over to the body and looked down at him.

Mat took out his service revolver and shot the man in the head to ensure that he was in fact dead. Having returned his pistol into his jacket pocked, the two of them lifted the body of the German up and put him into the rear of the van. Mat had laid some empty corn sacks across the vans floor, to place the body on.

"Very good shot Charles" Mat commended his man.

"Not bad yourself" Charles replied, with a broad smile.

"Right, let's get off and be ready to retrieve the second German." Mat said.

Both of them got into the van, after Charles had placed his rifle back into his bag and laid it in the back of the van, away from Steffen's body and the suitcase.

They were not in any hurry. It would be at least fifteen minutes before the second German arrived at the second of their ambush area.

David and Andy had been lying in the damp grass bank, by the River Cuckmere for an hour now. The man they were waiting for should have been here a long time ago. It was well passed half past eight and still there was no sign of him.

During their time there, they had seen five convoys of army vehicles going either up or down the road and crossing Exceat Bridge. This was not at all good, what if one came along, when the German arrived? What would they do?

As they were laying about twenty five yards apart, they didn't want to try and speak, in case anyone heard them. It was important that they remained hidden.

They had been told that it was expected that the German's boat would arrive at high tide, which was about nine o'clock. They would not have much time left now. David looked towards the bridge and he froze, for a moment, there, stood at this end of the bridge was a man, who looked very much like a tramp.

Was this the leader of the German spies? Andy so much wanted to change his point of aim and shoot the 'Tramp', rather than their assigned target but he remembered that Mat had said that, under no circumstance was the 'Tramp' to be shot, unless he was about to shoot one of their unit.

David lost sight of the 'Tramp' when yet another Army Convoy started across the bridge, headed their way and started up the hill towards Seaford. As the third of the Lorries passed by Andy, he turned and looked up the hill and saw that there was a man on a bicycle, heading towards him, about three hundred yards away.

He frantically signalled to David that their target was coming, but he had turned around and was trying to keep an eye on the 'Tramp'.

Andy picked up a stone, from in front of him and threw it at David, hitting him on his head. This brought his attention around to the job in hand, as soon as he realised what Andy was trying to tell him.

Most of the army convoy had passed David, by now and the last lorry was turning the corner to head up the hill. The German was still coming down the hill as the penultimate vehicle drove passed him.

Andy was hoping that the last one would have passed the German, before he had to jump into the road. All the time the German was coming nearer and nearer. They had their orders and now realised why they had practiced and practiced carrying out ambushes, time and time again, on their Auxiliary Forces training. They had to concentrate on the task in hand and then get the hell out of there.

Andy got himself ready to jump over the fence and confront the German. 'One... Two... Three...' Andy jumped over the fence and into the road. He took up a stance with his left hand held up, indicating that the cyclist was required to stop. His right hand held the butt of the Thompson, just out of sight, behind his back.

There was no way that Fritz did not understand what he was being required to do. He had to make up his mind very quickly. The last of the army convoy vehicles was just passing him. If he failed to stop he could have a troop of soldiers after him, very quickly. He jammed on his breaks and slid to a stop, just inches from Andy.

Having achieved his aim of stopping the German, Andy lowered his left hand and took a proper hold of his Thompson and bringing it around so that the German would realise that Andy was armed. Andy stepped to one side and walked towards the German.

"You are under arrest." Andy informed the German.

"Please get off your bike and walk down the hill, in front of me."

"Why are you arresting me?" Fritz asked, before moving off.

"You are one of a party of Germans who landed here on Friday morning. Your war is over." Andy informed him.

"I'm not German. I'm as English as you." Fritz said.

"Look, I've got my ration card and a driving licence."

"Keep your hands out of your pockets, please." Andy said.

"Let's go. I have a friend, down the road, waiting to meet you." Andy ordered.

By this time, David had also jumped over the fence and was walking up to road, towards the two of them. Fritz could see that he was also carrying a machine gun, the same as this man.

"You're not the police or army. You can't arrest me." Fritz said.

"You said that you're English. Have you forgotten that anyone can make an arrest in this country? That's what I'm doing." Andy said

Their luck had not lasted for long, as there were some soldiers sitting at the back of the last truck and they saw everything. They looked shocked and initially did nothing to stop their lorry.

The 'Tramp' looked at his watch. It was time that he should be along the river, waiting for Tobias. He had noticed that a fishing boat had already started to enter the mouth of the river. None of his men appeared to have made it to the bridge. He couldn't wait for them any longer. If they reached the boat then they would get home, if not, then they would have to hide out until the invasion. He turned and ran, without waiting any longer.

Andy noticed that the last of the army convoy had stopped, halfway up the hill. It appeared that some of the soldiers had seen what they had done and were informing their commander.

"Right, let's run the rest of the way. If you don't do as I say, my colleague, there, will shoot you." Andy said

The three of them ran down the rest of the hill and towards the bridge. They didn't go over the bridge but, instead turned up a small track that led up to some sheds. Andy was the first one to reach the shed door. It was not locked so he opened it and went inside and David ushered the German in, together with his bike.

"Make a sound and it will be your last." David said.

Andy was right, one of the men had jumped out of the back of the vehicle and ran along the side to the passenger's door and reported to his Sergeant, what he had seen.

The Sergeant gathered together two of the men and they walked back down the hill. From where they were, they couldn't see any sign of David, Andy or the other man. By the time the soldiers had turned the corner, there was no one in sight. The road was clear, the 'Tramp', the Sergeant had seen on the bridge was not there any more and there was no sign of the cyclist, who had passed by.

"I think you two should go and see the Doctor when we get back to camp, and get your eyes tested. There's no one about. Let's not waist anymore time here. This was our last run and I want to get back to the Mess for breakfast." The Sergeant said, turned around and marched back up the hill to join his vehicle.

As they turned the corner and headed back up the hill, to rejoin their lorry, they heard some firing. It sounded like a Bren gun and some other weapons.

"It's those bloody Canadians. You would think that they had better things to do on a Sunday morning than be on their range." The Sergeant said, but did not bother to turn around to confirm his thoughts.

Andy and David looked at each other, as the sound of the Bren gun could be heard, further down the river. Was someone trying to kill the 'Tramp'? Was this the reason why they had been told not to kill him? Someone else wanted the glory of that kill.

When the soldiers marched off, towards their vehicle, Andy and David relaxed. Once the lorry moved off they could extricate themselves from the shed and with their prisoner, make their way back to the bridge and await Mat and his trusty van.

As they started to walk on to the bridge, Mat's van appeared around the corner after descending the hill they had staked out.

"Andy, you go and get our bikes and I'll hand this German over to Mat." David ordered.

David waved out to Mat, who had already started to slow his van down to a virtual crawl. He was looking for both of his men and was happy that they were both up and about.

Mat and Charles got out of the van and walked over to join David and his prisoner.

"Well done, you've got him." Mat observed.

"Yes, he stopped, when Andy asked him to and then he arrested him." David replied.

Just at that time, Andy rode up, bringing David's bike with him. He wasn't going to ride David's bike, not with those doggy breaks.

"The pair of you better tie this man up; I don't want him to get loose in the van, before we can get him back to Newhaven." Mat ordered.

It took the two of them about five minutes to secure Fritz's hands and make a gag for his mouth so that he didn't call out. He was then loaded into the rear of the van. Not before Charles had removed his rifle, from the back of the van. Andy asked what they should do with the German's bike and the suitcase. Mat said that they would take the suitcase but they could leave the bike in the shed.

With everything tidied up, Mat and Charles drove away, towards West Dean and Andy and David walked their bikes up the hill and then rode off, back to Denton. They would meet up later, discuss the operation and then Mat could send in his report.

Chapter 26
Have you a light?

Tom Richards had been a first class student, on his latest Auxiliary Forces training course, at Coleshill House. This had been a specialist training course on silent killing. Tom had excelled in being able to get close to his targets without being either detected or suspected of being a killer.

His training included killing with a knife, a silenced pistol and how to break a man's neck. Tom was skilled in all those disciplines. He so much impressed his instructors that they had recommended that he be taken into active service.

The reason active service had been turned down was that Tom was fifty two years old. Although he had strength, he didn't have the overall fitness for the type of active service units his talents would be best served.

Tom's task, for today, was to take out the German, staying at the Star Inn, in Alfriston. Because of this he had got up early, about six o'clock. Gathered his weapons from his outside shed, where he had hidden them last night, after he returned from the units briefing.

His chosen weapons, for this mission were a 9mm Browning Pistol and silencer, His treasured Commando Knife, given to him for being the top student on the course, and his knotted rope. Although the rope had not been issued, Tom decided that he would make one for himself.

He had taken a five foot length of rope, tied a knot at each end and a further three knots in the middle section of the rope, about nine inches apart. He also had the shoulder holster, for the Browning. The one he had taken, from the Units store was the one that allowed the pistol to have the silencer fitted, while in the holster.

Happy that he had all the weapons he would need, for today's mission, he went back upstairs and entered his bedroom, walked over to the bed and bent down and gave his wife a kiss on her forehead.

This brought a small smile to her face but Tom didn't notice it, as he was already heading back out of the room and down the stairs. As he left the kitchen door, he picked up his hand held military radio. He would need that once he had completed his mission.

It was his aim to get to Alfriston, no later than seven o'clock so he planned his route to ensure that he was there in time. He was to walk up the track and then cross to Bullocks Barn, head up to the top of Camp Hill. From there he would turn right to Cradle Hill and then join the Alfriston road just below High and Over. He would walk down this part of the road until he reached Tile Barn, a large Sussex Barn, beside the road. There he planned to stop for a few minutes and take a rest.

He had not used too much of his energy, by the time he reached the road at High and Over but the steep hill, down to Tile Barn was a lot more energy sapping. He was used to walking over the hills, around here but never looked forward to this hill.

It was not only steep but long. Walking down hill was always more energy sapping than walking up hill. Once at the barn, the road then rose again, up a much shorter hill.

Tom stopped, when he reached Tile Barn and sat on a Milk churn stand, at the far end of the Barn. Here he took out a sandwich, he had made before he left his cottage. This was the first part of his breakfast. The second part would be taken, when he reached the spot he planned to stand, to watch the coming and goings at the Star Inn.

Having finished his sandwich he started off, along the road to Alfriston. Now he was rested he took the next up hill in his stride. He had just walked over the crest of this hill when he noticed a man, about two hundred yards ahead of him, walking in his direction. The man was dressed like a farm worker but, for some reason, was carrying a suitcase.

From last nights briefing, Tom had been told that the German, he was going after, would be dressed as a farm worker and that, when he was last seen, he had been carrying a suitcase.

By the time they were one hundred yards apart, Tom could see his features more clearly. He knew all the farm workers in this area and this man was not among the men he knew. Tom decided that this was his target and, also, how he was going to engage him.

As they closed with each other, Tom took out his packet of five Woodbine cigarettes, put one between his lips and, rather theatricality, felt for his, apparently non existent, box of matches. Having not found them, he cursed aloud, for not having brought any with him.

"Excuse me, have you a light?" Tom asked the man, as they were about to pass each other.

Tom had purposely walked so that he would be passing the man on the side that he was holding his suitcase. He needed that hand to be occupied, so that the German couldn't use it to defend himself.

"Yes, I have a lighter. Could you spare one of your cigarettes? Richard Hartmann replied.

With his left hand Tom offered him a cigarette from his packet of Woodbine's. Richard took one out of the packet, with his right hand, placed it between his lips and then felt in his pocket, for his lighter.

All this time, Tom engaged Richard's eyes, with his. Tom smiled and kept looking at him. Richard didn't understand why Tom was looking into his eyes and as a result, kept his eyes focused on Tom's.

Richard had retrieved his lighter and flipped the lid open and moved his thumb across the little wheel that would strike the flint and create sparks to light the wick. He felt the flame, as the wick ignited and started to bring the flame up towards Tom's cigarette.

It was then that Richard felt very worried, this was no farm worker. He dropped his lighter and quickly reached into his left hand inside pocket for the Luger, but he was too late. He suddenly felt an immense pain in his chest.

While Richard had been getting his lighter out, Tom moved his right hand around his back and under the tail of his jacket.

Here he felt for and extracted his Commando Knife. He took a good grip of the handle. Tom struck, at the moment that Richards realised something was wrong. The sudden realization of the danger he was in, was all too late.

Tom had brought his right arm around from his back, at some speed and had angled his knife so that it slid between the German's ribs and into his heart.

He pushed the knife in as far as the hilt, as taught on the training course. He was surprised how much force was needed to get it all the way in, but force was something Tom had plenty of.

All the time this was going on, Tom had been looking into the Germans eyes. As the knife entered his body, the German's look changed from a smile to disbelief and then a sudden look of surprise. His eyes widened and then they had a dead look about them.

Richard started to slump down on to the road and at the same time he let go of his suitcase. Tom held on to his knife and it came away from Richard's chest, as he fell away from him. As his suitcase hit the road's surface it broke open, as the catches were sprung, by the impact. Everything went all over the road.

Tom checked that the German was, in fact dead. If not he would have to use his Browning to end this mans life. He didn't want him to die in more pain than was necessary. There was no pulse from his neck and decided that he had done a good job, in killing his enemy well. The training had not been the waist that Tom had thought it would be, before he attended the course.

Although the order had been for him to arrest this man, it was made clear that if they found themselves in danger, they could kill the German and Tom knew that once he realised who he was, the German was about to draw his Luger pistol and would have killed him, given the chance.

He now had to clear up the mess that had been made. If anyone came along the road, there would be questions to answer and he was not in a very strong position to answer any.

After all, the Auxiliary Forces were a Top Secret organisation and very few people, outside, knew of their existence and, as they were all sworn to secrecy, they couldn't claim to be part of this organisation. Basically, he was a civilian who had killed another civilian. At that time, this was a hanging offence, even in the war.

The first thing he needed to do was move the body. Luckily it was at the side of the road so it would be quite easy for him to roll it over the verge and into the ditch, under the hedge row.

With that done, he gathered up the suitcase and put it onto the grass verge and then proceeded to gather up its contents that were spread all over the road.

He picked up all the clothes, but there weren't many of these, just a change of the things he was wearing, nothing much else. Once these were thrown into the suitcase, Tom then gathered up the Schmeisser and the four magazines that were spread about the road.

Tom saw that a couple of rounds had fallen out of one of the magazines, so he picked them up.

He walked back to the suitcase and placed the weapon inside. Before he closed the lid he searched the body, to see if he could find the Luger.

He found it in one of the jacket pockets', took it out and placed it into the suitcase and closed the lid. He then placed the case on top of the German.

In the meantime, Jack had been delivering Frank and Eddie over to the lane that led to Chryston Farm. He then drove up to High and Over and parked up, waiting for his next assignment.

It was now time for Tom to contact his leader, with his radio. He had carried that on a sling, under his jacket, so that it didn't show to any one he might have met.

"This is the shepherd. I have a dead sheep to collect."

"The tractor is on its way."

Was the only reply Tom received and the only message he expected to receive, anything else and he would have known that it was not Peter.

Tom, so much wanted to examine the Schmeisser but he knew that as soon as he got it out of the case, someone would come by. It would best be left until they got it back to their hide.

They could put it with all the other weapons they had at their disposal. Having a German weapon, may come in useful if the Germans did, in fact, invade.

It wasn't long before Tom could hear a vehicle approaching from Seaford. He hoped that it was Jack and his trusty van. He stood up and waited until the van came over the crest of the hill, so that he could be sure who was coming towards him.

The van reached the top of the hill and was now in full view. It was the van he had been expecting, with Jack behind the wheel. Tom stepped out into the road and waived him down. Jack got out of the van and walked up to Tom and shook his hand.

"Well done. Now we'll have to wait to see if the motor bike and possibly the fisherman also come this way." Jack said.

"Yes but we'd better get this body into the back of your van, first. You never know if anyone else will be along, we can't afford anyone to see what we've done." Tom said.

"It wasn't me my lord." Jack protested, with a big smile.

They exchanged a few more insults as they dragged the body out of the ditch and lifted it into the back of Jack's van. They threw the suitcase in with the body and then closed the rear door. With that completed, they both got in the van.

Jack started up the engine and they drove off towards Alfriston. Jack had noticed a place, just through the village, where he could, firstly park his van and secondly walk a short distance to a place that they could lay in wait for the man on the motor bike and the fisherman.

Once they had parked up, they both got out and Jack returned to the rear of his van, opened the door and reached in to retrieve the two Thompson machine guns that they would need to enforce an arrest or, if required, take out the motor cyclist.

They then walked along, beside the wall that separated the large house, behind it, from the road. They stopped one hundred and fifty yards short of the junction, leading across the river to Lullington.

They found a spot where they could lay up. It was on a bank, five foot above the road. This gave them cover and allowed them to see what was coming towards them.

It wasn't long before they heard the sound of a motor bike, coming towards them. Both of them readied their Thompsons and prepared to take action. It had been decided that Tom would jump down into the road while Jack would be in a position to give covering fire, if the need arose. As the motor bike reached the junction, it turned left and headed for the bridge that crossed the river.

They were a bit relieved and disappointed, at the same time. Still, they believed that he was now riding into another trap, laid by one of the other Auxiliary Forces units.

Everything went quiet for the next five minutes and then they heard the screech of breaks and a crash. Well the motor bicyclist had met his end. Now it was just the fisherman to wait for.

They were getting a bit board, just looking down the road, with nothing happening. Fifteen minutes had passed before they noticed anyone else on the road. Jack had his telescope with him and was looking around when he saw the fisherman, coming up the road. Right, now it was his turn to get one of the Germans, thought Jack.

Again they got ready to take on this German on. This time it was Jacks turn to jump down into the road and affect the arrest. Like the motor cyclist, the fisherman turned down the same road as the other German. Well they expected him to meet the same end.

Tom got out his radio and requested orders, now all the sheep had headed home. Peter told them to come back to the farm and await further orders.

The two men got up and walked back to Jacks van, got in and drove off back the way they had come.

In the meantime Frank Andrews and Eddie Turner had waked over to Seaford Head. Frank carried the Bren gun, in a corn sack and Eddie was carrying a box full of loaded magazines. They had not realised that there was likely to be a squadron of tanks, from the Canadian Tank Regiment, lined up along the Head, facing down into Cuckmere haven. As they turned a corner, around a hedge, they saw the tanks. Frank backed back around the corner and Eddie followed him.

"God, where did they come from?" Eddie exclaimed.

"Heaven knows. What are we to do?" Frank asked.

"Well we've got to get passed them and we'll have to get a bit lower down the hill, than we had planned." Eddie said.

We can't just walk passed them, carrying these." Franks said, indicating the box of magazines.

"I'll pop back to Chryston Farm and see if I can get a couple of sacks." Eddie said.

"When I get back, we'll put these in the sacks and say we're going to feed some cattle, further down the hill."

"Do you think that'll work?" Frank asked.

"Well we always have our Revolvers." Eddie said as he patted his, in his jacket pocket, and smiled.

It took Eddie about fifteen minutes to get to the farm, find himself a couple of corn sacks and return to Frank. In the meantime, Frank had been doing a little bit of scouting the area ahead of them. He had found that there was a track that would take them a bit away from where they wanted to go but it would skirt the squadron of tanks and hopefully they would not get challenged.

Once Eddie got back, they put the magazines into the corn sacks. Frank reported what he had found and Eddie agreed with his plan, so they set off for the track.

As they were going around the end of the line of tanks, they noticed that, in fact there were no soldiers about. The tanks appeared to have just been parked there, and left, over night.

That was good, they could relax now. The most important thing was to get them selves into position and ensure that their arc of fire ensured that they wouldn't have to move the Bren, once the firing started.

They had discussed how they were going to fire off all their rounds, at the fishing boat and try not to attract the attention of the Canadians. Once they were happy that the Canadians would not be able to immediately spot them, if they returned to their tanks, they got comfortable and settled into their firing positions.

Eddie got on his radio and called in to Peter.

"Fishermen in place." Was all he said.

"Boat in sight." Came the reply.

Eddie looked out to sea and, as said, the fishing boat was approaching the river mouth.

Chapter 27
Let's get us some geese

Graham had arranged to meet all the members of his unit, at the large barn next to West Dean church at seven o'clock, Sunday morning. Any later and they could run into the vicar and some of his congregation, going into the church for early morning communion.

Ian Badger was told that he had to stay in the barn and after nine o'clock, once he heard all the firing coming from the estuary, he was to open the barn doors and then keep well out of site.

He was not to interfere with any of the vehicles that would be arriving and was not to look at the men. After each had departed he was to check how many dead German's there were. If he had nine, he could close the barn doors. If not, he was to wait until Ten Thirty. Then he could close the barn doors.

Although the rest of the unit would be returning home, once the fishing boat had left, Ian was to stay around until a police car arrived. He was still to keep out of site but once they had left, he was to report to Graham.

Graham, Luke and Tommy all picked up their weapons and made their way out of the barn and headed to Exceat and the marsh land within the area of the original route of the river, to the sea.

This had long been cut off, since the big storm, several centuries ago, that initially sealed up the flow of the river, into the sea. It was the new channel that was cut, to allow boats up the river, well passed Alfriston, than that Germans would be using at high tide.

The quickest route, for Graham and his team, was up over the hill that separated the village from the main coast road. If they took the longer way, they may well run into people that they might not wish to meet, armed as they were.

Once they had reached the main road, they made sure that no one was about and ran over the road and hopped over the fence.

First Graham got over and then Luke and Tommy handed him their weapons, together with his weapon. Once this was done, the two of them also climbed over the fence.

They took control of their respective weapons and headed down the slope and onto the track that led along the valley, towards the sea.

Luke was carrying the Bren gun and Graham, the box of magazines. Tommy, being the best shot, carried the unit's sniper rifle, with its telescopic site. He was there to lay down more accurate fire, to actually hit the fishing boat, so that the Germans really thought that they were under attack. His more important roll was to ensure that only the 'Tramp' got on the boat. Any other Germans, who arrived with him, were to be killed, as they would have already escaped those trying to arrest them.

After they had walked about three hundred yards along the track they came off it and headed out to where the old river flowed nearest to the new channel. It was here that they intended to set up their Bren gun.

149

They were told that there would be members of another unit, on the opposite side of the river, so don't get involved in a fire fight with them.

Their target was the same as theirs, the fishing boat, but they would also be laying down fire at the 'Tramp' as he neared the boat.

Within fifteen minutes they had found the perfect site. They were close to the new river but on the far side of the old river bed. Here they had found some bushes and long growing reeds. Getting them selves settled into this area was good as they could not be seen from on the hill behind them and were well concealed from anyone in front of them. Now they hoped that the fishing boat would moor within their arc of fire.

It was as they were setting things up that Graham noticed that there were tanks, on the other side of the river, facing down towards the estuary. He was about to tell the others when Luke said that there were tanks, on the hill behind them, also facing down into the estuary.

What was going on? They hadn't been told about this. If the soldiers saw them shooting at the Fishing boat, would they open fire on them?

Just then, up behind them, on the road at the top of Exceat Hill, they could hear shooting and saw a couple of men, one appeared to be shooting the second one, and then they heard a second burst of fire, but not from either of the men they could see. In fact one of the two men was seen falling to the ground, before the second burst.

The three of them looked at each other, in astonishment. How big was this operation and how many Auxiliary Units were involved? They had better be very careful, when they left, in case they ran into one of the other units and got into a fire fight with them.

Tommy used his telescope to look at the tanks and see how prepared they appeared to be, for action. For the ones on the opposite side of the river, there did not appear to be any soldiers with the tanks. What he did spot was two farm workers and what appeared to be a Bren gun. They had set theirs' up and, it appeared to Tommy that they were looking down the river, towards the sea.

He swung the telescope to see what they were looking at and saw that the fishing boat had entered the river and was heading in their direction.

"Graham, the fishing boat's coming." Tommy said, pointing down stream at the boat.

"OK, let's get ready. Just remember the boat has to leave with just the 'Tramp' on board. Tommy, you watch out for anyone else trying to get a lift." Graham said.

The fishing boat was slowing down and the captain was manoeuvring the boat so that it was heading back towards the sea. It came to a stop, just opposite where they had hidden up.

They were now ready. All of them had their weapons at the ready and just waited for Graham to give the order to open fire.

Tommy looked along the bank, towards the bridge and noticed the 'Tramp' had suddenly started to run towards the fishing boat.

He appeared to be very frightened, running for his life. As the 'Tramp' got closer to the boat, Graham gave the order.

"Fire"

With that, there was a deafening sound of gun fire. That echoed along the valley.

None of the shots were designed to stop the boat leaving the river or any attempt to kill the 'Tramp'. The intent was that the Germans believed that they were very much the targets.

As they started to shoot, the two men on the opposite side of the river, started to shoot towards the boat.

The shooting lasted only a short while and ended as the fishing boat was about a hundred yards down stream, heading for the sea. It was now that Graham thought about himself and that of his team. If the Canadian soldiers or the tank crews had heard the shooting, they may well think that his team was the enemy and open fire on them. They were not trained to out run a tank's shell.

"Let's go, we've done our bit, now lets get the hell out of here before someone comes to investigate.

They gathered up their weapons and the discarded magazines and started to leave their position. Just as they stood up, a couple of shots came from behind them. Terry was the first to react. He saw the gun smoke coming from up among the Canadians tents. He quickly took aim and fired of a couple of shots. They were not aimed to kill but to make the soldier run for cover. He succeeded in that the soldier did dive for cover and decided that it was not prudent to get up again.

Graham said that they should get out of here before the Canadians got organised. This was not the easiest ground to run over, especially carrying a Bren gun. Terry took up the rear and kept a watch, behind them, to ensure that they were not being followed.

The final bit, to get out of the valley was quite hard as it was up the steep hill and over rough ground.

Still they felt that they were running for their lives and as such the effort was worth it.

When they got up to the road, just down from the top of Exceat Hill, they looked about and could see no evidence of any shooting in the area, there were no bodies, lying in the road, or anything.

What they hadn't seen, while they were firing at the fishing boat, was the Star Brewery van stopping at the top of Exceat Hill, as it picked up the two Germans, that the Eastbourne unit had been responsible for.

Chapter 28
Friston Church

Tom woke Will, at six o'clock as he needed to go down to East Dean and watch The Tiger Inn for when the two Germans came out, on their journey to Exceat. Will decided that he would leave his Thompson, here in the church. Once the Germans were on the move, he would need to travel light, so that he could get back to the church, to raise the alarm that things were happening.

It took Will about fifteen minutes to reach the spot, at East Dean village green, where he intended to stand and watch for the Germans. He had chosen the front garden of Major Swanson, the Eastbourne Golf Club Captain. He had been there before, to work on his garden, so knew the lay out of the area. That is why he had volunteered for this part of the mission.

Nothing happened for more that an hour and then all hell broke loose. Will heard two shots ring out from the direction of The Tiger Inn. One sounded like a pistol and the second was more like a double barrelled shot gun loosing off both barrels at the same time. This was closely followed by the two Germans coming running out of the Inn and heading up the green and, when they reached the road, they turned and headed for the main road.

This brought instant action from Will. He had to get up to the church, before these two arrived there. He knew of a short cut and he would be sheltered from their view. He ran along to the next house and entered the side of the house and headed for the rear garden.

He ran as fast as he could and leaped over the rear fence and landed in a farmer's field. Once there he headed up Hobb's Eares, which would allow him to come up to the church yard, more directly than the route being taken by the Germans.

He was the fittest of the unit and so it was a good job that it was he was making this journey. The others may have made it back to the church but they would not have arrived before the Germans.

At the time that Will had reached his watching point, Tom was leaving the church and walking down the lane, that lead to Crowlink farm. He didn't know which way the 'Tramp' would go, when he left the barn. He might head over the fields, towards Exceat. On the other hand he might head up the lane and join the main coast road and the other two Germans.

This gave Tom a problem. He needed to be able cover either eventuality. He looked around and saw that there was a narrow track, leading into a small wooded area, about two hundred yards from the farm.

Tom walked into the woods and found a spot where he could observe both sides of the barn. If he took the route over the fields, Tom could get back to the church and collect Terry. Between them they could soon catch his trail and follow him, from a distance, until he dropped down Exceat Hill.

Tom hadn't been stood there long when the 'Tramp' came out to the small door of the barn. Now where was he going?

To his amazement, he was headed back up the lane towards him. Tom checked to ensure that the 'Tramp' couldn't see him.

As the 'Tramp' walked passed, Tom held his breath and at the same time, took a hold of his revolver. Just in case he needed it in a hurry. The 'Tramp' walked by, without looking around.

Tom let him go, waited three minutes and then broke cover and followed after the 'Tramp', back up the lane. When he reached the church, there was no sign of him, so Tom went into the church. Terry said that he had just seen the 'Tramp' come up the lane and had then turned onto the main coast road and walked off towards Exceat.

They both gathered up their Thompson's and the magazines, from the pew they had placed them on earlier and told Luke that they were off.

Following the 'Tramp' was not going to be easy, the road was fairly open and in places, if he looked back, he could see for nearly half a mile, along the road.

They also needed to ensure that their Thompsons were not too openly exposed to onlookers. They had, once they left the church, placed a magazine on their Thompson's so they were ready for action.

The Thompson's had to be handled with respect. Luke had seen a man at the Auxiliary Forces training centre drop his, as he was climbing over a wall. The butt hit the ground. The shock moved the breach block back and when the spring forced it forwards again, it picked up a round from the magazine and as it reached the breach it automatically fired off the round. Luckily no one was hurt, but it was a lesson to them all.

As soon as Terry and Tom had the 'Tramp in their sight, as they walked along the road, over South Hill, they decided that they needed to get off the road, to their right. They climbed over the low flint wall that ran along this side of the road.

This area gave them cover but was not as easy to walk on as the road would have been. The important thing was that they were not to be noticed by the 'Tramp' or the soldiers, with the tanks. If the 'Tramp' did look back, he would only be looking back along the road, not over the wall. They ensured that they had regular views of their quarry, as they walked along the tree line.

Like the 'Tramp, they were surprised to see all those tanks, lined up in the field on the opposite side of the coast road. They were sure that they were not there last night. The soldiers were still moving the tanks into their positions and getting the camouflage nets over them. The barrels of the tanks were pointing towards the coast. Was this in preparation for the forthcoming invasion?

It was not too long before they had reached Newbarn Bottom. It was then that they saw the first of several Army convoys, they would see over the next few hours, travelling along the coast road, in both directions. Sam had not told them about this level of troop movements. Because of this and the tank crews, they had walked just a little further into the trees, as they followed their man.

If the soldiers spotted these 'civilians' walking along, carrying Thompson Machine guns, they may well come and investigate, as such they carried theirs on their right hand side, using their bodies to shield the Thompsons from the soldiers.

It had been hard work but they had gradually closed the gap between themselves and the 'Tramp'.

They were now less than one hundred yards behind him, as he reached the crest of the Exceat Hill. There he stopped to take in the view. They did not have the luxury of admiring the view; they had to ensure that he walked on down the hill, without seeing them, behind him.

The 'Tramp' started off, down Exceat Hill, and Tom and Terry moved up towards the road and ensured that they were hidden, behind the bank along their side of the road.

Here they could carefully watch him progress down the hill and turn the corner, towards Exceat Bridge. The first part of their job had been completed, now they had to prepare themselves for the second task.

On another training course, that they had all attended, they had learned how to set up an ambush. The most important thing to remember was, well second to their escape route, was to ensure that you had the element of surprise and that the targets would walk into your killing field, with out suspecting you were there.

For them they needed to find a place where at least one of them could see their targets coming and could signal to the other one, when they entered the killing field.

Another important element was to ensure that they did not end up shooting in a way in which they would end up shooting Luke and Will, who would be following the two Germans.

After five minutes they had found the killing field and also the two places where each of them could hide up, see each other and then attack, without endangering each other.

Tom would be back up on the bank, on the north of the road. This gave him an excellent view of the road, back towards Friston, with the least chance of being noticed. It allowed him to signal Terry, when they arrived.

It also gave Terry time to come onto the road and affect the arrest. In his position, Tom would be able to provide covering fire, if needed. They felt that this was a good plan and a perfect ambush site. Now all they had to do was to wait.

Will and Luke had left the church, in a hurry. With the two Germans due here at any moment, they only had time to gather up their Thompson's, magazines and get the hell out of there.

They knew that they couldn't go along the coast road as they were likely to be seen by the advancing Germans. They ran down the lane, leading to Crowlink Farm and quickly disappeared from the view of any one approaching the church. They needed to work their way back to the coast road, so they could pick up the trail of their targets.

The route that they were taking was longer than that being taken by the Germans, as they had to go down the lane and then circle round a wooded area, which would bring them back around to the road, just before it started to cross South Hill.

Although the route was longer, they were not to know that the two Germans had stopped outside the Church, to rest after their exertion in getting out of East Dean and getting up the steep hill.

Will and Luke arrived near the road and held back. They had a good view along the road, across South Hill and could see no sign of their quarry. It was as they were taking stock of the situation when Will noticed all the tanks, ahead of them.

It had been their intention to walk along this side of the road, as they followed but this changed everything. It would be like walking through a German Tank regiment, guns in hand. They wouldn't last a minute before they would either be arrested or shot.

The two of them felt lucky that the troop were more than likely to be British or Canadians.

Luke said that they should cross the road and walk along the trees, out of sight of both the Germans and the Tank crew. But first they needed to ensure that the Germans were ahead of them, along the coast road.

They could hear some people walking along the road, from the direction of Friston. From the sound of their voices, they were the Germans as they were speaking German, or what the two of them took for the German language. The two of them pulled themselves back into the bushes that they were stood beside. They didn't want to give them a chance of seeing their followers.

Once the Germans had trotted on passed, they allowed them time to get a couple of hundred yards ahead and then they broke cover and sprinted across the road, jumped the flint wall and moved along as quickly as both their fitness and the lay of the land allowed. A major consideration was their weapons. It was not easy to have them banging across their backs, as they ran. Will decided that he would carry his, down by his side, with the barrel pointing to the front and level to the lay of the ground. They were pleased with their progress.

By the time they reached Newbarn Bottom, they had managed to keep within about three hundred yards of the Germans. They saw that the Germans were walking up the last hill before they reached the crest at the top of Exceat Hill.

This gave them the chance to close the gap. They knew that Tom and Terry would have set up the ambush but they wanted to be in on it, after all it was they who had done all the work, following them and sheepherding them into the ambush. But they would be too late.

As the two Germans came into sight, Tom peered over the bank and watched as they moved towards the killing field. Just as he was putting up his arm, to signal to Terry to spring the trap, one of the Germans started to sprint away from the other, as if to race him to the Bridge.

Terry had been ready for the last ten minutes, he was like a coiled spring, just ready to leap out into the road and make the arrests.

Now the moment had come, Tom's arm was raised and so it was now time for him to make his move.

Terry jumped into the road, stood in the middle and raised his Left arm and ordered the two Germans to stop where they were. His Thompson was in his right hand and was pointed directly at the first of the Germans. Terry was initially surprised that this man was actually running towards him.

The same could be said for Karl. He had not expected anyone to actually arrest him. That is why they had moved this early on a Sunday morning, to avoid the local police.

Karl started to reach for his Luger. He had killed once this morning, a second killing would not be out of place. He had just taken a grip of the Luger's stock when Terry guessed, correctly, that Karl was trying to bring out his Luger.

Terry had already cocked his Thomson. All he had to do now was bring his left hand back onto the gun, to steady it. Aim and shoot. He sent a hail of bullets directly at the advancing German. Most of them struck him full in the chest and the force sent him spinning backwards and onto the road.

The second of the Germans was, for the second time this morning, taken totally by surprise. He didn't know what to do. He had never seen the war at close hand. The only shots he had seen fired or for that matter, fired him self, had been on the army ranges, back in Germany. It was then that Erich remembered he had his Barrette Pistol. Now he would prove the Hauptmann wrong. He would show him that he was right to bring this weapon along, on the mission.

Erich reached into his pocked and brought out his prized pistol and raised it towards the man ahead of him, who was shooting his colleague. He had forgotten the percularilities of this particular weapon. His finger slipped and pulled the rear most trigger and before he had raised the barrel towards his target, all the bullets from the magazine had been fired into the road.

He was now stood there with no way of defending himself. The first course of action would be to run for it. But from his left, he heard an English voice address him.

"You are under arrest. Put up you hands and drop you pistol." Tom said.

Erich turned to his right and looked up in the direction he thought the voice came from. There was now a man standing at the top of the bank, with an automatic machine pistol in his hands, aimed directly at him.

It didn't take him a moment to realise that if he didn't do as he was told, he would be killed, just like Karl, so he dropped his Barrette and raised his hands.

Will and Luke came running up, along the road. They were lucky that Tom and Terry recognised the men advancing towards them. With their adrenaline flowing they could have shot anyone at that moment.

Luke was the first one to react at the situation they all found themselves in. They had one dead body and a German with his hands in the air.

His police training came to the fore, he needed to take charge and get the scene cleared up.

They were not in a position to explain why a man had been shot, to any authorities. How four fully armed civilians came to be there and, what appeared to be two other civilians, either dead or arrested. This would be difficult to walk away from.

"Terry and Will, Get the arrested man up over the bank, and his suitcase. Tom, come down here and help me get the dead German up over the bank." Luke ordered.

Within a couple of minutes the dead German was hidden from view of the road and his suitcase was lying beside him. The arrested man was laying, face down and being searched by Will. He then tied his hands behind his back, ready for him to be loaded into the back of the Star Brewery van, when Sam arrived.

The next action that Luke did was to call up Sam, on his radio. It was well after eight o'clock, so Sam should be waiting for one of their teams to call in.

"All sheep accounted for, require tractor to collect sheep." Luke said.

"Tractor's on its way."

Tom moved forward, to the position he had taken earlier, so that he could watch for the Brewery van, coming along. What he did see was a lot of soldiers running around, trying to find out where all the shooting had come from. No one appeared to be in charge and there was no form of an organised search taking place. Hopefully Sam would be here before they got organised?

Five minutes later the Brewery van came into view. Tom called down to Terry to get into the road and signal to Sam, where he was to pull up. They wanted to get the body of the German into the back of the van and the man they arrested, alongside him, as quickly as possible. Then they could get away from here before anyone discovered the evidence of the killing. The one thing they hadn't had time for was to collect up the spent cartridge cases, which were scattered all over the place.

Sam drew up, as directed by Terry. He was told to keep the engine running and go when they told him to. He may have been the leader of this unit but they were more informed about the current situation, so he would do as he was told, he could get his own back at a later time.

He could hear quite a commotion going on, at the back of the van. In his side mirrors he could see the four of them rushing about and he thought he saw a body being carried towards the rear of the van, but could not be sure.

All of a sudden all the activity stopped, he heard the rear door being slammed shut and someone banging on the panel, behind his head and someone shouting for him to drive off, immediately. He did as he was told.

Sam drove carefully down Exceat Hill and he turned onto the road, leading to Littleington. After a short distance he turned right and drove into West Dean and headed for the large barn, by the church.

He pulled up next to the big doors and stopped. He was quickly out of the driver's door and went around and opened the rear door.

"Right get that body out of here and lay it out in the barn, in a dignified manner. Remember, he was fighting for his country, just as we have been, today, for ours." Sam ordered.

"Be quick about it, we need to get back to Eastbourne so Luke can lock this German up, in one of his cells. I've also got to get back for a church service. I'm reading the lesson today." Sam said.

It did not take the three of them long to carry the body of Karl into the barn and lay it on some straw. Luke gathered up his suitcase and placed it at the feet of the German, but not before he had opened the lids and removed the weapons and explosives it was carrying.

"These may come in useful, later." He said, as much to himself as to the others.

Chapter 29
I can't get involved in the actual killing

It was six o'clock in the morning when The Reverent David Cooper arrived at the main door to the Folkington church. He pinned up a notice, which would tell the few members of his congregation that expected Holy Communion at eight o'clock, that he was not available but he would take Holy Communion at the end of the eleven o'clock, Morning Service.

He could hardly tell them that at eight o'clock he would be part of an Auxiliary Forces unit who would be going out to arrest or kill some German spies. It hardly went with his outwardly peaceful facade.

David Cooper was one of only two vicars that became members of any of the Auxiliary Forces units. He was a very peace loving man and had preached that we should not be fighting and killing but on the other hand he did feel that, if it came to it, he would fight to protect his family and those of his congregation. It was for this reason that he had agreed to join the unit, based in his village.

After pinning the notice to the door he headed off to Bishop's Farm, to meet up with the members of his unit. When he arrived, Jack Abraham was already in the farm yard. Jack was getting the farm station wagon ready to take the unit over to Wilmington, to do their duty.

Very soon after David had arrived, Richard Younger joined them. He was carrying a large corn sack, over his shoulder. As he stopped by the car, he lowered the sack to the ground and opened it.

From the sack he took out three Thompson Machine guns and eight magazines. A Thompson and two magazines each for David and Jack and three magazines each for himself and Paul, all filled with the requisite number of rounds.

He handed David one of the radios that they would be taking with them. He kept one for himself and handed the last to Jack. As Paul would be working with Richard, he wouldn't need a radio.

"Jack, you do understand that I can't get involved in the actual killing, don't you?" David said to Jack, in front of Richard.

"Reverent, you made that clear, when you joined our unit. Nothing has changed, as far as I am concerned. Tonight we need the whole team and your task is as important, to the success of the operation, as that of any of the rest of us. With out you we would not be able to do it." Jack said.

"Where's Paul?" Richard asked.

"He left about half an hour ago. He should be outside the Inn, in Wilmington, by now. I gave him the other radio." Jack said.

"OK, let's go, before everyone wakes up or you have to give someone communion." Jack ordered.

The three of them got into the station wagon and Jack started the engine and drove out of the farm yard. He headed away from the houses in the village and off towards the main road between Polegate and Lewes.

At this time of a Sunday Morning there would be few if anyone travelling along this road. He was able to join the road, without stopping, turned left and headed of to Wilmington.

It was just over a mile, from where he joined this road and the junction, where he would have to leave it and drive through Wilmington.

Once they were on this new road and had left Wilmington village, they started up the road, to Littleington. David said that he had just seen Paul. He was behind a fence, opposite the Inn. Jack was pleased that he was there but unhappy that David had seen him so easily. He made a mental note to speak to him about that later.

As they went down the hill, passed Lullington church, Jack slowed down, ready to stop at the bottom of the hill, right by the junction with the road, leading over the Cuckmere River and on to Alfriston. Once he arrived at his first drop off point he stopped and let David out.

"Make sure they can't see you David, and in five minutes, give us a radio check, we'll be stuck if we can't hear you." Jack said.

"Yes, it would be a shame if he falls asleep." David said.

Whereby he quickly jumped out of the station wagon and missed being hit by Richard flailing hand.

With David dropped off, there was only Richard to leave at his assigned place. The spot they had selected, where Richard and Paul were to carry out the ambush. They did not know how many Germans would be coming this way. They knew, with some certainty that the two from Wilmington were bound to use this road, as it was the only logical choice. It was also possible that the German, on the motor bike, would also come this way, again as this road led directly to the Bridge. Where as, going through Alfriston would give him a longer journey and a greater chance of being seen or arrested.

There was a possible fourth man. He would be dressed as a fisherman, so should be quite easy to pick out, again he might go via Alfriston, as he could then walk along the river bank, to Exceat Bridge. Jack just hoped that there was someone in place, if he did that, but then it would not be his concern.

He had to wait for a few minutes, while Richard unloaded a few extras, from the back of the station wagon. They had thought carefully about what they would need, this morning. The motor bike presented different problems than men on foot. It would be going at a faster speed and could well get out of their ambush area, without being hit. Once Richard had closed the rear doors of the station wagon, Jack drove off and parked it in the farm yard of Church Farm, in Littleington, just about one hundred and fifty yards further along the road.

Jack had chosen this place for him self to be when the action took off. Although he had not intended to be part of the arresting party, that honour was assigned to Richard and Paul, He positioned himself so that if, for example the motor bike did get passed the others, he could step out and let fire with his Thompson.

162

Because of the likely number of Germans, that may come their way, they had all fitted silencers to their Thompsons.

In this way they could fire off as many rounds as necessary, without there being too much chance of the next Germans, hearing them.

If the next Germans did hear the shots, they could either run away or, being trained soldiers, could come at them, all guns blazing.

Once they were all in place, David made a short radio call to Richard. "This is Heaven, Radio check." David said

"This is Hell, A OK." Richard said.

Now was the very boring part, just waiting for something to happen. Richard did have something to do, before the action took place. He had to fasten the thin, but strong, wire that he had brought along, to a tree on the opposite side of the road, from where Paul would be hiding. He was careful to make sure that it was not too low or not too high.

It needed to be able to catch the German, on the motor bike, across the chest and drag him off his bike, if he failed to stop, when Richard put up his hand. Richard's job was to stop him and then arrest him. If Hans decided to drive on, then, with the help of the wire and Paul, he wouldn't get very far.

Once he had fastened it to the tree, he unwound the wire across the road, placing a stone on the wire, at the base of the tree it was tied to. After he had crossed the road, he placed another stone on the wire, to hold it in place, until it was needed.

He then climbed up the bank and attached a rope around the first tree he came to. The base of this tree was at the same height as where he had secured the wire, over the road. On the rope was a pulley, for him to thread the wire through. He then found himself the spot that he thought would be where Paul would need to be, to take on the German, once he was off his bike.

Because the spot he had chosen was quite high up, away from the road, it was not too likely that the Germans would be looking up, this high on the bank. They would have the element of surprise.

Happy that he had got everything ready, Richard settled down to wait for the Germans to appear. He was hopeful that Paul could join him before any of the Germans arrived, especially the one on the motor bike, as he would need to be back on the road, by then.

Paul would need both of his hands to pull the wire taunt while Richard was trying to stop the German.

It seemed like a long morning for them all. Paul was the first one to see movement. A light came on in one of the upstairs windows and he saw a man moving about.

He guessed that this was one of the Germans, as it was far too early for the Inn keeper or his family to be up and about, especially after a Saturday night drinking, taking place in his barroom.

Paul decided that he should move so that he was in front of the Germans, once they left the Inn.

As such he walked up the road and entered the church yard. Here he could see the Germans, as they started up the road. He would then be able to make his escape and get to join Richard, before the Germans arrived.

Paul didn't have very long to wait, just fifteen minutes. He had already put the unit on to readiness, with a coded radio message.

The next message would also be coded but would be to tell them that his two Germans were on their way. He could see the two of them, suitcases in hand, walking towards him. Now was the time to send the message.

"This is the poacher, rabbits running." Was all he said. He then switched off the radio, tucked it into his large, inside pocket, and moved off to the rear of the church yard. Paul stepped over the low flint wall and into the field at the back. He then started to run, at a steady pace.

He could not afford to be too noticeable to either the Germans or any locals. He was headed towards Milton Street, but was taking a route that would take him passed the hamlet, between it and the road.

The land had a gentle slope down, away from the road and on this side of the road was a fairly high hedge. That would lessen the likelihood of the Germans spotting him. He continued along this field until he came level with Lullington church.

He passed that by and soon reached the road, again. Now he was not far from joining Richard. As he was about to pass the road junction at the bottom of the hill, he looked into the small chalk pit and, behind one of the gorse bushes he saw David, waiving out to him. Good, he was in the right place.

It was not long before he reached the wire, across the road. He looked up to find where Richard was hiding and with some effort he saw his smiling face. Paul climbed up the bank and joined Richard.

"I think we should move a bit further towards David, for the first two Germans. That wire can easily be seen, from about ten yards away. If they noticed it, they would be off before we could get them." Paul said.

Richard realised that Paul was right so they left the wire, tied to the tree behind them and moved thirty yards, towards their on coming targets. Once they were happy with their positions they waited for David to signal that they were on their way.

Richard had turned the radio's volume down so that all he could hear was a slight murmur, when David called. He didn't want the sound to carry back to the Germans. Sound always carried further at night and early in the morning.

There was a sound coming from his radio. Richard gave Paul's arm a pat and they readied themselves.

"I'll do the first arrest. You can stop the motor bike." Paul whispered

With that said, Paul edged down the bank, onto the road. He kept close to the bank and waited for the two Germans to arrive. In the mean time, Richard had moved a little further towards the oncoming Germans. He did not want to be in a position where Paul came between him and any target.

Very soon they could both see the shape of two men walking along the road, on their side of the road. Both of them could feel the adrenaline starting to flow through them. They both took a deep breath and watched as the Germans approached.

Paul stood up and took three paces into the road, turned and faced the oncoming Germans.

"Halt." He ordered.

At the same time, he raised his Thompson's barrel at the Germans.

Jan and Simon looked at each other, in astonishment. This was not a Policeman or a soldier, who was this man? Why was he carrying an American gun?

While Jan was still thinking what to do, Simon reached for the Luger, in its holster, strapped to his belt. He undid the flap and pulled the Luger out.

Richard was prepared for this and before Jan could get off a shot, at Paul. He aimed a well directed volley of about four shots, at Jan. He dropped to the ground, before Simon had made his decision.

Simon's decision had been made for him, before he left the Inn. He had decided not to carry his Luger, on his person. He quickly raised his hands, in surrender. He saw no point in loosing his life, needlessly.

Paul walked up to him and told him to get down on his knees. Once he had done that, with the aid of Richard, the tied Simons hands, behind his back.

"Let's get this body off the road." Richard said.

Richard took out the radio and called Jack to collect their prisoner and one body.

It was only a couple of minutes before Jack arrived with the station wagon. They lifted Jan's body into the back and told Simon to get in and lay beside his comrade. He did not like doing this but with a Thompson pushed into his back, he decided to obey. After all he could well be lying beside Jan and as dead as Jan.

"Can one of you come with me? I need to lock this one up in one of the sheds, so need some help." Jack asked.

"You go, Paul. I need to reload my gun before the next lot arrive." Richard said.

Paul got into the passenger seat and Jack drove back to Church Farm. He had already found a secure shed, in case they did arrest any of the Germans. When they arrived, Paul told the German to get out and then he marched him along the path, which Jack was already walking down. Once they arrived at the shed, Jack opened the door and they took Simon inside.

Jack realised that this was not the most secure prison so had prepared some chains, by which he could secure the prisoners. Hopefully they would not be held in the shed for too long.

Once they had completed the job here, they would then be able to take them over to Hailsham and have them locked up, securely, in the local Police cells.

Richard climbed back up the bank. And found his stash of magazines. Instead of reloading this magazine, he decided to remove the one on the Thompson and fit a fully loaded one in its place. It was not long before Paul rejoined him.

They then discussed how they were going to address the issue of the motor bike. They had already set up the wire, but the problem was how they were going to stop him, before he reached there. They agreed that it was Richards turn to stand in the road and to flag him down. Paul would act as cover.

Richard turned up the volume of the radio a little, as next time they wanted to hear whatever David said, as it would tell them if it was the fisherman or the motor bike. That done they settled down to wait for the next piece of action.

After about fifteen minutes, Richard thought that he could hear the sound of a motor bike, heading in their direction. He was just about to mention this to Paul, when Paul turned towards him and mouthed 'motor bike'.

With that understanding, they both stood up. Richard gripped the wire and between them they pulled it so that it was taunt. They then secured it around the tree.

David, shortly, called "Speedy arrives."

Richard bent over and picked up his Thompson and slid down the bank, onto the road. He then walked off up the road, ready to hold up his hand to stop the German.

As the German had rounded the last junction, he had opened up the throttle, as the road straightened out. His bike picked up its speed about one hundred yards from where Richard stood.

Richard held up his left hand, in a signal for the German to stop but he was accelerating so fast that by the time he saw Richard he didn't have the control, over the bike that he really should have had. On seeing Richard he tried to pull on the brakes but he pulled on the front break, instead of using his foot to affect the back breaks.

Hans, lost complete control of his bike and the next thing he knew was that he was being tipped out of the saddle and he was flying towards a large tree. He had no way of controlling where he went. He closed his eyes and hoped.

Richard had never seen a man fly through the air, at such a speed. The German's head collided with the tree trunk and there was a sickening sound, as Hans head exploded.

He was not out of trouble. The motor bike was now completely out of control and careering along the road, towards him.

He was lucky that the main body of the bike was not about to take his feet from under him. He just had time to jump in the air, sufficient for the front wheel to pass under his feet.

Paul was up on the bank and could not believe what he had just seen. Richard had been very lucky not to have been hurt in this accident. He raced down the bank, to make sure that Richard was alright.

Once he was satisfied he was OK Paul said that he would go and check that the German was dead and that Richard should call up Jack to come and collect the body. There was little doubt, in either of their minds that he hadn't survived his crash, but he had to check.

While Paul was checking the German, Richard called up Jack, to come and collect the body. After he had done that, Richard climbed up the bank and unwound the wire from around the tree, where Paul had fastened it earlier. He knew that the tension in the wire could cause harm if he was not careful how he released it, so he walked forward until it went slack.

He then dropped it onto the ground. Richard then dropped back down onto the road and headed over the road, to remove the wire tied around the tree. He reached into his left hand jacket pocket and removed a pair of wire cutters, he had brought with him for this very task. He held the wire with his right hand and cut the wire, wrapped around the tree, with the wire cutters, in his left hand.

In the mean time, Paul had reached the body of the German. He was a bloody mess. Jack wouldn't be too happy to have this body in the back of his station wagon.

In the mean time Richard was now coiling up the wire, pulling it towards him and watching as the other end, came back through the pulley and crossed the road.

He bent over and picked up the end and wrapped it around the coil, to secure the whole coil.

While Paul and Richard were carrying out their tasks, Jack brought the station wagon back up the road, this time reversing it towards them.

With the motor bike lying against the side of the bank, he had an easy drive. He stopped, got out and opened the rear doors, to allow Paul and Richard to carry and place the second German body, in his station wagon. They put this body to the right of the other one but that was all the room there was, if they did have to load up a third body, it would have to go on top.

Jack told Paul to take the motor bike into the farm yard and hide it away and told Richard to get back on the bank, in case the final German arrived before Paul got back. On the way back up the bank, Richard removed the rope he had put around the tree, to hold the pulley. With this removed he went back to the place Paul and he had made their base.

He settled down and listened in to the radio, in case David called again. He just hoped that he hadn't missed a message and that the last of the Germans was not already headed his way. Paul wheeled the motor bike into the farm yard and took it over to one of the, apparently, disused sheds, at the end of the yard. He wheeled it in, shut the door behind him.

Jack, in the mean time was parking up the station wagon, so that it could be brought out, for hopefully, the last time, later, without having to manoeuvre it too much.

Paul was about to return, to talk to Jack, when he noticed the farm house kitchen door open and out walked Harry Sampson. This was a big surprise. It seemed early for him to be up and about, on a Sunday morning.

It was obvious, to Paul, that Jack had not seen Harry coming out of the house.

"Good morning, Mr Sampson." Paul called loudly.

This caught Jack by surprise. He turned around and watched Harry advance towards the back of his station wagon. Jack strode out so that he could intercept Harry before he could see into the rear of the station wagon.

"Hi Harry. You're up early this morning." Jack greeted his old friend, as he reached out his hand, to shake his.

"I know you said you wanted to park your car in my yard, this morning, but to keep driving out and back in again, woke Mary. She sent me out to see what was going on." Harry said.

"If Mary's up, I'd love a cup of tea." Jack said, ushering Harry back towards the farm house kitchen door.

"OK Jack, but you had better not be getting me in to some black market racket." Harry said earnestly.

"No nothing like that." He said, truthfully.

As Jack and Harry disappeared into the kitchen, Paul returned to the shed, where he had hidden the bike. He remembered that he had seen a stack of empty corn sacks, there. He walked in and collected four sacks and returned to the station wagon. He opened the rear doors and placed the sacks over the dead Germans, to ensure that if some one did look in, they would just assume that it was something to do with the farm.

Once this was completed, he closed the doors but, before he returned to Richard, he went and checked on their prisoner. Happy that he was secure, he returned to the road, walked up the road and rejoin Richard.

Richard and Paul sat on the bank, with their Thompsons lying across their laps, as they discussed the adventure they had already had this morning. The two of them had been sitting there for about twenty minutes when the radio rattled out a message, for the third and last time.

"Fish swimming up stream." David said.

Richard and Paul got to their feet and decided that they would both be in the road, when this man came along. They slid down the bank and lay against the bank, at the side of the road. They would stand up, as soon as one of them saw the German approaching.

Once they were in place they waited patiently for the fisherman to arrive. He was walking quite quickly and so was upon them sooner than they had expected. Paul saw him first. He touched Richard's arm. They were ready, now. It was judging the right moment to step out. Together they both stood up and stepped into the road and faced Hans.

Hans was surprised to see two men suddenly appear on the road, in front of him. What surprised him most was the fact that these men held Machine guns and they were pointed at him.

These two men shouldn't have such guns. They were farm workers, not soldiers. This thinking had delayed him reaching for his Luger but now he had returned to being a soldier. His right hand reached into his jacket pocked and his figures gripped the butt of his Luger pistol.

"If you bring out that pistol, I'll shoot you." Richard shouted at Hans.

Both the men in front of him raised their guns and were ready to shoot him. He had two choices and only the second left him alive.

"I surrender." Hans shouted.

He released his grip on his Luger and slowly brought his hand back into view. He dropped his suitcase onto the road and raised both hands and waited for the two men to approach.

Paul stepped to one side so that he could cover the German, while Richard approached him. He didn't want Richard to walk between him and the German.

When Richard reached the German he lowered his Thompson and reached into Hans's inside jacket pocket and retrieved the Luger.

"Now put your hands down and put them behind you, please." Richard said.

That achieved, Richard slung the Thompson over his shoulder and went around to the Germans back. He took out a length of rope he had brought along for this purpose and tied the man's hands together.

Just as Paul and Richard were beginning to relax, there was a sound behind them. They both spun around and aimed their Thompsons towards whoever was coming up the road.

"I'm a friend." David said, as he moved forward to greet his colleagues.

David was pleased to see that they had arrested this young German. He had heard firing on the first occasion, but was afraid to ask if they had killed both of those men.

How many young men's lives had been wasted today? He thought to himself.

"We had better get him away from here," David said.

David walked forward and picked up the German's suitcase and walked off towards Church Farm. Leaving the other two too escort Hans. They arrived, back at the farm yard, in time for them to take Hans to the shed, which held their other prisoner. They secured him, with one of the chains and then shut the shed door. Paul stayed outside while Richard and David returned to the station wagon.

Jack came out of the farm house kitchen door. "Thanks for the tea, Mary. Harry, remember you have not seen any one this morning." Jack said as he shook Harry's hand.

"I'm still in bed." Harry said with a smile.

Jack went back with his men. They organised it so that he and David would drive on to West Dean and deposit the two bodies in the barn. In the mean time Paul and Richard would guard their prisoners. Once they had returned. David and Paul would head back to Folkington, over the hills, while Richard and Jack took their prisoners over to Hailsham Police station.

Paul, being a poacher, knew all the short cuts and places to go, so as not to be seen, that would get them back to Folkington in plenty of time for David to change, for the eleven o'clock Sunday morning service.

Chapter 30
Shnell, Shnell

Frank Andrews and Eddie Turner were set up. They had been watching the fishing boat enter the estuary and it was now heading up river. They hoped that it wouldn't go too far upstream, otherwise they would not be able to ensure that only the 'Tramp' got on board. They then heard some shooting, coming from up at the top of Exceat Hill. They hadn't been expecting this.

No one had told them that any other unit would be operating in their area, other than across the river. They would have to keep a watch, to ensure that they didn't become targets, themselves.

Eddie saw the 'Tramp' first. He pointed him out to Frank, who acknowledged he had also seen him. He pulled back the cocking handle and made sure that the first magazine was sitting properly in place and that to hand was a further stack of magazines, all pointing the right way, so that he could pick them up and place them into the slot, after Eddie had removed the empty magazine.

They had practiced this many times and knew that they were a good team. On the ranges, at the training centre, they had won top prize, in a competition, in the use of the Bren gun.

They watched as the fishing boat slowed down and with considerable seamanship, the captain of the boat was turning it around, in mid stream, ready to pick up his passengers and head back out to sea.

Frank estimated where the 'Tramp' would be when he was about to get onto the boat. So he moved the gun around so that he had a good ark of fire that would cover the area he expected that he would be firing into.

He had just set up his Bren when there was shooting coming, towards the running 'Tramp', from the other side of the river. A few shots were from a Bren gun, others from a Thompson and, if he was not mistaken, a single shot from snipers rifle.

It would appear that whoever had planned out this ambush had thought of everything. Frank felt that it was time for him to join in the fire fight. He would target the boat.

He knew that the boat had to be able to sail out of here, so it was no point in making a hole in the keel, so the boat would sink. He aimed at the wheel house, trying to hit the side and base. He then racked the deck, with a full magazine. With skilled practice, a new magazine was in place before anyone could have notice the break in shooting, coming from his Bren.

The German boat's captain was shouting at the 'Tramp'. He appeared to be urging him to hurry up. With every stride, the 'Tramp' was running faster. He didn't want to die, before he could report on the mission. He was sprinting now and as the boat came as close as it could to the river bank, the 'Tramp' swung his bag onto the deck of the boat and then leaped over the gap and landed half over the gunwales and half hanging towards the river.

Simon got himself up the side and eventually got onto the decking. He made no attempt to stand up with shooting coming from both sides.

"Shnell, Shnell," Simon called to Tobias

Tobias didn't need to be told to get out of there quickly. He realised that they were deserting the other members of the team, but their lives were important, to them at least. He opened up the engine and using all his skills he took the boat out into the English Channel.

What now bothered Tobias was that the English were waiting for them, in the open sea. Had they sent a navy vessel after them? There was no time to bother about something that may or may not happen. He had to get the Hauptmann back to France, so that he could report about the English and their preparations for the Germans Invasion.

Once he had gone about half a kilometre, the firing stopped. He didn't think they were out of range as the guns firing at them were machine guns, not pistols. Their range was sufficient to still be shooting at them for at least a kilometre. Still that was of no concern of his, providing they were not shooting at him, he felt safe to ensure that the Hauptmann was safe and had not been hit.

Tobias turned around and saw that Simon was lying on the deck, but did not appear to have been injured.

Simon started to get up and walk towards the wheel house. He was not at all happy. He kept looking back towards the river and the bridge. He was looking, in hope, for some of his men but there were none in sight.

Chapter 31
You're POWs now

Now that Mat Palmer had delivered the first body into the barn in West Dean, his next job was to take his prisoner to his local police station, in Newhaven.

What worried him most was that by the time they arrived in Newhaven, there would be a lot of people about, mostly going to church. He could not see that handing the German over, in front of the locals would be very secure. Word would soon get out.

Mat discussed this with Charles and they decided that if they caught up with Dave or Andy, they would ask one of them to go into Newhaven and arrange with PC Ken Proctor that they would bring their prisoner to his police station at ten thirty.

In that way those going to church would already be there and those waiting to go to the pubs or inns would not yet be about as they wouldn't be open until at least half an hour after the church services had ended. It was also important to get the message to Ken before he attended church.

They were in luck. Dave and Andy were stopped, near the junction that went up to Denton village. Having a smoke and, most likely, waiting for Mat and Charles to return.

"Andy. Can you go into Newhaven and contact Ken Proctor and tell him that we have a prisoner for him. We'll bring him to the police station at ten thirty." Mat asked.

"Why can't Dave do it?" Andy asked.

"Because I need Dave to come with us and guard the German until we can hand him over to Ken." Mat replied.

Andy rode off, towards Newhaven while Mat drove off, towards his farm, with Dave following, on his bike.

Andy was in luck, the bridge was open and so he was able to ride directly to Ken's home. He passed on the message to Ken but his wife, Lilly, wasn't at all happy. Sunday was their day.

No Police work, just a family day and the Sunday morning church service was the centre point of their day. It took Ken some time to placate her but she eventually realised that occasionally, his work had to come first. She didn't have to like it though.

Having delivered his message, Andy rode off home. He could have a cup of tea with his wife, before he would need to go and join the rest of the team, for a debriefing about today's goings on.

At quarter passed ten, Mat, Dave and Charles got back into the van. Being the smallest and fittest, Dave climbed into the back of the van, with their prisoner. They had all left their other weapons hidden at the farm, but retained their service revolvers. After all, their prisoner was a German soldier and his duty was to escape, theirs was to stop him.

The town was virtually empty when they arrived in the high street. Their timing was just right. They drove up to the small police station, which was also Ken's house.

As well as having a small office in the front of the house. In the back garden they had built a small cell block. It looked very much like an outside toilet, except that the door was metal and the small window had a grill, instead of glass. Its intention was that it would only hold the occasional prisoner, over night. They would then be transferred to Lewes's main Police station, where they could hold the prisoners in slightly more comfort.

Once they had drawn up outside, Mat got out and knocked on the door. Ken answered it more or less instantly.

"What can I do for you, Mr Palmer?" Ken asked.

"We have a prisoner for you."

"No, Andy said he had a prisoner." Ken said.

"Andy works for me." Mat said.

"Bring him in."

Mat returned to the van and with the aid of Charles and Dave, they got the prisoner out of the back of his van and into Kens house. Mat dismissed his two men, before Ken could see who was with him.

"What is he being charged with?" Ken asked.

"You keep no record of this man. You just ring Lewes and tell them that you are holding a German spy." Mat said.

"I can't do that. I have to keep records of everyone I put in my cell." Ken protested.

"In that case, give me your keys and I'll put him there. Then your records won't lie." Mat said as he reached out his hand, for the keys.

While Ken was finding the keys to the cell, Mat took out his revolver and waived it in the face of Fritz.

"If you try to escape, I'll use this and then take your body and dump it with your colleagues." Mat warned.

"Here are the keys. I'll take you through to the cell." Ken said, as he handed over the bunch of keys and then walked off, through the house, to the back door.

"Before I lock him in the cell, would you search him? I don't want him to take any weapons into the cell." Mat said to Ken.

Ken carried out a thorough search and as well as finding his English identity, he found his dog tags. He handed them all over to Mat, who looked at them and was surprised to see his German name and army number.

"So you are Fritz Jung." Mat said to his prisoner.

"Yes." Fritz said as he stood to attention.

"Well Fritz, you're a Prisoner of War now."

"Only until the Fuhrer orders the invasion of this country, then I will be free to celebrate his victory over Churchill." Fritz said proudly.

"Well your Generals don't know about us, do they? You didn't get passed us, so what makes you think the rest of your army will?" Mat said.

With that he gave Fritz a push, backwards, into his cell, closed the door and turned the three locks on the door.

"He's all yours Ken. Remember, I wasn't here." Mat said as he handed back the cell keys.

With that done, Mat returned to his van and the three of them went back to the farm, to join up with Andy and get their report ready to send.

Once Ken had ensured that everything was safe and locked up, he opened the small window, in the cell door and told Fritz that he was leaving this open so as to let some light in. If he made any noise, he would close it. He would bring Fritz a meal later and, if he needed it, there was a bucket under the bed.

When he had returned to his office he picked up the telephone and asked the operator to put him through to the Lewes Police station. It was not long before he was listening to the voice of his friend, Bob James.

"Hi Bob. I'm holding a prisoner in my cell. I need him collected." Ken reported.

"He'll have to wait until tomorrow, Ken. We've no one about who can process him today." Bob said.

"Look, he's special." Ken said, quietly.

"Like how?" Bob asked.

"He's a German spy."

There was silence at the other end of the phone. At first Ken thought that he had been cut off but he could still hear the sound of the radio that was playing in the background.

"Bob. Are you still there?" Ken shouted.

"Look Ken. I'm going to have to get back to you about this. Inspector Littlewood needs to know about this before I can arrange for a pick up." Bob said.

In the mean time, Jack Abraham had delivered the two bodies that were lying in the back of his station wagon, to the barn in West Dean. It was then time to collect his two prisoners from the shed in Church Farm. That is of course if Dave and Paul had managed to keep them under proper guard and not allowed them to escape.

He backed his vehicle into the farm yard and as close as he could to the door of the shed, were his prisoners should be.

Dave and Paul were stood in the shadow of the next building. They were trying to keep out of sight of the farm house, in case Harry Sampson or his wife came out. So far they hadn't ventured out into the farm yard.

"Right lets get those two into the back of the car. Ensure that they are still tied up." Jack ordered.

Hans Schmid was the first of the Germans to be brought out, soon followed by Simon Baecker. They were both checked to ensure that they had not been untying their bonds. When it was confirmed that they were still secure, they were ordered into the back of the station wagon and told to lie down, side by side. Richard said that they were to be covered up with corn sacks.

"Please don't cover my face." Hans asked.

"OK, provided that you don't try to escape or make a noise. If you do the sacks go over your face as well." Richard said.

With that said, he covered them both up as far as their chins but with enough spare, that if the need be he could just reach over and cover them up, completely.

"David, you had better get back or you'll be late for the morning service. Paul will take you the quickest route. You may learn something about one of your parishioners." Jack said.

"What time do we meet up?" Paul asked.

"The service should be over by twelve thirty, unless David's sermon is all about 'Though shall not kill'. Lets say one o'clock, then we can be home in time for dinner." Jack suggested.

Before David could retaliate about his sermons, Jack had started moving off, with his prisoners and Richard.

"The Genever Convention says that all prisoners of war have to be treated with dignity." Hans said.

"If you don't shut up, I'll cover the two of you with the sacks." Richard retorted.

It didn't take Jack too long to reach Hailsham. The Police Station was not far from the station, so was easy to find.

Their problem would be to find a place to park, out of site of the entrance. They wanted to get their prisoners into the Police station with the fewest people seeing or being able to identify those taking them in.

Jack turned up, behind the Police station and found the gate that led into its court yard, used to park the few cars and vans the police possessed.

"We'll drop them off here." Jack said. "If we stand them just outside the rear door, you can keep guard of them from the gate, while I go around and tell the Desk Sergeant that he has some prisoners at his rear door."

They both got out of the car and opened up the rear doors. Richard uncovered the Germans and told them to get out. Both Jack and Richard drew their revolvers and made sure that the Germans could see that if they tried to escape, they would be shot.

Once they were safely out of the car. Richard closed the doors and told the Germans to walk towards the rear door of the Police Station. As they approached the door, He told them to stop one yard from the door.

If they got any closer they could well be hit, when it was opened. In the mean time, Jack turned around the car, ready for them to drive away, hopefully without being noticed.

With Richard guarding the prisoners, Jack walked around to the main entrance and walked in. There was just one Policeman on duty today. Well it was a Sunday. The man on duty today was PC Leatherhead.

"Good morning Sir. How can I help you?" Norman asked.

"You will find two German spies in your back yard." Jack said.

"This is no time for silly games." Norman said.

"They are to be secured, in your cells, until you received orders on what to do with them." Jack said and turned to leave.

"I can't do that. Without them being formally charged!" Norman said.

"You have two minutes to get to your back door and take them in. If not, they'll be shot." Jack said and continued to leave the Police Station.

Norman didn't know what to do. Should he phone the Inspector first but if he did, these two Germans could very well be shot and how would he explain that?

Norman decided that he had better go through to the rear door and see if what this man had said was true. If they were there, he could telephone his Inspector, once they were in the cells.

He opened the rear door, into the yard and, there before him were two men, with their hands tied behind their backs. One was dressed as a fisherman and the other as a farm worker. How could they be spies?

He looked passed the Germans and saw a man, stood in the gateway of the yard, holding a revolver. He appeared to be pointing it at the backs of the Germans. For their safety, he decided it would be better if he got them into his cells quickly.

"We're not Germans." Hans protested.

"Well I'll let my Inspector see about that." Norman replied

"We're not spies, either." Simon protested.

"My Inspector will decide that."

Norman told them to turn into the corridor that led to the cells. He instructed them to go to the end and stand by the rear wall. Norman had been alert enough to pick up his truncheon and the cell keys, before he had opened the rear door. There were three empty cells today so Norman would give them one each and to be sure, he would leave an empty cell in between them.

"Right, you whose not German, get into that cell." Norman said.

Hans did as he was instructed.

"And you, who isn't a spy, can get in that cell." Norman told Simon.

He had left the one cell, between them, for any miscreant that may arrive, later today.

Having secured his prisoners he returned to the front desk and picked up the phone and asked to be put through to Inspector Hayman. The Inspector was not at all happy at being disturbed, just before he was going to church. After Norman had explained what had happened, the Inspector said that he would be there in about fifteen minutes.

Sam Carter and his team had delivered the body of Karl Braun to the barn at West Dean and, while he was leaving the village by one route, Mat had been arriving, in his van, along the other road that ran through the village. It was very lucky that the two teams did not run into each other. Someone had not foreseen this eventuality.

At the road, he decided that he would head for Wilmington and then take the main road into Eastbourne. This would be safer, considering what he was carrying in the back of the Brewery's van. The rest of the team, were sat on the van's floor. Each one was holding on to the various weapons they had taken with them.

Terry had been given the job of guarding their prisoner. He put Eric in the corner of the van, with his back against the dividing partition between the van and the driver. He sat in the opposite corner and held his Thompson on his lap, pointing towards his prisoner. This allowed 'Uncle Tom and Will, to be sat close to the rear doors.

The reason Sam had Luke in the passenger seat was that, being a Police Sergeant, he would be able to get them out of there without the van being searched, if they were stopped.

Once they reached the Old Town, Sam pulled up about fifty yards away from the Police Station. None of them wanted to be seen by the duty policeman. Luke took the prisoner in and ensured that he was put in one of their two cells, until they were told what to do with him.

"George, I have a prisoner for you." Luke called out as he escorted Erich Drechsler into the Police Station.

"Where did you find this one, in church?" George asked

"It doesn't matter where I found him. He needs to be locked up."

"What's the charge, Sarg?" George asked.

"He's a German spy, that's what he is." Luke said.

While George was taking the prisoner into the rear of the station to lock him in a cell, Luke picked up the telephone and asked to be put through to the Main Police Station. Once through he asked to speak to Inspector Roberts.

"Sergeant Davies, what do you want?" The Inspector asked.

"Sir, you remember the 'Tramp'?"

"Yes."

"Well, I've arrested one of his men. He's locked up in one of my cells." Luke reported.

There was a short gap before Inspector Roberts replied.

"I'll have to get back to you about that."

"Well I'm not on duty today. Constable Edwards has him under lock and key." Luke said and before the Inspector could answer, Luke put the receiver down.

Before Luke left the station, he went through to the cells to ensure that George had his prisoner secured. Satisfied that he wasn't to record this arrest or who brought him in. Having made sure that George spoke about this to no one, Luke left and returned home, for his Sunday dinner.

"Constable Proctor, how can I help you?" Ken said when he answered his office telephone.

"Constable, Sergeant James reports that you have told him that you have a German spy, locked up in your cell. Is that correct?" Inspector Littlewood asked.

"Yes Sir, I have." Ken replied.

"How do you know he's a German spy?"

"Because the person who brought him in said he was and he has been swearing at me in German." Ken said.

"Who brought this man in?" The Inspector asked.

"I don't know who he was." Ken lied. "But he had a service revolver and seemed very important."

"Right, I'm sending Sergeant James over to you and he'll escort your prisoner back here." Inspector Littlewood said.

"When can I expect him?" Ken asked.

"He left here about a quarter of an hour ago, so he should be with you in about fifteen minutes."

"Thank you Sir. I'll be pleased to have him out of here." Ken said, as much to himself as to the Inspector.

"You've done a good job, Constable." Inspector Littlewood said.

Inspector Hayman walked up the steps towards the main entrance of the Hailsham Police Station and was met at the door by Constable Leatherhead.

"I'm sorry for disturbing your Sunday, Sir." Norman said, as he saluted his Inspector.

"If, what you reported to me is correct, it'll be worth it." Inspector Littlewood replied.

He walked over to the desk and turned around the Incident book, to examine what had been written in it, about the arrests. There was nothing there!

"Why is there nothing here?" The Inspector pointed to the Incident Book.

"I was given the impression, by the man who dropped them off, that there was to be no records of their arrest." Norman explained.

"We'll see about that." Inspector Littlewood said.

"I need to see the prisoners."

Norman led the way to the cells and told him that he had one in the first cell and the second prisoner in the far end cell. The Inspector went to the first cell door and opened the viewing hatch and looked in. There on the far side of the cell was a man dressed as a farm worker, sat on the mattress. He shut the hatch and walked on to the last cell. In this one he saw a fisherman standing with his back to the door, looking out of the small window, at the rear of the cell.

"I'll interview this man." He ordered.

179

Ken had the keys with him so he unlocked the cell door and called the man out of the cell and ordered him to follow the Inspector. When they reached the interview room, Inspector Littlewood opened the door and walked inside the spacious room. He headed for a chair behind the only desk in the room.

"Come in. Before we get around to talking, I need you to take off all your clothes."

"That is against the Genever Convention." Hans said.

"The Genever Convention only applies to Prisoners of War. Are you a Prisoner of War?" He asked.

"I don't know. The men who brought me here were only farm workers."

Inspector Littlewood looked at Constable Leatherhead to get some confirmation of what he had just been told.

"They looked that way to me, Sir." Norman reported.

"Your name, please?" The inspector asked.

"David Smithers."

"No, your real name"

"Unterfeldwebel Hans Schmid." He said, as he stood to attention.

"So your Sergeant Schmid, then" Norman asked.

Hans looked around at the Constable. He was surprised that such a man would have understood his rank."

"What was your mission, Sergeant?" Inspector Littlewood asked.

"You are only entitled to know my name and service number. I will tell you nothing else."

"Right, Constable, take this man back to his cell and bring the other one here."

Norman escorted Hans out of the interview room and back to his cell. Once he was secure, he went along the corridor and unlocked the cell door and told Simon to come with him.

As Simon was passing Hans's cell, Hans called out to him.

"Tell them nothing about our mission." He said in German. He had forgotten that Norman understood German.

It did not take him long to get Simon to the interview room.

"My arrest is against the Genever Convention." Simon said.

"So you're another German soldier, just like your friend." The Inspector observed.

"I'm English, just like you."

"Constable, search this man and let's see what identification he has with him, which will prove what he says."

Norman started his search, in his trouser pockets but found nothing there. He then transferred to the jacket pockets. His first find was a ration card. He passed that to the Inspector. He then continued to search the other pocket but there was nothing there. Lastly, he felt for the pocket inside his jacket and this time he found a driving licence. As he was bring this out, the back of his hand brushed against something hard, under his shirt.

"Sir, there's something under his shirt. Can I open his shirt and see what it is?" Norman asked.

Seeing the man's face suddenly going red, the Inspector agreed.

Norman unbuttoned the shirt, from the second button, as the top one was already open. By the time he had reached the forth button, what he was looking for, came into view. It was a necklace, with a difference. Norman took it off, over his head and placed it on the desk, in front of the Inspector.

"Well, what have we here?" The Inspector said as he picked up the necklace.

"If I'm not wrong these are a set of military ID Discs." He said as he looked up, into Simons face.

Simon did not know what to say.

"Simon Baecker. But your Ration card says you are Simon Baker. Which one am I to believe?"

"Simon Baker, Sir."

"You do realise that as a spy, you will be shot but if you're a soldier, you would come under the Genever Convention?" Inspector Littlewood pointed out.

Their training had not been long enough to tell them how to act or what to say, if they got arrested.

Simon was in a pickle. The one thing he remembered was that as a soldier he could not be shot as a spy.

"I am Obergefreiter Simon Baecker." He finally answered.

"In that case, what was your mission, here?"

"I can't tell you that. Under the Genever Convention you can not make me tell you." Simon said as he stood tall.

"In that case, take this soldier back to his cell, Constable."

Norman took Simon back to his cell and locked him up. Once he had checked on Hans, Norman returned to the front desk, to await his Inspectors order.

Chapter 32
There are bodies to identify

Sir Thomas Murray, Chief Constable of East Sussex and his wife Mrs Diane Murray were just leaving their house in Ringmer, when a Police car came roaring into the village, headed around the village green and screeched to a stop, just by the Chief Constable.

Inspector Keith Mannering stepped out of the police car. Saluted the Chief Constable and asked to have an urgent word with him.

"I'm sorry Inspector but my wife and I are going to church. It will have to wait until after the service." Sir Thomas replied.

"I'm sorry Sir but this is very important. There's to be a telephone call for you, from the Home Secretary, at eleven fifteen, at your office in Headquarters." Inspector Mannering said.

Sir Thomas realised that he would have to miss church today. He had only spoken to the Homes Secretary, just the once. He knew the man to be very single minded and did not take to the Chief Constables working against his policies or demands. He was not a man to cross,

"I'm sorry my dear but I have to go. I'll be back for dinner." Sir Thomas turned and said to his wife.

"I'm sorry Madam but it's unlikely that Sir Thomas will be back before nightfall." Inspector Mannering cut in.

"What do you mean, Mannering?" Sir Thomas snapped.

"I can't say out here, Sir. While we are on our way to Lewes, I'll brief you of what has been happening." Inspector Mannering said, as he escorted the Chief Constable to the Police car.

Once they were in the police car, Sir Thomas sitting behind the driver and Inspector Mannering, in the front passenger seat. The driver was told to get them back to HQ as quickly as he could. He switched on the bell and drove off as quickly as was safe to do so, considering all the people walking towards the church, for morning service.

"Well Mannering, tell me what all this is about."

"This is not firm information, but, on the grapevine I have been hearing that some Germans landed near here on Friday. It appears that they have been followed and, this morning some of them were killed and some arrested and handed into various Police stations." Inspector Mannering informed the Chief Constable.

"Why weren't we told about this?" Sir Thomas asked.

"I don't know. It appears that it has something to do with the Army, is what I'm hearing."

"Right, as soon as we get back to the Headquarters, I need you to contact Brigadier Palmer and find out what his men have been up to. They or the Canadians can't go around killing people, willy-nilly. Not in my County, they can't".

183

The driver was first rate, by the time the two officers had finished their conversation, he was swinging into the main entrance of the Sussex Police Headquarters and drew up at the main door.

Inspector Mannering thanked him and told him he was on stand by to take the Chief Constable out, at a moments notice. With that, he got out of the car and followed the Chief Constable into the Headquarters.

Sir Thomas, headed for his office but before they parted told the Inspector that as soon as he had the information, from the Army, he was to come, directly to his office and report.

Keith ran off to his office and even before he had sat down, picked up the telephone and told the operator that they were to get Brigadier Kenneth Palmer on the phone, immediately.

By the time he had taken his seat the telephone rang and he picked it up.

"They said that he's not there any more. Colonel Downing, his replacement's also not around." The operator told him.

"Then get me the Duty Field Officer. Don't take no for an answer. Tell them that the Chief Constable needs to talk to them immediately." Keith said and put the telephone down.

While he waited for the operator to connect him, he got out a note pad and pencil. He needed to write out a few questions to ask the officer and space to write his replies. The telephone rang again, after about five minutes.

"Lieutenant Colonel Harris, can I help you Sir." Came a very upper class voice.

"Colonel, this is Inspector Keith Mannering, from the Sussex Police Headquarters. Sir Thomas Murray has asked me to contact you about a very urgent problem that has come to our notice." Keith said, introducing himself.

"I thought it was Sir Thomas that I was asked to talk to?, not you, Inspector."

"I'm afraid he's talking to the Home Secretary, at the moment, about this same problem. He needs to be able to brief the Home Secretary on the Army's involvement." Keith said.

"What's this problem then, Inspector?"

"We have just been hearing that a bunch of German's landed in this area, on Friday. It is also coming to our attention that some of them have been killed." Keith informed Colonel Harris.

"The reason that I took so long getting back to you is that there were reports, coming in to us, that there had been some shooting, going on, around Exceat." Colonel Harris replied

"Were any of your soldiers involved or did they see anything?" Keith asked.

"Two of them reported seeing two men, with machine guns, trying to stop a man riding a bicycle, towards Exceat Bridge. By the time they had managed to get their truck to stop and, with their Sergeant, walk back to where all this had been going on, there was nothing to be seen." Colonel Harris reported.

Keith was about to ask some more questions when the Colonel said for him to hold on for a moment. Keith was getting very impatient. He needed to get this report up to Sir Thomas, as quickly as he could.

"Harris here, I've just had a visit from the Canadian Duty Officer. He said that some of his men have reported seeing men firing at a fishing boat, at the mouth of the River Cuckmere. When one of his sentries fired on one of the groups of men, shots were returned. He then saw the men running off. They also heard shooting coming from the top of Exceat hill."

"So they weren't your men then?" Keith asked.

"No. What is going on?"

"We don't know, but with the Home Office involved, it must be very important. When I find out, I'll tell you what I can. Thanks for your help." Keith said and put the telephone down.

He quickly made notes of what Colonel Harris had just told him.

Keith wanted to know how many of these Germans had been arrested and where they were being held. He ran down to the reception desk and asked the duty Sergeant to ring around all the local Police stations and find out if any Germans have been handed in to them. He told him to find him, as soon as he had this information. He would most likely be in the Chief Constable's office.

This done he returned to his office, picked up his papers and then ran up two flights of stairs and continued running until he was outside the Chief Constables office. As the Chief Constable had told him to bring the information directly to him as quickly as possible, Keith did not bother to knock and wait to be told to enter, he just entered the office.

The Chief Constable was on the telephone. He looked up and beckoned for Keith to sit down, on the chair, opposite him.

"Yes Sir.....But why weren't we told? ....Oh.....We should have been told. ..... The Police can keep secrets you know. ..... You want me to do what? .... Where? .... Alright I'll call back when I return to my office." With that he put down the telephone.

"Those bloody politicians. Someone had been countenancing some skulduggery in our area and we have to clear it up, without anyone knowing." Sir Thomas said, as much to himself as to Keith.

"What do we have to do, Sir?" Keith asked.

"Well, it appears that there are about five bodies, laying in a barn, in West Dean. I am informed that they were from a troop of German soldiers, sent over here to cause trouble, when the German's invade. It would appear that someone has taken it on themselves to arrest those they could and eliminate those they were unable to arrest. We have to clear up their mess."

"I know where that barn is. I'll take some men and secure it." Keith said as he stood up, to leave.

"No, I have to do this and no one is to know, just you and me."

"But we can't leave them there." Keith protested.

"You're right but we have to, for now. Get a couple of men to come over there, about half an hour behind us. They will guard the barn, until we know more, but they must not look in the barn, under any circumstances." Sir Thomas ordered.

Just then, there was a knock on the door.

"That'll be Sergeant Upton. I asked him to check all the Police stations to see how many Germans had been handed in."

With that said Keith walked over to the door and opened it and invited Sergeant Upton into the hallowed grounds of the Chief Constable's office.

"What have you been able to find out?" Keith asked the Sergeant.

"Well Sir. Two Germans were handed in at Hailsham. Another one was handed in at Eastbourne Old Town and a further one more was delivered to Newhaven." He reported.

"Sergeant, get hold of the Duty Inspectors responsible for those Police stations and make them understand that these prisoners are to be kept very secure and are to have no visitors, without my permission. Do you understand?" Sir Thomas said, sternly

"Yes Sir." Sergeant Upton said, saluted and left the office.

"I'll get the car and detail off the men to follow." Keith said and walked back out of the office.

Once in the corridor he sprinted to the stairs and ran down them until he reached the reception area.

"Sergeant; I need you and two men to report to Sir Thomas, at the large barn, in West Dean, just by the church, at." He looked at his watch, "Eleven thirty."

"But Inspector..." Sergeant Upton started to protest.

"Sergeant; this is an Order, not a request." Keith said sternly.

"Get someone else to phone these Police Stations. I need you out there." Keith ordered.

With that he left the reception and walked down the outside steps and beckoned the driver to bring the car over to him. There he would wait for the Chief Constable to arrive.

He only had a few minutes to wait, when Sir Thomas started down the steps and got into the car. Keith got in the passengers seat again and instructed the driver where he wanted to go.

"I don't know where that is, Sir." He said.

"Just head for Polegate and I'll tell you where to turn off that road." Keith replied.

"Right what did you find out from the Brigadier?" Sir Thomas asked.

"The Brigadier's has been replaced by Colonel Downing, Sir. I couldn't get hold of him but I did get hold of the Duty Field Officer, Lieutenant Colonel Harris. He told me that he had just received a report from the Canadian's that some people, with machine guns, had opened fire at the top of Exceat Hill. By the time they investigated, there was no one there.

He also reported that they had spotted a group of men firing on a fishing boat, in the River Cuckmere and that when their man fired at them, these people returned fire." Keith reported.

Sir Thomas sat back and was in deep thought. He still had not said anything when Keith told the driver to take the next right turning. This would take them towards Alfriston.

After a short while he told him to turn left, and head over the river.

He said that at the end of this road, he was to take another right turn and follow the road towards Exceat.

Still Sir Thomas had said nothing, this concerned Keith as, normally he would engage in a conversation, on a long journey. Either about the reason for the trip or he would ask about any gossip going around. Today he looked very worried.

Sir Thomas was worried. How was it, that he and none of his senior officers knew what had been going on, in his area, this weekend.

He hadn't had time to read all the Friday reports, Saturday morning, had he missed something? He realised that it was a weekend but still someone should have known. It was then that he remembered on Saturday morning, he saw a short report from Eastbourne, about them looking for some tramp.

But surely that had nothing to do with what had happened this morning. He was brought back to reality, when the Police car drew to a stop, outside a very large Sussex barn. He presumed that they were in West Dean. Inspector Mannering was too good an officer to have brought them to the wrong place.

Inspector Mannering got out of the car and opened the door, so that the Chief Constable could get out. Then he followed him over to the barn's large doors. The driver had got out of the car and was starting to follow his superiors, when Sir Thomas told him to stay in the car.

With the two of them pulling, the right hand door opened and they were able to step inside and look around. Although they had been told what to expect, they were still shocked at what was laid out behind the left hand door. Starting from about three feet inside that door was the first of the bodies and then they counted four other bodies, placed side by side.

What surprised them was the amount of blood.

"You had better get out your note book and take down what I tell you, Inspector." Sir Thomas said.

Keith took out his police note book and pencil and made a note of the date, time and place they were in.

He then waited for Sir Thomas to dictate what he required him to write down. In the mean time, Sir Thomas had started to examine the first body.

"First body: Male about thirty, six foot, dressed like a travelling salesman, shot once between the eyes. The suitcase contains a change of clothes, explosives, a Luger and two magazines."

Sir Thomas checked out his clothes and found a Driving Licence in the name of Steven Cook, 33 Cox's Drive, Tunbridge Wells.

"Second body: Male, about twenty five, about five foot seven, dressed like a farm worker, appears to have been stabbed.   Suitcase contains a change of clothes, three magazines and a Luger pistol."

Sir Thomas then foraged through the pockets of his clothes and found a Ration Card in the name of Richard Harrison, 2 Slade Cottages, Ripe. He passed that over to Keith and then moved on to the next body.

"Third body: He appears to have had his head caved in.   He is dressed as a Farm worker. In his suitcase is a Luger pistol and four various magazines.   Two were for the Luger and two for a different weapon." Having searched his pockets he found a Driving Licence for Henry Long, 5 Tudor Road, Dover.

"Whoever it was, diffidently wanted them dead." Keith observed.

"They knew what they were doing, that's for sure." Sir Thomas replied.

"The Fourth Body: He has been shot many times in the chest and arms. In his case he had a Schmeisser and four magazines, three for that gun and one appears to be for a Luger." He felt around his pockets and found the Luger, but no English identity documents.

As he was about to move on, something caught his eye. He didn't know what it was or its significance, at that moment, but he did as soon as he reached under the man's shirt and pulled the thing towards him. It was a military ID Disc. He took a close look at this and discovered it had a name, stamped on it, together with a set of numbers. The name did bring Sir Thomas to realise that these bodies were, in fact, all German soldiers. This one was Karl Braun.

"They're Germans."   Sir Thomas said as he stood up and turned towards Keith. "Look I have a German ID Disc." He said as he handed it over to Keith, to record.

"We'd better go back and check the others." Keith said.

"You do that while I move on to the last one." Sir Thomas ordered.

"The Fifth Body: Male, about twenty, five feet seven inches tall, again dressed as a farm worker. This one has been shot from the side, lucky he wasn't cut in half, the number of wounds he's got. His name is Jan Martin and Ration card for John Martin.

Having taken down the details on the last one, Keith returned to the first body and felt around his neck and pulled at the string to see what it would revile. Out popped an ID Disc.   He turned it around to see who this one referred to. The name shown was Steffen Koch. He moved to the second, his disc showed Richard Hartmann.

The next was Hans Lange. The third body was harder to find but he eventually discovered it, tucked into his shirt pocket, this one was for a Karl Braun.

"Well sir, what do we do with all this information?" Keith asked the Chief Constable.

"We get it back to HQ and send the information back to the Home Office, that's what we do." Sir Thomas replied.

With that, the two of them walked out of the barn and Keith closed the large barn door and fastened the two doors shut.

Just as he was about to join the Chief Constable, The Sergeant and his two constables arrived, in a second Police car.

The Sergeant got out, saluted the Chief Constable as he was getting into his car. He then moved over to ask Inspector Mannering, what their duties were to be.

"Sir, I have the two men you asked for. What do you want them to do?" The Sergeant asked.

"Sergeant, the three of you are to guard this barn. No one is to go in, under any circumstances. If anyone tries, you are to arrest them. Do you understand?" Keith asked.

"What are we guarding?" he asked.

"That is not your business. You are to ensure that none of your men peer into the barn. If I hear any talk about what is in there, around the Headquarters, I'll have you busted down to Constable and send you to Rye. Do I make my self very clear?" Keith said.

"You can be assured that no one will get near the barn, Sir." The Sergeant assured him.

"Good. I'll be back out here later today. Hopefully we won't have to be looking after this barn for too long." Keith said.

The Sergeant saluted the Inspector as he turned to walk back to the Chief Constable's car. He then returned to his car to brief his men. He knew that they would not like not knowing what was in the barn but he would need to make them understand what would happen to them if they not only looked into the barn, but then told colleagues about it. They understood and promised not to look. They then settled in for a long, boring afternoon.

In the mean time, the Chief Constable's car departed from West Dean and headed back to Lewes and the Police Headquarters. Neither the Chief Constable nor Keith spoke about what they had found in the barn. They didn't want the driver to be privy to that information.

Once the car drew up, outside the Headquarters, Keith told the driver that he was to remain on standby. He then followed the Chief Constable back into the building and up to his office.

"Right, Inspector, I will be ringing the Home Office, once I get to my office, you go and get those details typed up and bring them to me ASAP." Sir Thomas ordered.

Keith returned to his office, and put a sheet of paper into his typewriter. He also decided to make a copy of what he was writing so took the sheet out and picked out a second sheet of paper and a sheet of carbon paper. The Chief Inspector hadn't told him to make a copy, but he knew that one may be needed.

When Keith had finished typing up his report he separated the papers and put the second copy into his right hand draw. He got up and walked back up to the Chief Constable's office, Sir Thomas had managed to get through to the Home Office.

"... Yes five bodies and four handed in to three of my Police stations... All of them had German names but English Ration cards with English names and addresses. .... I have placed a guard on the barn. .... When? .... I haven't got the men for that long. ..... What about the prisoners? ... I can get them all to Eastbourne Main Police Station by Ten o'clock. .... You need them there today... Alright, by five o'clock. I will inform the Chief Inspector to expect someone to collect them... And the bodies... Tomorrow lunch time, no later... Good bye Sir." Sir Thomas said as he put the telephone receiver down with some force.

"Give me that list." Sir Thomas said, reaching out his hand.

"And your Note Book." He said.

"But Sir, I have other notes in this book. I need the notes for some other cases I'm dealing with at the moment." Keith protested.

"Well you'll have to remember what you wrote. All these are being collected by a despatch rider, in half an hour, and taken up to London. I doubt if you'll get your Note Book back, what you have written in that book has been classified as Top Secret, so the whole book is deemed as Top Secret and you don't have clearance for that level of security." Sir Thomas explained.

What Sir Thomas did not realise was that as part of Keith's remit, he did have clearance for Top Secret documents. He was the county's liaison with the Secret Services and many Top Secret documents passed over his desk, each week.

Chapter 33
All at sea

Simon Krause was just getting himself together as the Fishing Boat exited the River Cuckmere and entered the English Channel. Simon was not a good sailor and was not looking forward to the next few hours, bobbing about on the waves, with the boat also rolling from side to side.

The first thing he needed to do was to use the boat's radio and contact his headquarters. He was not going to bother about coding his message, he would keep it short and to the point, but he would not give out any locations, as that would tell the enemy not only where he had been, but the likelihood of his current location.

Once he was in the wheel house, with Tobias, Simon switched on the radio and tuned it in to the required frequency. Being a German radio he had no trouble getting through, he just hoped that it had the desired range, to be picked up back in France.

"This is Tramp." He called.

"Location?" They requested.

"Away." He replied.

"All present?"

"No. All others presumed dead." Simon said, using an educated guess.

There was silence for several minutes, before the radio crackled back to life again.

"Explain?"

"Ambushed, each one, they are ready for us."

Simon meant to say 'they were ready for them' but it was taken that the English were ready for the German Invasion.

Again there was silence and shortly he was told to report to Area Headquarters, as soon as he returned. This worried Simon. Up until now all his reports were directed to the small camp, where their training took place, where Obersleutant Weissmuller was stationed.

He had heard that when the last group were captured, all the officers, in charge of that operation, were all court marshalled and shot. Was he in line for the same fate?

For the rest of the journey, Simon said nothing more to Tobias. His mind was filled with the possibilities of what was going to happen to him, when he reported to Generalmajor Emmerich Eberhardt, at the Area Headquarters.

If he is the only one present, when he gives his report, then he should be alright but if there are other Generals present, that will be a different matter. Simon left the wheelhouse and went and sat on the deck then lent his back against the wheelhouse.

Simon had not realised that he had, in fact, fallen asleep. At about two o'clock Sunday afternoon he was suddenly brought back to reality, when Tobias bent over and shook his shoulder, to wake him up.

"Are we there yet?" Simon asked.

"Yes, we are just coming into Calais harbour." Tobias replied.

"Tobias, when we get along side, I will jump onto the quay. You turn the boat around and get the hell away from me." Simon told him.

"Why?" Tobias asked.

"The mission failed.   Anyone connected with it will be Court Marshalled, then shot." Simon said sternly.

"You're joking!"

"No I'm not. Just get away from me, get back to your unit and keep your head down. Never mention this mission to anyone, deny ever seeing me or my men. Do you understand?" Simon said.

"Alright, if you think I'm in danger, I'll do as you suggest." Tobias said, reluctantly.

It took them fifteen minutes to arrive at the quayside, where a staff car was waiting to take Simon to his meeting. Also on the quay were three, heavily armed, SS soldiers. It was then that Tobias realised what Simon had said earlier, was correct. He had to get away as soon as he had landed his passenger.

"Look after yourself Simon." Tobias shouted, as Simon jumped from his boat, onto the quay.

"And you." Simon shouted, as he fell into two of the SS soldiers, his aim was to ensure that they didn't engage Tobias.

The third SS soldier stepped to one side and made to apprehend Tobias by jumping onto his boat and arrest him. The only problem was that Tobias was already swinging the wheel around and revving his engine to get the boat back into the main stream, as quickly as he could. The soldier jumped, at a spot he had decided would bring him onto the boat's deck, it was not there. In fact there was nothing underneath him but water.

There was a loud scream as he hit the water, which brought the attention of his colleagues, to his plight.

The first SS Solider raised his machine gun to fire on the fishing boat but Simon hit him in the stomach and he lost his aim and fired high into the air. By the time he had remonstrated with Simon, Tobias was well out of range. Now it was time for him to get out of the harbour, up the coast and back to his home port of Bremerhaven.

Simon may outrank the two SS soldiers but they grabbed him and bundled him into the waiting staff car. They then walked behind the car and got on to their motor bikes. It was their duty to escort the car to Area Headquarters.

Simon looked around and found that there was another passenger, in the back of the car. It was Obersleutant Klaus Weissmuller, and in the passenger seat, sat an SS Officer. Klaus signalled for Simon to say nothing, he was to leave his talking until they were in front of Generalmajor Emmerich Eberhardt.

192

Chapter 34
Stand down

After a very long morning, all the Auxiliary units returned home, from their various assignments. None of them had been seen. Or at lease, close enough to be identified. They had all cleared up any evidence that could tie them to any of the killings of the German spies.

Police investigations were not as thorough as they are today and as such, what little they left behind was very unlikely to be found by the police. If, by chance, it was spotted, it could be taken as things left around after a Home Guard practice exercise.

They weren't to know that the police would be instructed not to carry out any investigations as to whom and how, the bodies in the barn were killed. The Police were also told that no records, of the prisoners, were to be kept.

By ten thirty that morning, all of the Unit leaders had sent in messages, to the 'Pheasant', informing them that they had carried out their missions and detailing which of the Germans they had killed and which had been arrested. All confirmed that the bodies had been deposited in the barn at West Dean and the prisoners delivered to the appropriate Police Station.

That night, each of the Unit leaders gathered their members together in the local public house and toasted the success of their mission. They also had a silent toast to the dead Germans, as fellow soldiers.

On the Monday morning, 16th September 1940, each of the units received a message telling them that they could stand down.

Chapter 35
You Failed the Fuhrer

Obersleutant Weissmuller and Hauptmann Krause sat in silence throughout the journey from Calais harbour until they reached the Area Headquarters.

This was, in part, because the driver of the staff car and his front seat passenger were members of the SS and secondly they were busy trying to find the right words to ensure that they wouldn't be Court Marshalled.

After two hours of, frankly, dangerous driving, they arrived at the main gate to the Headquarters. The driver just flashed his headlights and the two motor cycle outriders drew up alongside the car as it drove up the driveway to the Château, which had been taken over by the German Army for their purposes.

Once the car had reached the steps, leading up to the main entrance of the château, it stopped and the two SS Outriders opened the rear doors and told the two officers to follow them. Klaus and Simon got out of the car and followed the first of the SS soldiers up the steps, while being followed by the second SS soldier. It would appear that they were under arrest.

When they reached the reception area, there was Viktor Junker waiting to greet them. That was not actually true. He was as much under arrest as the two of them. His duty was to lead them into the main office, where Generalfeldmarschall Eberuardt and Generalmajor Eberhardt (his cousin) were seated behind the large and imposing table on the far side of the room.

The three officers marched up to about three metres from the desk, halted and saluted the Generalfeldmarschall. They then stood there and waited until one of the officers, in front of them spoke.

Emmerich Eberhardt was the first to speak, after looking from one to the other of the officers in front of him.

"Hauptmann. Give us your report as to how you failed in your mission." He asked.

This took Simon by surprise. He had expected that Obersleutant Junker would give his report first.

"Sir, it appeared that the British had been tipped off about us. We did nothing wrong. Our English was perfect and we appeared to have been accepted as what we were saying we were." Simon reported.

"Are you saying that there are spies here? This Headquarters is the only place, other than Obersleutant Junker's training unit, that knew about the mission."

"With due respect Generalmajor but SS General Wannemaker was present when Obersleutant Junker outlined his plan at the meeting in Berlin. He was not at all pleased that he had been shown to have caused the failure of the previous mission." Emmerich Huber put in.

195

He was trying to divert the blame from his Officers. If they got any of the blame, then it could very easily spill over to him and he would receiver the same punishment as them.

"I'll not have you ducking your responsibility for the failure of this important mission. Because of this, it is likely that Operation Sealion will be cancelled and that will not be good for any of us. The Fuhrer will be very angry with all of us." Lars Eberuardt said sternly.

"Well someone must have told them. We were all spread out, over a large area and each of my men, on Saturday, told me that they had either overheard men taking about their arrest or been spoken to and told that German spies were to be arrested on Sunday morning. How else could anyone have known, other than being told?" Simon asked.

"It is obvious to us that you have been very careless and that because of this, you put your men in danger. Their lives were your responsibility and as such you will pay the price of failure." Lars Eberuardt said to Simon.

"Guard" Emmerich called

The two SS soldiers entered the room.

"Take this Officer to the garden." He ordered the Guards.

Before Simon knew what was happening, he was being frogmarched out of the office and, via another room, out into the garden.

At first he didn't realise what was happening but as he was marched further into the garden and into the walled garden, then he realised his fate.

To the left side of the walled garden was a post that had been driven into the ground, about two metres from the wall. Behind this post was evidence that shots had been fired at whoever had been stood in front of the post. He was now going to join his dead comrades. Maybe then, he would find out what really happened to their mission.

By this time he had been taken over to the post and his hands had been tied behind the post and he was facing across the walled garden. In front of him were stood, five SS soldiers and an SS Officer. Simon was given no time to gather his thoughts before the Officer told the soldiers to take aim and fire. His death was as quick and unreal as was the deaths of some of his team, in England.

Back in the large office, the other two officers heard the volley of shots and knew what had become of Simon. If they were not careful, they would be the next to suffer the same fate.

"Obersleutant Junker. This was your plan. Explain how it failed." Emmerich ordered.

Viktor needed to think quickly, one of the Officers, who entered the room with him had already faced the firing squad. He didn't want to be the next. He would put the blame firmly on to Simon. After all he was already dead and could not answer back.

"I had been very specific on how Hauptmann Krause and his men were to act and how careful they were to be. Major Wolf was in charge of their training and I had instructed him to ensure that they only spoke good English. He reported that they did. It would appear that he gave me a false report. If I had known that they were not up to the task I would have cancelled the mission." Viktor reported.

"Obersleutant Junker. This was your plan. It was your job to ensure that it worked. You assured us that you had chosen the right men. Had you not done so, we wouldn't have agreed to the plan."

"Guards" Emmerich called.

The two SS soldiers re-entered the room.

"Take this Officer to the garden." He ordered.

Chapter 36
Where can we dig the Graves?

One Monday 16th September 1940, Sir Thomas Murray rang the Home Office and asked to speak to the Home Secretary. He was told that he was not available as he was in a meeting and could not be contacted today, try again tomorrow.

Sir Thomas knew that what he was about to say may well get him into a lot of trouble but the problem had to be sorted today.

"Tell the Home Secretary that if I don't hear from him by lunch time, I will be ringing The Times and be telling them about my five dead Germans."

"I'll give him your message Sir Thomas." The lady at the other end of the line said.

At eleven thirty, his telephone rang and his assistant said that the Home Secretary wanted to talk to him. He told him to put him through.

"I'll not stand for blackmail, Sir Thomas."

"I have five dead Germans, under guard, in a farmer's barn. I need to get them moved before they start to smell and too many questions are asked, that I'm not in a position to give answers to."

"Get them into the local hospital morgue."

"I can't do that without the proper paperwork and there would be questions asked, seeing the way they died." Sir Thomas replied.

"What do you suggest?"

"We take the bodies to the ferry terminal at Port Tennant in Swansea. There we hand them over to the German Consulate, from Dublin. They could take them back to Dublin and then have them shipped back to German." Sir Thomas suggested.

"And if they won't come and collect them?"

"We burry them in the grave yard, near where they died." Sir Thomas said.

"I'll get on to the Foreign Office and see what I can do but in the mean time, see if you can arrange a burial in that village." The Home Secretary ordered.

"Sir, if I don't hear from you, by six o'clock tonight, I'll burry them at midday tomorrow." Sir Thomas said

"What will the villagers say to have Germans buried in their church?"

"We'll use their English names. That way they won't know where they came from." Sir Thomas replied.

Sir Thomas was please with what he had achieved this morning. He thought it would be harder than that.

Now he needed to get the burial planned as he didn't expect the Germans to want their men back. To agree to get them would amount to admitting that they had invaded our country.

"Pat will you get me Brigadier Palmer on the phone please. It is vital that I speak to him and only him." Sir Thomas said.

199

"I'll try my best." Pat replied.

"No. You get hold of him, chase him around the country if you have to but I must speak to him today."

Pat had never been spoken to like that by Sir Thomas. She knew that this must be very important. It didn't take her long to find out that Brigadier Palmer had been posted away, at very short notice. He had been replaced by Colonel George Downing. As Sir Thomas needed to talk only to this officer, she instructed the military operator to put her in touch with Colonel Downing.

After twenty minutes she had tracked him down. He was in a meeting but would call her back in about half an hour. She gave this information to the Chief Constable.

While she waited for the military operator to get back to her, she informed Sir Thomas of the change of command and gave him the name of the new Officer in Command of the area.

They were true to their word, after thirty two minutes the army telephonist call her back and said that Colonel Downing was on the line for the Chief Constable. Pat then put the call through to Sir Thomas.

"Colonel Downing, I'm Sir Thomas Murray, Chief Constable of East Sussex, we haven't met."

"No, I only arrived last week and haven't got to know everyone yet. By the way, I'm George." He said.

"I'm Sir Thomas."

"Sir Thomas, what's so important?" George asked.

"George, have you hear the reports about some shooting at Exceat, yesterday morning?"

"Yes, that came up at our meeting. The Duty Field Officer read out his report."

"What I'm about to tell you is Top Secret. A party of ten Germans landed on Friday morning at Exceat. I don't know how or why or by whom, but with the exception of one, the rest were either killed or arrested and I have the bodies to dispose of."

"You're joking." George said.

"I wish I was." Sir Thomas replied.

"Right, what is it you want from me? I presume you do want something?" George got straight to the point.

"Yes, I need a platoon of men to dig the graves and the use of one of your Chaplin's to conduct the service." Sir Thomas requested.

"I'll get the Canadians to provide the men and you can have my Chaplin. Where and when do you need them?"

"If I do need them, I'll need the Platoon to report to one of my Inspectors at Exceat Bridge at eight o'clock tomorrow morning and the Chaplin, at the same place, at midday."

"What do you mean, if you need them?" the Colonel asked.

"I'm trying to get them moved out of the county. If I succeed then we won't need to burry them."

"The Exceat Bridge is a funny place to burry these bodies." George said.

"No your soldiers will be met and then taken to where the burials will take place. By the way, the platoon with need picks and shovels."

"When will I know if it's on?" George asked.

"No later then half past five, this evening." Sir Thomas said.

Sir Thomas thanked him for his help and then rang off and got on with the normal work of the day, but he got Pat to cancel all the scheduled meetings for the afternoon, as he felt that he might be quite busy later on.

The afternoon seemed to be dragging on for Sir Thomas. He detailed off Inspector Mannering to contact an undertaker, away from this area. They would need to provide five coffins and be present to put the bodies into the coffins, tomorrow morning. In fact they would still need the coffins, even if they were to transport the bodies to Swansea.

Sir Thomas explained to Keith what the plan was, but he couldn't remember the English names of the dead Germans.

It was then that Keith told the Chief Constable that he had kept a copy of their names. Sir Thomas was about to rebuke Keith when he realised that he was glad that he had kept the list.

At five fifteen Sir Thomas's phone rang. It was to Home Secretary, informing him that the German Consulate, in Dublin, had denied that any German Soldiers had landed in England and as such they were not responsible for them. Sir Thomas asked if it was alright to burry the men? He was given permission.

Before asking Pat to get the Colonel Downing on the phone, he also asked her to get Inspector Mannering to come to his office ASAP. After the phone call he made a few notes of what needed to be done over the next twenty four hours.

"Colonel Downing is on the line for you."

"George, we need your men. Is that OK?" Sir Thomas asked.

"Yes, the Canadians have agreed to provide about twenty men and the Chaplin has been briefed. I've told them both that there was a training accident and that we couldn't expect the Regiment involved, to burry the men. They have all accepted that." George said.

"That's great George. Inspector Mannering will meet both the Canadians and the Chaplin at eight and twelve o'clock, respectively. You realise that none of this can appear in any of your reports?" Sir Thomas said.

"I've forgotten about it already." George said.

"Many thanks. We'll have yourself and your wife around for dinner, sometime soon." Sir Thomas said, as a way of a thank-you.

Just as he was putting the phone down, there was a knock on his office door and Inspector Mannering walked in, without waiting for an invitation.

"Right Mannering, I need you to go out to West Dean and find the local vicar. Tell him that a group of Canadian soldiers were killed on a training exercise and it has been decided that, as they can't take the bodies' home, they were to be buried in a small village, like the small town they all came from."

"What if he doesn't buy that?" Keith asked.

"Well that is up to you, but he has to agree to them being buried in his grave yard. Then get him to show you where we can dig these graves." Sir Thomas was insistent.

"By the way, tell him that a military Chaplin will be performing the funeral service."

Keith noted this all down in is new Police Notebook.

"I contacted an undertaker, in Uckfield. He has agreed to have five coffins ready, by nine o'clock tomorrow morning." Keith reported.

"That's good."

"Tomorrow morning, at eight o'clock, you're to meet a platoon of Canadian soldiers, at Exceat Bridge. Take them to the grave yard and set them too digging the five graves. Then go and collect the undertaker."

"I'll send Sergeant Upton to collect him and the coffins, in the police van. He knows where to bring him. I'll also tell him to put the undertaker in the back of the van, so he doesn't know where he's going." Keith said.

"Once the Canadians have dug the graves, you can use them as pallbearers, for the funerals. Oh by the way, they are to be buried using their English names, not their actual German names." Sir Thomas said.

"Will you be attending the funerals, Sir?" Keith asked.

"Yes. I'll want to say thank you to those who take part."

"How will you get there, Sir?"

"I'll drive my own car. You'll be using my police car, I presume."

"Yes, if that's alright. I'll use your driver as well, he knows the way there and also a little of what is going on. No need to let more than necessary into what has been going on, this weekend." Keith said.

After leaving the Chief Constables office, Keith went down to reception and asked for the Chief Constables driver to be found and told to bring the car over to reception.

When he arrived, Keith told him that they would be taking the Chief Constable home and then he was to drive Keith to West Dean. He said no more, in case others, in the reception area were listening in.

By half past six, they had delivered Sir Thomas home and were on their way to West Dean.

"Fowler, tomorrow morning you're to pick me up from my house at seven o'clock. You won't be picking Sir Thomas up. He's driving himself into the Headquarters." Keith said.

Constable Fowler said nothing. The last few days had been strange, not like normal days. He had decided to just do as he was told and not ask too many questions. He had found that over time he would find out what was going on by just listening. It took them only about twenty minutes to get to West Dean village.

"Park up by the church, please. I've to go and find the vicar. Once I've talked to him, we can both go home. We'll have a long day tomorrow."

It was seven o'clock, before they arrived at the church. Constable Fowler found a safe place to park up, after Keith had left the car, in search of the Vicarage.

It was not far from the church so within a few minutes he was knocking on the front door.

"Reverent Upton" Keith asked of the elderly man who answered the door.

"Yes."

"I'm Inspector Mannering, from the County Police Headquarters, in Lewes. Can you spare me a few minutes?"

"Yes, please come in, Inspector. What is it I can do for you?" He asked.

"Can we talk in your study, please Sir?" Keith requested.

"Right this way." He said, leading the way into a room to the right of the large reception area.

The room they entered was very large, hardly a study, more a meeting room, which of course it was. He held many meeting of his parishioners in this room, together with communion classes for the village youngsters. There were four large windows, reaching from the ceiling to the floor on two sides of the room, bringing large amounts of light, to make this a very airy room.

Keith was invited to sit in the arm chair, to the right of the fire place and Reverent Upton took his seat on the left of the fire.

"What can I do for you, Inspector?" Henry Upton asked.

"Reverent, this is an important request and I have already spoken to the Bishop of Chichester, about this and he has agreed." Keith lied.

"Some soldiers, far from home, were killed on a training exercise and their families would like it if they were buried near where they were stationed. Your church is the nearest." Keith said.

"I haven't heard of this." Henry said.

"It only happened on Sunday and it is being kept secret, because the War Office doesn't want it to get out and reduce moral." Keith lied again.

"Was that the shooting that I heard Sunday morning, during communion?" Henry observed.

"Yes Sir, I believe it was." The truth for a change!

"I was wondering if you could show me where, in your grave yard, we could burry these poor men." Keith asked.

With that, the two of them got up and the Vicar led Keith out of the room, via one of the large windows. That doubled as a door out into the garden. It was just a short walk to the church and even shorter around to the rear of the church where the current grave yard was.

"This is where the next grave is due to be dug." Henry pointed to a plot of grass, next to a recently occupied grave.

"Would it be possible to use that space, over there? That way their families could visit them away from your local dead." Keith asked.

"That's a good idea, Inspector. How many graves will there be?" he asked.

"Five." Keith said.

"It would take Jack a couple of weeks to dig those." Henry noted.

"That is alright, I'll bring in a group of soldiers who'll do the digging." Keith replied.

"If you could just show me where we can dig these graves? I'll make sure that they are dug properly and your graveyard is left tidy." Keith said

With that they walked over to the area Keith had pointed out and Henry showed Keith where they should be.

"When do you want me to arrange the funeral services?" Henry asked

"The Army will provide a Chaplin to take the services."

"I think this is all very strange, Inspector. I'll write to the Chief Constable about this." Henry said.

"There'll be no need for that Sir, He'll be at the funerals himself and I know that he'll want to come and thank you for your help in this sad matter." Keith said.

With that said Keith shook the Vicar's hand and walked off, back to the police car and home for the night.

Tuesday morning was going to be a very busy one for Keith. Firstly he had to be up, washed, dressed and eaten breakfast by seven o'clock.

This was an hour earlier than was his norm. He was just tipping the last drops of tea into his mouth when there was a knock at his front door. It was Constable Fowler, with the Chief Constables police car.

Keith said goodbye to his wife and thanked her for getting up early to prepare his breakfast. With that done he picked up his cap and ran out and got into the passenger's seat, beside the driver.

"Right Fowler Exceat Bridge we have to be there, no later then eight o'clock. Can you make it there in time?" Keith asked.

"No trouble Sir. If I have to, I'll ring my bells." He said with a big smile.

They arrived at the bridge at ten to eight. Fowler parked up and they waited for the arrival of the Canadian soldiers. They didn't have long to wait. Like the British Army, they were used to parading five minutes before time.

When the first of the two Lorries had pulled up, a large soldier got out of the cab, supporting Sergeants chevrons on his arms, Keith got out of the car and walked over to him.

"Sergeant, I'm Inspector Mannering." He introduced himself, as the Sergeant saluted him, which he naturally returned.

"Good morning Sir. I'm Sergeant Delamare; I understand that you have a little digging for us to do." He said with a big smile on his face.

"Yes, I have. Will you get your vehicles to follow my car and I'll take you to the place I need you to dig. Sergeant, if you would come with me I'll brief you on what I need your men to do and by when." Keith said.

The Sergeant told his driver to follow the car and then he returned to the Police car and sat in the rear seat, behind the driver. Now that his passengers were seated, Fowler got the car back on the road, the two army Lorries followed on behind him. He realised that he would have to drive a bit slower then usual, as the Lorries were not a fast or agile as his car.

It would only take the convoy about ten minutes to reach West Dean church.

"Sergeant I need your men to dig five graves, in a village church yard." Keith said, and let that sink in.

"It needs to be completed no later then midday, today."

"You're joking. That can't be done."

"It has to be done. The funeral services start at Midday."

"What's the hurry?" the Sergeant asked.

"I'm afraid it's vital that this task is completed by then."

The Sergeant sat back and thought things out. He had eighteen men, including him self, plus two drivers. That was twenty in all. With five teams of three men each, he should be alright.

With the Corporal and himself in charge, they seem to have the right number of men. One thing that did bother him was the ground that they would be digging. This area was chalk and interspersed with flint. Still they would show these British Police, what Canadians could do. It may get them some slack, when some of their men get into trouble in the local towns?

Fowler parked his car further along the road, so that the army vehicles could park nearer the church entrance. Keith and the Sergeant got out of the car and the Sergeant told the Corporal to get the men and equipment out of the Lorries and fall in on the road, to await his return.

It was now time for Keith to show the Sergeant where the graves were to be dug. It took them a few minutes to reach the far end of the grave yard.

"This is where you are to dig the graves. The first one should be here and then the next one four feet away from the last, until you have completed them all." Keith instructed the Sergeant.

The Sergeant paced out the distance that these graves would take up, there was plenty of room to get them all in before they reached the end, and the fence that separated the church grounds from the small field next door.

"Right Sir we can do this. The time might be a bit tight though."

205

"Oh Sergeant, I forgot, one last thing. I will need twelve of you men as pallbearers, for the funerals." Keith said with a smile.

"That's OK Sir, I have some good big men here and they are strong enough for the job." He replied.

Keith left the Sergeant to get on with his job, while he walked over to the low flint wall that ran along the road and separated the church yard from the road. Towards the far end of this wall, away from the church gate, they had built a gape and some steps down to the road. He took this route out of the church grounds. He needed to get to the barn, before Sergeant Upton arrived with the undertaker, from East Grinstead.

It was not long before Sergeant Upton arrived, with the Police van. He pulled up and asked where he wanted it parked. Keith said that he needed it reversed towards the barn doors. It took him only a few moments to achieve this and stopped the engine and walked around to the rear door. In the mean time, Keith was opening the right hand barn door, but not to far. He didn't want others to see inside.

"About bloody time too. I'm not a criminal, you know." Mr Wellington said as he faced the Sergeant.

"Sorry Sir but I was told that you were not to see where I was taking you and you refused to wear a blindfold." Upton stated.

"Sergeant, bring Mr Wellington in here, will you." Keith called.

"This way Sir" Sergeant Upton said as he took the right arm of the undertaker, as if to 'escort' him to the Inspector.

"Good morning Mr Wellington. Thank you for coming. I presume you have the five coffins with you." Keith greeted.

"Yes I have the coffins, but I had no choice in coming, especially at such an early start." Mr Wellington complained.

"Right Mr Wellington, these are the bodies I need you to put into the coffins." Keith said as he moved his arm in the direction of the bodies.

"I'll need to see the Death Certificates, before I can put them in the coffins."

"I'm sorry but they haven't been sent to me but I'll have them brought to your office, as soon as I receive them." Keith lied. It seemed that he had told more lies over this case than in his whole Police career.

"All right but make sure you do."

"Sergeant, you and I'll unload the coffins, while Mr Wellington examines the bodies."

"By the way, Mr Wellington, please place the suitcases over there." Keith pointed to a spot away from the bodies.

As Keith was walking out of the barn, with Sergeant Upton, for some reason he turned his head and glanced back at Mr Wellington. He saw that he was just about to open one of the suitcases.

"If you do that, Mr Wellington, I'll have you arrested and you won't see the light of day until this horrible war is over. Do I make myself clear?" Keith said.

Mr Wellington stopped what he was doing, looked around at Keith and saw that he meant every word he had just said.

He took his hand off the lid, fastened it down and picked up the suitcase and moved it to where Keith had asked him to stack them.

It took the two of them about fifteen minutes to unload the coffins and place them at the foot of each of the dead Germans.

"I must go and see how they are getting on with the graves." Keith said. "Sergeant, please help Mr Wellington. Oh by the way, here is a list of the dead men's names. It starts from the one nearest the door. I'll need that list back. The Chaplin will need it for the service. Make sure their names are written on the lids." Keith said as he handed the list to Mr Wellington.

Keith had no intention of allowing Mr Wellington to take the list away with him.

Keith looked at his watch, it was now ten o'clock.

He thought that they had enough time for the bodies to be put into their coffins but he was worried about the digging of the graves. Could they be completed in time?

As he approached the grave yard, there was a lot of swearing and cursing going on, some in Anglo-Saxon and some in French. It would appear that things were not going along too well.

"How's it going Sergeant?" Keith called.

"Not to good Sir. There are a lot of flints here. I can see why they hadn't buried their own people over here." The Sergeant reported.

"Will it be done in time?"

"I think we'll have four dug by midday but not the last one."

"That's alright. We can start this end and do one funeral at a time. That should give your men time to complete the last one." Keith said, as much to himself as to the Sergeant.

"Corporal McKean, When can we release half of the men for pallbearer duties?" The Sergeant asked.

"We should have the first four graves dug in about half an hour. Provided we do not hit any large flints, then we can release twelve men." Nathan replied.

"Good, make sure that they have a quarter of an hour rest, then send them over to the barn." Keith asked the Sergeant.

"I hope their relatives appreciate all this work we're doing." The Sergeant said.

"I'm sure they will." Keith said as he walked off, back to the barn.

Sergeant Upton and Mr Wellington had been busy, while he was away. They had already filled four of the coffins and written their English names on the lids. Good everything was coming together well. In half an hour all the coffins were filled and the lids fastened down.

In the mean time, Keith had been moving all the suitcases into the back of the Police van. They were to be stored in the evidence room. You never know when it may be decided to actually find out who killed these men.

What Keith hadn't realised was that, although the barn had been under Police guard, Ian Badger had crept into the barn, via a secret doorway, he had recently built, at the far end of the barn. He had been tasked to get all the weapons, ammunition and explosives out of the suitcases and hide them away behind a stack of bales, until the barn was released back to the farmer. Then they could move them out of the barn and into their hide. Ian had completed this task last night, while it was still being guarded by the police.

"Mr Wellington. Thank you very much for your hard work yesterday and today, it is much appreciated." Keith said as he shook his hand.

"I'll send my bill to the Police Headquarters then." He replied.

"Yes, address it to the Chief Constable, if you will."

"Sergeant Upton, please take Mr Wellington home now."

"Mr Wellington, the list please," Keith said as he held out his hand.

Having received the list of name, Keith again thanked Mr Wellington for his help.

"This way Sir, do you want to go in the back or will you wear the blindfold?" He asked.

"I'll wear the blindfold, if you don't mind, Sergeant."

With that agreed, the two of them climbed into the front of the van and after a few minutes, after Mr Wellington had had the blindfold fitted, Sergeant Upton started the van's engine and drove off. Once they were passed Lewes, Sergeant Upton told him he could take the blindfold off., much to Mr Wellingtons relief.

It would soon be time for Keith and his driver to return to the bridge and meet up with the Chaplin. He walked over to his car and sat in the rear. He took out his notebook and made some rough notes as to what they had done, this morning.

Before he left the village he got out of the car and walked over to the flint wall. Here he stopped and shouted over to Sergeant Delamare.

"Sergeant, when your men come over to the barn, can you get them to carry the coffins out of the barn and lay them along this wall? That will make it easier for later on." Keith said.

"OK Sir. I'll get Corporal McKean to organise that, in a couple of minutes." The Sergeant said and waived as Keith turned away and returned to his car.

"Right Fowler, we'd better fetch the Chaplin." Keith said.

With that Constable Fowler started up the car's engine and they drove off, out of the village and along to the Bridge. He parked up, as he had done earlier. It was not long before a battered old car drew up next to their car. Out got an Army Officer and he walked around to the rear passenger door and got in.

"Captain Hamilton." He said as he sat down next to Keith.

"I'm Inspector Keith Mannering. Please to meet you."

"The Colonel said that you have a few bodies that you need me to burry."

"I've told my driver to follow your car, so he can take me back home later."

"I'm sorry but he'll have to wait here, we'll bring you back after the services." Keith stated.

"Fowler, go and tell the Captain's driver not to follow us, then we can go." Keith instructed his driver.

"Yes Captain, five men who lost their lives on a training exercise." Keith replied.

"I hadn't heard about this."

"No it was a secret one, so I understand. That is why it is all clock and dagger stuff, to burry the men." Keith was really getting into this lying thing.

Fowler returned from giving the driver the message and drove off, towards West Dean.

"This is the list of the men who you'll be burying, Captain." Keith said as he handed him a piece of paper, listing all the names that had been written on the coffin lids.

The Chaplin looked through the list and then, used it as a book mark, in his book of common prayer, at the start of the funeral service.

As the driver was about to turn into the narrow road, leading up to West Dean Village, the Chief Constable's car preceded them into the turning. They followed it towards the village church.

Both cars stopped near the church gates. All those attending the funerals, got out of their respective cars.

"Sir Thomas, this is Captain Hamilton. Captain, this is Sir Thomas Murray, Chief Constable of East Sussex." Keith said.

"Thank you for coming at such short a notice, Captain." Sir Thomas said as he held out his hand to shake that of the Chaplin.

"Death doesn't have a time table, Sir Thomas."

"Gentleman, if you'll come this way, I'll lead you to the special area we have been given. We can start the service, as soon as Captain Hamilton is ready." Keith said.

He led the two men up the path, towards the church door but did not enter the church, instead they turned right. He was taking them directly to the graveside, for the first burial. Once they had arrived, Keith left them, to see how things were going with the final graves.

"Nearly finished Sir, we only have this last one to complete. There's a ruddy great flint down there but we'll have it out soon and then we can get the last foot dug, quite quickly." Private Mason reported.

"Unless you strike another flint," Keith said with a smile.

"I'll just go and check with the pallbearer party, Sir, and then we can start." Keith reported to Sir Thomas.

Keith walked over to the low flint wall and noted, before he arrived that all five coffins had been brought out of the barn and were propped up on the low wall. That would make it easier for the men to lift each of them up and get them on their shoulders. He also noted that there were about twelve men standing by the coffins.

"Corporal, are these men the Pallbearers?" Keith asked.

"Yes Sir." Corporal McKean replied.

"That's very good. We should be able to get out of here much quicker than I thought." Keith said.

"Corporal, will you supervise your men, as they lift the coffins. We will start with the first one, now. I will signal you when I need the next one brought over to the grave side." Keith said

"Fine Sir, right Number one section, you'll take the first coffin. Remember what we practiced earlier."

Once the men had taken their places, The Corporal told them to 'Lift' and as one they all lifted up the coffin and, once they were steady, with a practice movement raised it up on to their shoulders, as they turned to face the grave yard.

Corporal McKean had detailed off a Lance corporal to escort the coffin and ensure that the men kept in step and did not drop the coffin. Once all was ready, the Lance Corporal gave the order to march.

When they had arrived at the graveside, they placed the coffin onto the wooden slats that had been laid across the grave, for just this purpose. Keith checked off the name, against the Chaplin's list of burials, so he knew who was being buried.

When everything was in place, the Chaplin started the service. Although their actual religion was not known, they used the service from the Book of Common Prayer for each and every one of the five burials.

Everything went like clock work. The soldiers did a very good job; it was if they had done this many times before. The final grave was completed as the Chaplin was ending the forth service.

Once all the services were completed Sir Thomas retrieved the list of names from the Chaplin and escorted him back to his Police car.

"Thank you very much Captain."

"Fowler, take the Captain back to his car, please."

With that he shook hands with the Chaplin and returned, back to the grave yard.

In the mean time, Sergeant Delamare had organised his men to fill in the remaining graves. He had the men, who were not acting as pallbearers, coming behind the Burial party, filling in those buried, once the Chaplin was two graves away. In this way, once the last one had been buried, they only had his and one more to fill in.

"Fall your men in, please Sergeant." Sir Thomas asked.

"You heard the Gentleman. Fall in." Sergeant Delamare shouted.

Once they were all stood in three ranks, Sir Thomas walked out, in front of the men, to address them."

"Men, I know that you are all far from home. The men who you have helped to burry, today, were also far from home. I just want to thank you all for the excellent work you have done today and I'll be writing to your Commanding Officer to express my admiration and praise for the way you have carried out your duties."

"Sergeant, if you can arrange for your men to visit the Eight Bells, in Jevington, tomorrow night, Inspector Mannering will be glad to buy them all a drink." Sir Thomas said and smiled at Keith.

"Squad, Squad, Attention."

"Officer on Parade, to your duties, Dismiss"

With that said the soldiers turned to their right, saluted and took three paces forward and then broke off, some of them running to get to the truck first, so that they could get the best seats. The rest just walked down the path, carrying their tools and were too tired to use so much energy.

"Sir, would you like me to introduce you to Reverent Upton?" Keith asked Sir Thomas.

"Yes, I'd better thank him for allowing this burial in his church yard."

"Sir, I told him that the Bishop had OK'd this." Keith admitted.

"You will just have to say a few more 'Hail Mary's' next Sunday." Sir Thomas replied with a broad smile.

Chapter 37
The final solution

Yesterday had been difficult for Lars Eberuardt. He didn't like having to execute those good Officers but to save his own neck someone had to pay for the failure of Operation Tramp.

Today he had to report to Berlin, at the German Army High Command. He had a meeting with Field Marshal Gerd von Rundstedt. What surprised him was that Grand Admiral Dönitz and the Reichsmarschall were also present.

Lars gave his report about how prepared the British appeared to be. The reported that troop movements, were going on along the coast. Also from nowhere, they appeared to have a secret force that had not only taken on their advance party, but had wiped them out.

"We've heard nothing about such a force." The Field Marshal said.

"Nor had we Sir, but they exist and it appears they are well trained and well equipped."

"You can go now Lars." The Reichsmarschall ordered.

After Lars had left the room the High Command gathered around the large table and they had to decide what recommendation they were to put before the Fuhrer at the meeting at midday.

The Reichsmarschall spoke first.

"Hitler had laid down three main things that must be in place before Operation Sealion can proceed. Firstly: Air Superiority. Secondly: The Royal Navy being kept out of the Straights of Dover and lastly: Good weather. Well where are we with these?"

"We have never been able to guarantee that we could keep the Royal Navy out of the straights of Dover. Since the Norway operation, we have lost too many ships. There are ten that are far too damaged, to be fit for battle." Grand Admiral Dönitz said.

"Your Luftwaffe hasn't been able to destroy the RAF, Reichsmarschall." The Field Marshal pointed out.

This remark brought about an outburst, from Hermann Göring, which lasted for several minutes.

"Until we know more about this secret force, it would be foolhardy to go on with the operation." Field Marshal Rundstedt stated.

The others were in agreement and it was decided that the Reichsmarschall should advise the Fuhrer. He agreed but the other officers were to accompany him to the meeting. It appeared that he didn't want to face the Fuhrer by himself.

At that meeting, on the 17th September 1940, Operation Sealion was postponed, indefinitely.

The End

Prologue

The Auxiliary Forces never existed, as far as the British public were aware. As a result, it was very many years, after the end of the war, that word of its existence started to leak out.

Although the Germans tried to find out about the men who had scuppered their final plans, there was nothing to find. As far as they could find out, they didn't exist.

The hardest bit, for the members of the Auxiliary Forces, involved in this operation, was that it was a secret that they would have to keep to their grave. They couldn't even tell their families, in case it got out. Even if they spoke about it with the members of their own unit, it may be overheard. For some, they tucked it away deep in their memories and filed them under 'forget'.

For others they just lived with it. But for two of them, the memory of it would drive them into the local mental institution, at Hellingly. They never recovered from the guilt of what they had done that Sunday morning.

Acknowledgements

East Sussex County Library

For the loan of many books for my research.

Special note:-

The Secret Sussex Resistance by Stewart Angell
Published by Middleton Press

Advice on starting a WWII motorcycle

Cosmo Classic Motorcycles Ltd.
St Leonards on Sea
(www.comoclassic.co.uk)

Made in the USA
San Bernardino, CA
19 January 2014